I0524930

LEAVING FIRE

BY PATRICK MCKENNA LYNCH SMITH

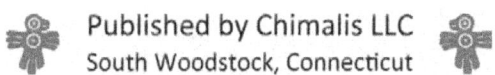
Published by Chimalis LLC
South Woodstock, Connecticut

www.PatrickMLsmith.com

Copyright © 2020 by Patrick M. L. Smith.
All rights reserved. No part of this book may be
reproduced or transmitted in any form or by any means,
electronic or mechanical, including photocopying and
recording, or by any information storage and retrieval
system, without the express written permission from the
author, except for the inclusion of brief quotations in a
review.

None of the people, places or events described in the
following pages are real. The author and publisher do not
assume, and hereby disclaim any liability or responsibility
to any party for any loss, damage, or disruption caused, or
alleged to have been caused, directly or indirectly, by
content, errors or omissions contained in this book,
whether such result from negligence, crummy editing,
accident, or any other cause.

Published by Chimalis LLC
PO Box 206, South Woodstock CT 06267
Printed in the United States of America

First edition, April 1, 2020

Library of Congress Control Number: 2020935410
Cataloging-in-Publication Data
Smith, Patrick McKenna Lynch, 1950-
Leaving Fire
/ by Patrick McKenna Lynch Smith. – 1st ed.
p. cm.
1. Fiction   2. Hunting   3. Young-Adult—Fiction
4. Adventure   5. Smith, Patrick McKenna Lynch   I. Title
Paperback ISBN   978-0-9890086-0-0
eISBN 978-0-9890086-1-7

For William Kerr:
My godfather, best man and lifelong friend

TABLE OF CONTENTS

Chapter 1 THE NARROW WAIST 2

Chapter 2 THE GAME BEGINS 8

Chapter 3 GOOD FEET 14

Chapter 4 NO TAKE 29

Chapter 5 NONE TO KEEP 44

Chapter 6 LIKE AN OX 66

Chapter 7 ALWAYS THE SAME 71

Chapter 8 CONSENT 80

Chapter 9 CIVILITY 96

Chapter 10 ALL WEARS AWAY 102

Chapter 11 WITNESS 111

Chapter 12 TIME 121

Chapter 13 THE TRUE PRIVILEGE 125

Chapter 14 THE CHARGE 131

Chapter 15 MUNDANE AND PROFOUND 157

Chapter 16 GO! 160

Chapter 17 COLLECTIVE MEMORY 167

Chapter 18 THE WOLF TREE 170

Chapter 19 CRAFTING THE WEAPON 184

Chapter 20 FIRST FRIGHT 188

Chapter 21 SECOND FRIGHT 201

Chapter 22 TASUKETE 208

Chapter 23 DUMBFOUNDING 217

Chapter 24 PREY NOT PREDATOR 226

Chapter 25 LOSING POISE 243

Chapter 26 MINE TO MAKE 253

Chapter 27 LITTLE GHOST DEER 266

Chapter 28 NO LONGER A PLACE OF PURSUIT 270

Chapter 29 OUT OF BOUNDS 273

Chapter 30 AMBER EYES 285

Chapter 31 HARD TO HOLD 292

Chapter 32 ON THREE LEGS 300

Chapter 33 FIRE 310

Chapter 34 LIKE THE REST OF US 314

Chapter 35 WHOLE THAN FIRST 317

Chapter 36 FIRELIGHT 338

ABOUT THE AUTHOR 339

A Message from the Publisher 340

MASHENTUCK MOUNTAIN, Burwick, CT

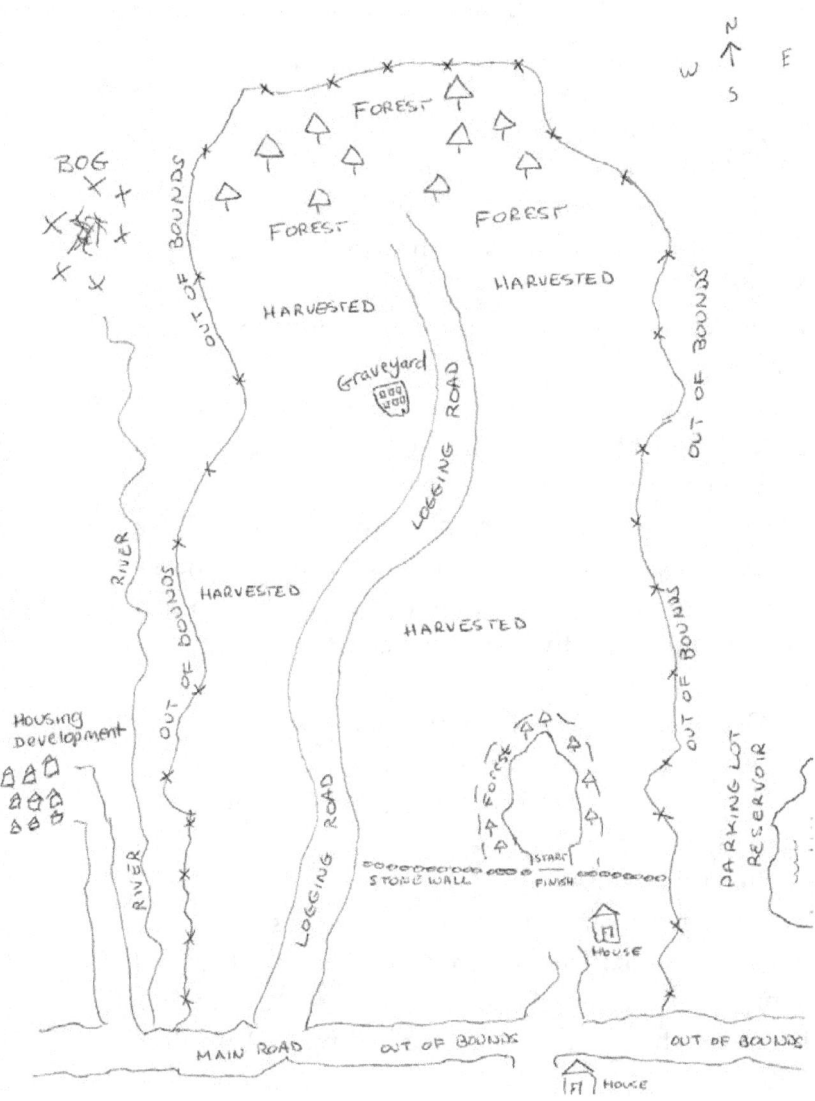

CHAPTER 1

THE NARROW WAIST

Of course they would try to kill him.

That was part of the game.

"Just part of the game," he muttered.

Leaves tumbled across the parking lot in the harsh November wind.

He was at the Hearthstone Inn, sitting alone in his car.

He watched the hotel entry. No one came or went. Everything was going according to plan.

Except for Sarah.

Sarah should have been with him. She used to be so encouraging, so in favor of it all, and then, abruptly, she was pleading with him not to go. He didn't understand. She refused to even accompany him. She no longer wanted any part of it.

"The whole thing is barbaric," she said.

"Primitive and foolish," she said.

He thumped the heel of his hand against the steering wheel.

But she knew! All along, she knew.

He closed his eyes as he sat back in the seat, forcing himself to relax. He was tired. Anxiety and fear had kept him awake, night after night. Wrestling with who he used to be. That's how Sarah had put it. Wrestling with....

The car trembled with a particularly strong gust of wind.

He opened his eyes.

"Enough!" he said.

He looked to his left, then to his right.

He turned abruptly in the seat and scanned the area behind the car.

All clear.

He grabbed the gym bag, opened the door and got out of the car.

He pressed the coat collar to his neck. When he lowered his head against the wind, he couldn't help noticing the bedroom slippers. They were absurd. But he had not been able to find anything else to wear. His feet were distorted with calluses between his toes; and each sole was as thick as leather, even the arch, the part of the foot that never touched the ground. If needed, he could run barefoot across glass. But he had ruined the proportion. Shoes no longer fit. So he wore leather bedroom slippers, size XXXL. But even these could barely contain his feet. Where the stitching had burst apart, it was plain to see that he wore no socks.

He crossed the parking lot.

The wind was horrendous.

He pulled on the glass door, entered the vestibule, passed through the second set of doors and was now in the hotel lobby.

Other than the clerk at the front desk, no one was about. The clerk sat on a stool. He was chewing gum, mouth open; an incessant jaw. A newspaper was spread out on the counter in front of him. He did not look up. "Unless you're here for the running," he said, "there aren't any rooms available."

"For the running."

"With the press?" the clerk asked.

"No."

"One of them foreigners?"

"American," he said.

"Name?"

"Russell Bowen."

The clerk looked up from his newspaper. He grunted. "You're Bowen?" There was disbelief in his smile. "But... you're just a kid!"

Russell said nothing.

"No wonder they don't give you much of a chance," the clerk said. He tapped the newspaper with his finger. "Odds makers favor the...."

"Can I please just check in?"

"Nope," the clerk said. "Too early. Security guards are only just getting into position, and...."

"But I requested early check-in," Russell said.

"Oh? Well, let me check on that. But first you need to show me some ID." The gum chewing made smacking sounds. "Rules," he said. "For your protection. You understand."

No, Russell did not understand. But neither was he going to make a scene. He planned to keep a low profile. His was a type of forced humility, like the turtle withdrawing into its shell so as to decrease the possibility of injury. Let the world prod and probe. He would reveal himself only as much as was absolutely necessary. And revelation seemed necessary in order to meet the desk clerk's request. He removed his license from his wallet and held it out toward the clerk.

But the clerk shook his head. "Go home, kid. You don't want any of this. It's insane, that's what it is. Do you know how...."

Russell made a motion with his hand, a gesture of insistence.

The clerk shrugged, took the license, briefly studied it and handed it back.

"Something else I just read in the paper," he said. "About life insurance and health insurance. They go into...what was the word...default. That's the word. All insurance policies go into default until this thing's over. Because of the statistics. Too many injuries." He stared at Russell and said, slowly, "Too many *deaths*."

Russell cleared his throat. "So is my room ready?"

"Yes, yes, all right," the clerk said. He moved to the computer and typed on the keyboard. "Bowen... Russell Bowen...Here it is. Okay. Let's see. Yup, early check-in requested. Also says here that you also asked for a room with a view of....?" And now he cast a suspicious look at Russell. "This place is known for its scenic views of the forest and river, and the manicured grounds at the rear of the hotel. Yet you asked for a room with a view of the front *parking lot*?"

Russell looked about. He saw two men coming through a doorway down the hall. Fortunately, they were not within earshot. He looked back at the clerk and said, "The room key, please."

The clerk rolled his eyes and then pointed to the guest register. "Okay. Sign, please." He typed on the keyboard; a coded key-card came out of the slot. "According to the file, there's supposed to be two people. Mrs. Bowen arriving later?"

"I'd be surprised," Russell said, as he signed the register.

Sarah was probably still asleep. But tomorrow at this time she would certainly be awake. Tomorrow she would be among people all over the world who would rise early so as to light a fire at dawn. Doing so was one of the traditions associated with the competition. For Sarah, though, lighting the fire would not signify participation or support, but hope. That, she had told him, would be the extent of her involvement.

Hope?

Absurd.

Hope doesn't win.

The clerk handed him the key-card.

"Second floor," the clerk said. "Room 232. And there's a video on your TV. Compliments of the Committee. Channel 3."

"Channel 3. Okay. Thank you."

"That Canadian seems like a piece of work, eh?" the clerk said.

Russell had a good idea of what the man was referring to, but didn't want to know the details. Not yet. So he simply nodded and turned away.

He rode the elevator to the second floor. The doors opened. He peered out. He looked left, looked right, then moved into the hall.

He put his ear to the door of room 232. He listened. He knocked and waited. Then he slid the key card into the slot, and a light blinked green.

He pushed the door open and again waited. He moved cautiously into the room, looking to the left and right. He checked the closets, pulled back the shower curtain, looked under the bed.

All clear.

He shut the entry door.

He took the desk chair and leaned it so that its crest was propped beneath the doorknob.

After pushing the bed up against the wall by the window, he drew the curtains until there was only a narrow gap between them.

Wind rattled the windowpanes.

He put his gym bag on the bed, opened it and removed the clock and the catalogue. The clock had belonged to his grandmother. It was old, but reliable. No batteries required. He wound it and placed it on the windowsill. He could hear it softly ticking away the seconds.

Then he sat on the bed and peered out between the curtains to the parking lot.

He wasn't sure what he would learn, if anything. But, for the moment, the advantage was his.

Maybe.

He had arrived early and, from this position, he would be able to observe the others as they arrived. Perhaps they would reveal something about themselves when they thought no one was watching.

He glanced over at the clock. A phrase came to mind and it made him think of sand passing through the narrow waist of an hourglass.

Time was running out.

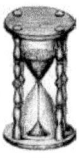

CHAPTER 2

THE GAME BEGINS

*W*hile still sitting on the bed in his hotel room, Russell Bowen continued to keep an eye on the parking lot. Over an hour had passed. A few people had left the hotel, but no one had arrived.

He used the remote control to turn on the television. He selected Channel 3, as the hotel clerk had instructed.

A video began to play.

Russell saw a tall, lanky man seated at a long wooden table in what appeared to be the great hall of a castle. A fire burned in an enormous stone fireplace. But there were also the makings of an office: file cabinets and computers and desks, lamps and stacks of paper. To one side, a very thick, open book rested in a glass case. Now a title appeared on the screen:

A Brief History of The Kincaid

At home, Russell had shelves full of books on the history of The Kincaid. He had books by people describing how they had survived the competition. Books about tactics and strategies, about cultural and socio-economic impact, about anything and everything associated with the competition. He considered himself somewhat of an expert on the subject. But this video was new to him.

He turned away to once again face the parking lot. He had a job to do. But even as he watched for signs of activity outside, he listened to the narrator's voice from the video:

"Hello. Welcome to Kincaid Castle in Buckshaw, Dorset, England.

My name is Ian Rushmore, and I am Chairman of The Kincaid Committee. I'd like to take you on a brief trip through the history of the famous game known as The Kincaid.

We know surprisingly little about the early years of James Kincaid, the man for whom the competition is named. We do know he was born in 1451, in Somerset, England. We also know that he was well-educated, which was a true privilege at that time. He could read and write in English, French and Latin. He knew mathematics and law.

His first act of historical significance occurred during the Wars of the Roses, a civil war that came about when both the House of York and the House of Lancaster claimed the throne of England. This was a time of confusion in England, a time of relative lawlessness, heavy taxation and fluctuating loyalties. Who was the legitimate king? Who deserved the people's trust?

James Kincaid sided with the House of York. He rose through the ranks to serve as second in command under Richard, Duke of Gloucester. Through bravery and cunning, Kincaid proved himself indispensable in a key battle with the Lancastrians at Tewkesbury in 1471. In part due to that victory, Edward IV was restored to the throne. As a reward for his services, Kincaid was not only paid a considerable amount of money, he was also knighted and given a grant of land in Dorset.

Sir James Kincaid, as he was now known, married and set about to build a home with his newly acquired wealth. He chose to build a castle. At that time, cannons were in use, so a castle no longer offered an impenetrable defense. Thus, in retrospect, the effort and expense of constructing a castle seems a peculiar choice. In fact, Castle Kincaid would be one of the last castles built in England. It also depleted much of the owner's finances. Soon, Sir James was in need of additional funds.

He had an idea.

On November 10th, 1476, just outside these castle walls, Sir James Kincaid gathered together some of the local townspeople. He lit a great bonfire, and announced that he was going to hold a contest. For the duration of this contest, his land would be considered a 'common chase.'

A 'chase' was a piece of land delineated by boundaries; unlike a park, it was not enclosed, nor was it as undefined as forestland. Typically, only those of high social standing could hunt a 'chase,' but a 'common chase' was open to hunting by any and all.

Kincaid explained to the townspeople that the rules of his contest were quite simple: the first person to bring a deer to the bonfire would win a portion of the venison, as well as a prize. Sir James would wait by the fire for the winner to come in, and the two of them would then share a meal of venison. The winner would return home with the remainder of the meat, as well as a sack of wheat flour. At that time, wheat flour was quite valuable. Barley and rye were typically used by the poor to make bread, whereas wheat was generally reserved for the upper classes. Venison was also a rare treat for peasants, because most deer were considered 'royal deer,' and only those of high social standing, such as Sir James, were permitted to hunt them.

Kincaid explained that there would be no restrictions on how the deer could be captured. People could go on foot or on horseback, hunt in groups or individually. There were no restrictions with regard to weapons either. People could use long bows, spears, knives, lances, crossbows and nets.

After the first event in 1476, the hunt became an annual event, held on the tenth of November each year. But it was too easy. There were years when the contest ended only a few hours after it had begun. The rules evolved. The use of horses was banned. The crossbow was eventually eliminated, due to its range and accuracy.

The contest soon became so popular that Sir James saw his chance for what many historians believe was his original intent for creating the competition: profit. He announced that the winner would now receive a cash reward, but there would also be an entry fee. This payment to compete could be in made in coin, goods, or the promise of services to the castle. This changed the overall tenor of the contest, because a competitor not only had a chance of winning something, but now also risked losing something.

Competition stiffened. Over the years, the prize money increased, but it was always less than the total amount laid down for entry fees. Thus, Sir James profited, and his coffers were full once again.

People from neighboring towns, having heard of what had become known simply as The Kincaid, began to arrive in Dorset each year for November tenth. A record was kept. Each entrant made his mark. Those who could write signed their name. Once the competition was over, the winner's name or mark was circled. This record, captured in a massive leather bound book, became known as The Book of Kincaid.

The contest continued to be held every November tenth. Sir James lit the bonfire to signify that the game had begun, and then people sat around the fire, eating and drinking as they waited for the winner to return with a deer.

In 1482, Sir James was notified that someone had been killed during the game. He went to investigate. The body lay in the woods. The man had been shot in the back with an arrow.

Whether the killing was accidental or intentional could not be determined, but the archer had certainly made an attempt to cover his traces. The feathers at the notched end of an arrow were often of a particular design and color that identified the owner of the arrow. In this case, the arrow had been broken; the notched end was missing. The local sheriff was called in, but the culprit was never identified.

Another man died during the following year, 1483. Whether this man had been killed intentionally or not was also unknown. Once again, the sheriff's investigation was inconclusive.

Sir James realized he could not possibly police the activities of those in the forest during the contest. He was also well acquainted with the rules of law. He knew that if the sheriff had to be called in every year, or the courts became involved, the contest would be brought to a halt and this source of income would end.

To prevent this, he devised an agreement that would become known as The Kincaid Covenant. Beginning in the year 1484, this Covenant was written across the top of each page of the massive book. In modern parlance, the Covenant was essentially a 'release' or 'waiver.' "

"Neither in benefit nor in burden...," Russell said out loud, without turning from the window.

The narrator continued:

"Here is the original Covenant followed by a modern translation. As you can see, the rules of the English language have certainly changed over the centuries."

Russell momentarily averted his eyes from the parking lot to the television, and saw these words on the screen:

Whee of thys gamen are of na Lawes betwene us, neyther in bunfyte ne in burthen, excepte thoos of God, of Consyens and of Natour.

(We of this contest are of no laws between us, neither in benefit nor in burden, except those of God, of Conscience and of Nature.)

The narrator went on:

"Most people in 1484 could neither read nor write, but being illiterate did not prevent them from understanding the rules of the game. The Covenant was simply read aloud to each person at the start of the contest. By doing so, Sir James believed that he could keep himself out of legal difficulty.

He was wrong."

Russell pushed the pause button on the remote, stopping the video.

All his attention was now focused on an expensive looking car that had just pulled into the hotel parking lot. He watched as the car came to a stop. The doors opened and a man and a woman got out.

Russell felt his pulse quicken.

The game had begun.

CHAPTER 3

GOOD FEET

From the window of his hotel room, Russell studied the man and woman as they moved to the rear of their car.

The man had short black hair. In his dark overcoat he looked trim, fit. His trousers flapped in the relentless wind.

The woman kept her hand pressed to the red, broad brimmed hat on her head. The hat obscured her face. Her long overcoat was also red, with large brass buttons.

Perhaps these two people weren't contestants after all. The fancy car and stylish clothes suggested they might be sponsors. Everything about them indicated wealth and class, not really the type to be....

"Hold on," Russell said, softly, barely a whisper. He brought his face closer to the window. "Maybe that's Ortiz."

He recalled the day when he first learned about Ortiz.

Last April, a letter had arrived with The Kincaid catalogue. Sarah had gone down to get the mail and returned with a bulky white envelope. She had pushed the envelope across the kitchen table at him. And he had pushed it back at her.

"You read," he had said, and resumed rubbing sandpaper between his toes and along the soles of his feet.

"Hey, I thought we agreed you wouldn't do that in front of me anymore."

He set the sandpaper aside, looked at her and nodded. "Yes," he said. "Sorry."

She sat down at the table across from him. She opened the envelope and removed the contents. "Holy guacamole!" she cried in mock surprise. "The Kincaid Catalogue!" She looked at him. "Now, why on earth would we be getting one of these?"

"Sarah...."

She opened the catalogue. She read aloud from the index:

"Entry Fees and Prize money for 2020.

Rules and Regulations.

General Site Area for 2020.

Potentials.

Sample Covenant."

Russell nodded. "Fees and prize money?"

She turned several pages, and then read aloud: *"Entry fees must be sent in the form of a certified bank check to the Committee and postmarked no later than July 15th, 2020. The entry fee is $250,000 U.S."*

"Doesn't matter," he said. "Sponsors pay the fee."

She continued reading: "The prize money for this year has been increased to $2,500,000 U.S."

He laughed, incredulous. "What? How much?"

"You heard me."

"But wait...yikes...after taxes and expenses, and reimbursing the sponsor for the entry fee plus their percentage of the purse, the winner walks away with...about...okay, okay...about a million dollars!"

She frowned. "It's *not* enough."

"Sarah, just imagine what we could do with that kind of money! Between your job at the Town Hall and mine at Ricky Dee's, we couldn't save that kind of money in a hundred years. We could pay off the house, free and clear. We could…."

"A million dollars to risk your life?"

"Okay then. So how much *would* be enough?"

"It doesn't matter," she sighed. "You're going to do it no matter what anyone says or does."

"It's called commitment."

"Ahhh…the magic word," she said.

He rolled his eyes. "Here we go again."

"Russell, please…just listen to me for a moment," she said. "Okay?"

He sat back, his arms folded across his chest. "Go."

"In this town," she said, "on any given morning, some old lady at her breakfast table might look out of the window and see a nearly naked young man running through the woods. Even in the middle of winter. Would that old lady sound the alarm? No. Why?

'It's just that Bowen boy again. He's in training, you know.'

That's who you've been, Russell. Something familiar, and yet …I don't know…distant and removed. Even though you spent most of high school set apart from the group, everyone knew what you were planning. Always training for The Kincaid, pushing yourself, so strange and wild, yet focused, so unlike other people your age. You were the most disciplined of them all, Russell. And in the years since high school, you've kept to your… commitment. But you need to acknowledge that, along the way, you made *other* commitments. We got married. With my parents' help, we bought this house."

"So...once again: you knew what you were getting into. Even before we got married and even before we bought this house, you knew."

She shook the catalogue at him. "This?" she asked. "We were only 16 years old...."

"Actually, we were 15."

"That's even worse," she said. "We were 15 when you first heard about this game. You swore an oath: you would run when you were old enough. I thought you were so brave! Since that day, how many times have I waited for you at the edge of the woods? How many times have I tended to your wounds? My support for you has been unwavering."

"Yes, it has. Unwavering."

"But things are different now, Russell. Back then, we were just kids, full of childish anger and defiance. We were incapable of grasping the true nature and risks of this game. But now we know better: it's insane. Absolutely crazy. It doesn't make sense anymore. You're letting the past control our future...!" She paused. She sat forward in her chair. "What is this really about, Russell? Are you afraid to back out? Afraid to say no?"

"No. Are you?"

She nodded. "Actually, I am. I'm afraid to tell you that I don't want to help you in this anymore. Who knows? What if it upsets your rhythm of training and distracts you? You might get injured. I'd be letting you down, backing out on an agreement. And I'm also afraid to let go of it all, to say goodbye to something that was such a big part of our youth. The game seemed so thrilling back then, Russell. For years, I've dreamed of standing at the line one day to watch you cross.

But now that we're here, so close to it, and we're older, my perspective has changed. It's not what I want anymore. The game seems foolish to me now. Primitive and barbaric. And yes, of course we need the money. But the risk is simply too great. You're willing to…." She slumped in the chair. "Oh, forget it. I'm wasting my breath."

"All right," he said. "Then can we get back to the catalogue and…."

"To win is to leave the wounded where they fall," she said. "That's the rule, isn't it, Russell?"

"I didn't say that."

"But you did," she countered. "I learned it from you."

"Okay, okay," he said. "If you want to win at anything, then…."

"And so now I am one of the wounded," she said, and slid slowly, dramatically from her chair to the floor.

"Oh for goodness sake Sarah," he said.

She looked up at him. "Going to leave me where I fall?"

"Very funny."

"Oh?" She got back up into her chair. "Actually, I'm being quite serious."

"You knew, Sarah. You've known all along…."

"You keep telling me that," she said. "Is that the best defense you can come up with?"

"I don't need a defense."

"Okay then. What if you *are* seriously hurt during the game? Oops! Health insurance won't cover it. How will I take care of you? You end up paralyzed like Malkovich or whatever his name was, and you think I'm going to spoon-feed you oatmeal for the rest of your life? Oops! And no money. Oops! We lose the house." She sucked her tongue against the roof of her mouth, making a clicking sound. She said, "And *I'm* the one being silly?"

"You're upset because I'm keeping my word. Think about that."

"And you always said: commit to something larger than yourself."

He shrugged. "And?"

"Just that."

"Look, Sarah…we agreed to do this," he said. "But if you've changed your mind, then I'll…."

She smacked the catalogue down flat on the table. "I don't know what to do!" She lowered her head. After a few moments she said, "To the end of training. I will be there for you until the end of training. How's that? But not one step beyond. I'm not going to travel to Arizona or Alaska or wherever. I'm with you until the last day of training and then I'm *done*. Fair enough?"

"Fair enough."

"Okay then."

"Now you probably want to know about the Victor's Realm, right?"

Sarah knew that the present champion, an American, had won the game in Japan last year. The Rule of Victor's Realm dictated that the competition always be held in the homeland of the champion. So, obviously, it would be in the United States this year. But it could be anywhere in the United States, from Maine to Florida to Hawaii.

She thumbed roughly through the catalogue to the appropriate page. "Let's see…where will my stubborn spouse have to go? To Oregon, for black tail deer? Or to Nebraska, for mule deer? Oh...."

Once again she lowered her head, as if in defeat.

"What?" he asked.

"Oh my God. I can't believe it. It's going to be held right here." She looked up at him. "In Connecticut."

"Don't joke about this."

"I wish I were joking."

"Connecticut?"

"Yes."

"Seriously? I can't believe it! *Connecticut*?"

"Don't make me to say it again."

"No travel?"

"That's right," she said. "No travel."

He smiled. He stomped his feet in rapid succession, a heavy drum roll on the kitchen floor. He sang out: "Hallelujah! Hallelujah!"

The catalogue did not reveal specifically where in Connecticut the competition would be held. Only The Kincaid Committee knew the exact location. As a matter of fairness, information about the exact location would be released piecemeal so that, ultimately, all competitors would encounter the site for the first time, at the same time.

Sarah said, "The Kincaid in Connecticut." Her smile was weak. "What more could a fool Connecticut Yankee ask for?"

"How about a supportive Connecticut wife?"

"Oh, I'm supportive, all right," she said. "Just not of this."

He turned to leave. "I know, I know. I'm sorry, but I have to get ready for work now."

She reached out, put a hand on his arm and said, "You don't have to run this year, Russell. Why not wait until next year?"

"All athletes die young," he said. "That's the rule. Another year of training? Another year of...."

"Russell...."

They stared at each other in silence.

She drew the back of her hand across her cheek.

"I'm running," he said.

"I know." She nodded.

He sat back down. "I can do this, Sarah. I can win! I can change our lives forever."

"But maybe not in a good way," she said. She sniffled and looked down at the open catalogue. "I know this is what you've always wanted to do. But it's not a childhood fantasy anymore, Russell. And this isn't baseball or golf or tennis."

"Thank God."

"Russell, please...This is so...dark...and just look at all these potentials from India and Japan, England...so many of them."

'Potentials' were people in search of a sponsor to pay the entry fee for them. Their photographs were in the catalogue. Beneath each photograph was a short listing of pertinent information that would, they hoped, spark a sponsor's interest. Russell knew that the vast majority of those listed in the catalogue would not make it. Some would not be able to prove themselves and thus would not be able to raise the money for the entry fee. Some would get injured. But most would back out due to fear. Fear ruled this game.

When he was younger, Russell sent away for the catalogue every year and studied it in detail, particularly with regard to the potentials. But now, as part of his strategy, he would not read it.

Not yet.

"They are from all over the planet," Sarah said. "This is a veritable rogues' gallery. They all look so...menacing." She held the catalogue out to him.

"You know I don't want to see it."

"Just look at your own picture," she said.

He looked, and was startled by his appearance.

He had taken the photograph himself by setting the timer and then rushing to get in the front of the camera. That had been in January. Now, he barely recognized himself. His eyes appeared deeply set and this made his nose seem longer and narrower than it really was. The picture was black and white, so it was not possible to tell that his eyes were brown and yet, even so, there was something unsettling about the eyes, something dark and evasive. Did his jaw always show so much strain? And there was a slight tug at the corner of his mouth, not hinting at a smile but more of a suggestion of some secret that was his. The overall effect was indeed that of a sinister cunning, intense, someone to be feared.

Below the photograph he read:

RUSSELL BOWEN
Age: 21
Height: 5' 10"
Weight: 158 lbs.
Nationality: United States (Connecticut)
Trainer/Coach: Dan Lowry
Notes: Good feet

He said, mockingly, "Good feet."

"You're the one who wrote it."

"And I'm embarrassed by it."

"As you should be," she said. "But you didn't mention that you were All-State Cross Country Champion three years in a row. As a matter of fact, you really didn't mention anything revealing at all."

"Just part of the overall strategy."

"Ah, yes," she said. "The turtle in his shell. Blah, blah, blah." She began stuffing the catalogue back into the envelope. "Here's a strategy for you. Come out of that shell and do something else entirely. Go to college. Become a fire fighter. Or...why won't this darn thing go back into the envelope? Hang on. There's something else in here."

She pulled the catalogue back out, felt around inside the envelope and pulled out a piece of paper. A small card had been stapled to it.

She read in silence.

He drummed his fingers on the table.

Finally, she looked up at him. "It looks like you're going to have to learn something about one of the other potentials. Now."

"But I don't want to..."

"Just listen to this letter," she said, and then read out loud:

'Dear Potential,' ..."

She laughed. "What kind of absurd greeting is that? Is that all you are?"

"Would you please just read it, Sarah?"

"Fine. Here you go."

Dear Potential,

The committee wishes to inform entrants that, for the first time in the history of the competition, a woman has obtained sponsorship. Her entry fee was received with her application. Her name is Adriana Ortiz, of Mexico. She is listed on page 28 of the catalogue.

Ms. Ortiz has asked for an exception with regard to the second rule. She asks that she be permitted to cover her chest. She says this is not for added warmth or protection, but out of modesty.

After much deliberation, the Committee has decided to allow the entrants to decide this issue. Should you obtain sponsorship, please fill out the attached card and send it back to us before August 15th. Your vote will not be considered unless we receive the card by that date.

Our apologies for any infringement this may have upon your strategy and/or timing.

Sincerely,

Ian Rushmore

Chairman, The Kincaid Committee

Russell wondered aloud, "But how could she have possibly gotten a sponsor this early?"

"Maybe she's rich and paid the entry fee herself."

"Maybe," he said. "What does the card say?"

"Check the appropriate box, either 'Objection' or 'No Objection.'" She looked at him. "Do you object?"

"Heck yes, I object!" he said. "I want her to run buck naked!"

"You're such a jerk!"

"Seriously, I really don't care what she wears. A tutu, bikini...whatever she wants. But...a woman?"

"What difference does that make?" she said. "Women can be just as vicious as men."

He smiled at her. "Finally, you're making some sense."

She laughed. And tossed the catalogue at him.

That had been six months ago, back in April.

Now, in his hotel room, as he looked down at the parking lot, Russell wondered. Was it possible that the woman down there in the bright red hat and coat was a competitor?

The man who had arrived with her was pulling suitcases from the trunk of the car. The woman stood by and continued to press her hand against the stylish hat. Russell watched her and saw the fine lines of a dignified, elegant bearing.

Then, for whatever reason, she removed her hand from the hat. The wind took it at once. She moved with graceful yet sudden speed toward the hat, but stopped almost immediately, as if realizing the chase was futile.

The glamorous red hat was gone, rolling on its brim along the pavement, rising up and suddenly dropping back down, turning rapidly end over end as it entered traffic out on the main road, where it was crushed by a passing car. There it remained, a dark blemish in the road, as car after car ran over it.

Russell studied her as she moved back toward the car. She was leaning into the wind and yet somehow retained a dignified posture. She was symmetry in motion, as if all her parts were more than mildly familiar with one another.

Was she smiling at her friend? It was difficult to tell. Maybe she was grimacing. Or was she merely squinting against the wind? Without her hat, Russell could see that her dark hair was cropped short. Very short, almost a crew cut. Her skin was somewhat swarthy. She was beautiful, stunning. He doubted very much that someone like that would cross the line. But maybe....

For over six months he had resisted the temptation to open the catalogue and learn about the other contestants. He thought of this as a common sense tactic. True, forewarned was forearmed, but there was also a risk in preconceived notions.

Learning of the other competitors before meeting them might be dangerous, because it could interfere with the actual encounter once it took place; assumptions that had been made might prove to be without substance. Once made, however, assumptions were difficult to dispel. This might make a crucial difference later on. Thus, his approach had been to assume nothing about the other competitors, and the best way to do this was to learn nothing about them before the initial encounter.

Another part of his plan was to do exactly what he was doing right now: observe. Between the car and the hotel, when they thought no one was watching, he might be able to discern something useful about them. He figured that once they were inside the hotel, posturing would begin. There would still be things to decipher, but the discernment would have to be made through a haze of potentially false signals and cagey responses. Sitting here, on the bed by the window, he might just catch a glimpse of unguarded personality traits that would prove valuable later on.

It was part of the game.

He picked up The Kincaid Catalogue. Folded inside was a letter that had arrived two months ago. In part, the letter contained the "site notice," naming Burwick, Connecticut as the town where the competition would be held. The letter also contained the final list of those who had attained sponsorship.

Now he unfolded the letter and, for the first time, read about the other contestants:

"This is to advise you that, as of August, the following people have achieved sponsorship for this year's competition:
Christopher Alden, prior year Champion, U.S.A.
Russell Bowen, U.S.A.
Albert Girard, Canada
Yuri Kozlov, Russia
Mishima Nakamura, Japan
Adriana Ortiz, Mexico
Please refer to the catalogue for further information about the contestants."

He turned to the heading of "Mexico" in the catalogue.

She was not difficult to find. She was the only woman on the page, probably the only woman in the entire catalogue. Even though her hair was longer in the picture, there was no doubt. This was the woman he had just seen down in the parking lot.

His heart sank as he read her entry.

Not just a woman, but an Olympian. And not just an Olympian, a marathoner. She could probably run like a deer.

He watched out the window as she and her companion moved toward the hotel entrance.

Why would such a woman play this game? Her appearance was alluring. Her manner of dress was refined. Everything about her suggested femininity and elegance.

ADRIANA ACEVEDO ORTIZ

Age: 22
Height: 5' 6"
Weight: 118 lbs.
Nationality: Mexico (Puebla)
Trainer/Coach: Juan Flores, contestant in the 2002 running of The Kincaid
Notes: As of this printing, Ortiz has qualified for the Mexican Olympic Team: track & field, marathon.

"Look about," he said, cautioning himself.

He lay back on the bed, thinking of the beautiful woman who had just arrived.

Point of assumption: she would kill to win.

CHAPTER 4

NO TAKE

*A*t the moment, there was no activity in the parking lot. A few people had arrived after Ortiz, but they carried no luggage, so Russell figured they were probably hotel employees arriving for work.

He pushed the play button on the remote to restart the video. Once again, he heard the narrator's voice.

"In England during the fifteenth century, the Court of Oyer & Terminer was a commission of judges sent out twice a year from Westminster to visit each county. "Oyer & Terminer" is from an Anglo-French phrase meaning "to hear and determine."

The duty of this court was to preside over trials concerning treason and felonies, as well as to confront issues of both new and old law being considered in the higher courts back in London. The judges of this court arrived in Dorset in 1485. They had heard stories of people dying under suspicious circumstances on land belonging to Sir James Kincaid. They summoned him to court. The judges read The Kincaid Covenant, the contract Sir James had devised for his annual contest. A contract wherein contestants agreed that there would be no laws between them.

Whee of thys gamen are of na Lawes betwene us....

The judges were outraged. They accused Sir James of using the Covenant to suspend the King's laws. They demanded that the practice stop at once. But Sir James maintained that those who took part in the contest had agreed to the risk. No one was forced to enter the contest, and no one was at risk who had not agreed to the

Covenant. Surely, he argued, after consent there could be no crime. The contest was also confined to the limits of his own personally created "common chase," and in no way threatened or sought to dishonor the King.

But the Court of Oyer & Terminer countered that the contest was inherently wrong. It was "contra bono mores," contrary to moral good. Besides, they added, "Hyt acomptes natht for the Kynge." (It accounts naught for the King.)

Sir James understood the implication. A tax might make The Kincaid Covenant legal.

After much discussion, the judges stated that the contest would be allowed to continue in exchange for a tax of one hundred pounds sterling per year. For Sir James, this was too much. Paying such a high tax would have defeated his purposes.

He would not be denied.

He went to London.

Sir James was well acquainted with Richard, Duke of Gloucester. As mentioned earlier, he had served as Richard's second in command at the battle of Tewkesbury, a battle that had played a significant part in restoring Edward IV to the throne.

Edward had since died. Richard was now King Richard III. Because of their past affiliation, Sir James was permitted an audience.

He told the King of his dealings with the Court of Oyer & Terminer. He asked permission to hold the contest, but with a reduced tax. The King consented.

Though Richard III had consented by rule of "Rial Prerogatyue" (Royal Prerogative), it was only a verbal approval. Sir James not only requested something in writing, he pushed the issue even further. He knew that King Richard's hold on the throne was, at best, tenuous. Rumor had it that Richard had come to the throne by means of deceit. And murder. His nephew had been the rightful heir to the throne. Reportedly, Richard had the boy and his younger brother smothered as they slept in the Tower. As a result, Richard III was not looked upon with any great favor by the general populace or those in political power. Even as he met with Sir James, Henry Tudor was gathering forces to overthrow him.

So Sir James Kincaid did not want King Richard III's seal on the document. There was a good chance that seal would soon be worthless. Sir James wanted something more durable. He asked that the document be signed and sealed in the "Corte of Concente" (Court of Consent), a court that remained in place regardless of who was on the throne, and whose sole purpose was to see to "Wrytts of Rial Agreament." (Writs of Royal Agreement.)

Sir James' timing could not have been better. His request may have been a blatant affront to the King's political standing, but it was obvious that Richard III was in need of all the allegiances he could muster, even if that constancy had to be bought. In agreeing to the request, Richard is said to have told Sir James, "For nane bot a loyall." (For none but a loyal.)

By this time, most court proceedings were held in English for the benefit of the common man, even though the documents of those proceedings were recorded in Latin. Sir James knew Latin and seems to have had a hand in the actual wording of the document, for it would appear to grant permission not to him, but to the contest itself. This document would become known as the Writ of Kincaid. The translation of part of it is as follows:

"...for the sum of one-pound sterling per year, those of Contest Kincaid shall, to each and other in bounds of said Contest, be pardoned of offense to Law, and this privileged jurisdiction so persist for as long as Kincaid, in name and practice, shall be."

The document was signed and sealed, the twelfth of April, 1485.

Sir James returned home with the writ, confident that no judge or sheriff or any other magistrate could now stop him from holding the contest. He was called to military duty again later that year. On August 22nd, 1485, he joined with King Richard III to fight at Bosworth Field in yet another battle in the Wars of the Roses. But Sir James, along with many others who realized that the battle was lost, defected and fought against the king. It was during this battle that Shakespeare attributes Richard with crying out 'A horse! A horse! My kingdom for a horse!'

Richard was killed.

The Wars of the Roses finally ended and Henry Tudor ascended to the throne.

Sir James returned home yet again. He continued to hold the contest every November 10th. The Covenant was read aloud to the participants before they signed or made their mark in the book. Sir James paid the annual tax, and to this day the Committee pays the same tax to the royal coffers. This is done with little fanfare, in a quaint and quick ceremony. I, as Chairman of the Committee, bow before the Queen, and then hand over the sum of one-pound sterling so as to honor to the terms of agreement made so long ago."

Russell saw an enormous white van with a satellite dish on the roof pull into the hotel parking lot. A peacock, with its tail spread in colorful display, adorned the side of the van. The van moved to the far end of the lot and parked. A television crew emerged from the front and side of the vehicle. Russell watched them as they struggled against the wind with their gear.

Meanwhile, the video continued to play.

"Sir James Kincaid died in 1506, during the reign of Henry VII. Kincaid's son, Alexander, (1478-1530) continued the tradition each November, as did Alexander's son, Culver, (1513-1551), as did Culver's son, James II, (1534-1573.) As each generation continued to hold the event, word of the competition spread.

It was now the age of Tudor. Elizabeth I was on the throne. The common view of the universe was that of the Great Chain of Being. Power descended from God and diminished in strength as it passed through various stages, all the way down to the smallest of creatures. Social standing was also seen as divinely prescribed; there was no social mobility; a person died on the same rung of the ladder on which he had been born. Thus, certain economic freedoms were prohibited, for if competition were allowed to exist, social stability might be disrupted by people daring to move from one echelon to another by means of acquired prosperity. This would constitute a violation of God's Order and His Great Chain of Being. Laws and social programmes, such as The Statute of Apprentices of 1563, sought to stifle any urge toward unacceptable individualism. After all, man was put on earth for spiritual growth, not material gain. In the absence of competition, economic distribution was, in essence, controlled and guided by the state.

Contrary to this philosophy, and perhaps even in rebellious reaction to it, The Kincaid competition prospered. By 1569, people were coming from Cornwall and Somerset and Wiltshire to compete. It was not the gentry who entered the competition, but peasants, the people of the land. That a man might step outside his "divinely apportioned" place and actually gain, not by birth or inheritance, but by ability, was a revolutionary concept. To many, anything that could be achieved in this manner was an ill-gotten gain, a violation of the order of church and state. But to others, The Kincaid offered opportunity. It even appealed somewhat to the gentry, for here was a chance to improve their own lot as well, by gambling. Grain and gold and silver and sheep and horses and casks of ale were wagered by lords and earls, knights and sheriffs, in short, by anyone of means.

This, in turn, gave rise to sponsorships. For instance, if a nobleman wanted to bet on someone he believed stood a good chance of winning The Kincaid, he might pay their entry fee to ensure that his favorite would be able to compete. This kind of sponsoring became increasingly popular and served to further bolster the level of competition. It also increased the rivalry among those of noble standing who wagered on the contest.

Soon, pigs and sheep and the promise of services were no longer accepted as entry fees. Only coin of the realm would do. But when those with money began to lose their money in the wagering, complaints began. Some losers felt it was unfair that the competition was always held on the land surrounding Castle Kincaid. Locals obviously had the advantage of knowing the land better than people from other areas.

A meeting was held, here at Kincaid Castle, in 1608. Marcus, then heir to the Kincaid name, reluctantly agreed to a new rule: if an individual from another village won, then the next year the competition would be held in their village. This became known as the 'Rule of Victor's Realm.' In 1613, the competition was held outside of Dorset for the first time. It moved to Glastonbury, Somerset, and The Book of Kincaid went with it.

Word of the competition continued to spread. In 1678, the first foreigner competed. A Frenchman, Jacques Boucher, sponsored by the court of Louis XIV, crossed the Channel with a purse of gold for his entry fee. An uproar ensued. A Frenchman would try to kill an English deer. The competition was delayed while the Committee deliberated. It was decided that Boucher could indeed enter. His gold coin was as good as anybody else's.

Boucher not only entered; he won. He demanded, under the Rule of Victor's Realm, that the contest move to France the following year. But it was decided that no, it would not move to France. Victor's Realm pertained only to sites on English soil. And so it was, for many years.

But eventually a dilemma arose.

Competitions similar to that of The Kincaid had sprung up across the continent. But they lacked the prestige of the original. Little could compare with defeating the English on their own soil, and so The Kincaid attracted premier competitors from all over Europe.

In 1737, the contest was held in Kent. A man named Richard Wayland had sponsored the previous year's champion, and so assumed the duties, and garnered the profits, minus the fees due to Sir James Kincaid's heirs, of hosting the competition.

At this time, England was on the verge of another war with Spain. Tensions had risen over Spain's protectionism of her trade system in the West Indies. The English had been pirating Spanish ships. Treaties had been violated. King Philip V of Spain, in an attempt to wound English pride, sponsored not just one Kincaid contestant, but twelve. It was a tactical as well as a political ploy: to flood the competition with Spaniards. There were more foreigners than Englishmen. But the Spaniards, as instructed, would not put their money down without being guaranteed, in writing, that the Rule of Victor's Realm would apply to them as well.

Richard Wayland realized his quandary. If he refused their demand, the Spaniards would leave and take their money with them. But if he let them all enter and one proved victorious, he would then be known as the man who let the famous tradition slip from English soil. But perhaps he could get their money and also keep the competition in England.

He offered a deal.

Certainly, the Spaniards could enter. Yes, Victor's Realm would apply to them. But there were also two new rules. He enforced a time restriction. The competition would last only from sunrise to sunset. But he also instituted a far more severe constraint: no one could enter the forest with a weapon.

The Spanish coalition was at a loss. There was no time to send home for further instructions. Catching a deer without the use of a weapon was considered impossible, but it was equally doubtful that they would survive their king's wrath should he disapprove of their refusal to compete. Hoping to appease the potential royal anger, the Spaniards decided that six of them would compete and six would not.

Richard Wayland agreed.

The six Spaniards put their money down.

The competition was held.

By the time the sun set that evening, neither Englishman nor Spaniard had brought a deer to be placed at the feet of Richard Wayland. In future years, this would become known as a "No Take." It was considered a tie, a draw. As far as the gambling was concerned, no sponsors won any money, and no sponsors lost any money. Richard Wayland, however, did get to pocket the entry fees.

For the next seven years, the competition ended in a "No Take." But, in 1745, a German named Karl von Heinrich entered the forest without a weapon, yet returned with a deer, which he set at the feet of Richard Wayland. There was immediate questioning as to whether the man had cheated. Had someone gone into the forest and given him a weapon? Nothing could be proven.

Wayland had no choice. He surrendered The Book of Kincaid, and the contest moved to Germany."

Russell pressed the pause button on the remote.

Another car had pulled into the parking lot, moving quickly, tires screeching. The vehicle stopped abruptly. Two men got out. They were both short, but the size of each man was distorted by their matching bulky blue parkas; thin below the waist, sumo above. The man who exited from the driver's side looked much younger than his passenger. Even above the wind, Russell could hear the driver shouting. The words were indistinct, but the tone was obviously that of anger. Russell saw him kick the car door. Twice.

The two men moved to the trunk. The driver gesticulated wildly with his parka-puffed arms. He stomped a foot. His mouth did not stop moving. Suddenly, he folded his arms across his chest and gave a single firm nod to the other man. But the other man seemed to be paying little attention. He pulled the suitcases from the car, put them on the ground and closed the trunk. The driver watched, his arms still folded across his chest; a stance of defiant pouting.

Then the two men walked toward the hotel. The man who had exited from the passenger side of the car carried all three suitcases. The other still had his arms folded across his chest but moved with a sure, steady gait, ramrod straight, rigid against the wind.

Both men stopped at the hotel entrance. The older man put down the suitcases and held the door open. The younger man kicked over the suitcases and then, with his arms still folded across his chest, entered the hotel.

Russell wasn't sure what to think. The driver may have been in a genuine rage about something. Or maybe he was simply putting on a show, leaving a false trail for others to follow.

Russell looked again at the list of those who had achieved sponsorship. He chose the one that seemed the most appropriate.

"Mishima Nakamura, Japan"

He flipped through the catalogue until he found the listing for Japan. Well over thirty Japanese men were listed alphabetically.

"Nakamura...Nakamura...here it is."

MISHIMA NAKAMURA
Age: 22
Height: 5' 4"
Weight: 142 lbs.
Nationality: Japan (Yorimichi)
Trainer/Coach: Nagai Tanaka—Kincaid
Champion—2000.
Notes: Nakamura is a professional baseball player: shortstop; Yomiuri Giants. He was temporarily released from his contract with the Giants this summer in order to train for the competition.

Russell shut the catalogue and moaned in despair. "From the land of the rising son of a bitch!"

First, an Olympian. Now, a professional athlete. These people probably had access to world-class equipment and top-notch training programs. He imagined an entire team working alongside each athlete, everything being analyzed, from sleep habits to the proper angle of foot impact while running. He saw coaches and trainers with stopwatches and notebook computers. He envisioned sports medicine experts tending to the slightest injury, offering advice on healing and therapy. He saw dieticians with charts and graphs, ascertaining the proper levels of hydration, calculating proteins and carbohydrates ingested, calories burned. These people weren't mere athletes. They were products of science. These people were machines.

Russell's training paled in comparison. True, it had been grueling, but it lacked sophistication. Some of it had been positively bizarre.

After graduating from high school, Russell worked as a prep cook at Ricky Dee's Restaurant. Ricky Dee's was a small family eatery, nothing fancy, but the food was really good.

When he was not working, he was training. He ran barefoot on pavement. He ran barefoot through the woods. Ice, snow, summer, fall, he ran wearing nothing but shorts. He took freezing cold showers to stimulate his body to send more blood to his organs; he broke through the thin lake ice of December and swam about; all to harden himself to the elements.

He worked the night shift at Ricky Dee's. Often, after the restaurant had closed, he went into the walk-in refrigerator. When he closed the door, the light went out. It was cold and dark in there. A strange thing to do, but that's how the game would begin, in the cold and dark.

He spent countless nights in that refrigerator, running in place, doing pushups, sit-ups, and chin-ups. It was 38°F inside. He struggled to stay warm, to stay alert, to endure. He imagined all sorts of villains pursuing him. Sometimes he stayed in there until the massive steel door opened, the light went on and warm air rushed in, and there was Rick, puffy-eyed from having just gotten out of bed to open up the restaurant.

"Still in here, you maniac?" Rick would say. "Want some breakfast?"

Russell's "breakfast" would also be considered bizarre by most people. But he was serious about nutrition as one of the keys to success. He usually started the morning with a smoothie concocted of beet juice, bone broth, blueberries, kale, dried coconut, brown rice powder, chia seeds and bananas. He also practiced intermittent fasting three days a week to prepare himself for the inability to bring food along during the competition. On other days, he needed at least 3,500 calories a day, mostly sticking with pasta, grilled fish or chicken, and lots of vegetables.

On nights when he wasn't working, he ran in the woods. Running through a forest in the dark was dangerous. Low branches were a threat to his eyes. He ran with his hands held close to his face. He tripped on rocks and tree roots. It was insane. And necessary. After about two years of practice, he was surprised at his success. He had learned how to manage it instinctively, almost with a sixth sense. Somehow he sensed where to step, when to leap and when to duck.

When he ran on pavement, he did so until his feet bled. This was part of a long, slow process of forcing calluses to develop. He also used sandpaper between the toes and on the soles of his feet. That part had been excruciating. But his feet needed to be as tough as possible.

And then there had been the standing still. During summer months, he would stop in the marsh and just stand there while mosquitoes feasted on his blood. This was pure misery. He slowed his breathing. His chest rose and fell imperceptibly. He kept his eyes open, but didn't blink. The mosquitoes bit his lips and crawled into his ears and nostrils. He didn't swat at the bugs or allow himself the relief of scratching countless bites. He did this so as to learn to be still, regardless of aggravation.

"Still is a skill," he liked to tell Sarah.

Yes, absolutely still, because in the frenzy of motion, stillness goes unnoticed.

Maybe.

There were a lot of 'maybes' in this game.

And then there was working with Dan Lowry. That had not exactly been a joy either. Lowry taught self-defense at the high school. At least, it was called self-defense. But for Lowry, to defend was to attack and to attack was to defend. After all, he said, the War Department and the Defense Department were one in the same. So for three years after graduating from high school, Russell paid some of his hard-earned money to Dan for private lessons in boxing, Tae Kwon Do, wrestling and other methods of attack and defense.

Lowry was 40 years old, a former Green Beret. He was only slightly over five feet tall; but was fit, abrasive and officious; Napoleon with a migraine. Lowry was a tightly wound knot of discipline. And he could fight. He did his best to make the training as demanding as the competition itself. He tripped Russell, choked him, punched him, kicked him, threw spears and stones at him. He made Russell carry a sandbag around on his shoulders. 40 pounds. Then, 60 pounds. Finally, an 80-

pound bag of sand across his shoulders as he ran, dodging spears and stones, jumping hurdles out on the track, running, always running.

"Don't let me get behind you," Dan said, again and again. "Never let anyone get behind you."

The training was rough. And Russell had the scars to prove it.

Lowry also constantly warned him about fear. "Only the dead aren't afraid," he said. "Make the fear work for you," he said. "Lose your fear, lose your rear," was another of Lowry's growled ditties. Don't waste energy being ashamed of it, he said. Don't try to repress it. Fear was necessary, a survival mechanism. Courage lives in fear. So don't run from it or deny it.

The paradox, however, was that ultimately it did not matter what others did or did not do. From working with Lowry, Russell had learned the truth of all perils: the threat is from within. From *within*. Here was the greatest source of menace, for from within came laziness, fatigue, complacency. From within came arrogance and misplaced trust. "You are the most dangerous person in your life," Lowry told him, again and again. "Pay attention. Look about. Protect yourself from yourself, at all times."

This was more than a practice; it was a way of being. Looking in was looking out; looking out was looking in. This was the challenge, the test, the endless demand.

Endless.

What he had learned, he was now beginning to understand.

After the two Japanese men had arrived at the hotel, Russell felt an inner shift, as he recalled his training and Lowry's warnings. The fear, for so long a vague and distant turbulence, now appeared as a dark whirlwind coming closer, closer.

He braced himself.

Fear would not stop him.

He wasn't going to let anything stop him.

CHAPTER 5

NONE TO KEEP

ussell continued to watch the parking lot as the video continued:

"By the early part of the nineteenth century, The Book of Kincaid had traveled to Germany and to Italy, to Switzerland and Spain. The objective remained the same: to catch a deer. And Richard Wayland's rule remained intact—no weapons were allowed. Surprisingly, this had the opposite effect of what one might expect, for the rule served to heighten the mystique of The Kincaid in comparison with similar contests that had sprouted up across Europe. It was a rare competitor who could enter the forest without a weapon and yet come out of the forest with a deer.

The Industrial Revolution was underway, spreading across Europe and to the United States. The effects permeated all aspects of human interaction, even war.

In 1846, the Geneva Convention was created in order to establish rules of war. War would no longer involve raping and pillaging at will. There would be restrictions as to what soldiers could do with regard to the enemy wounded, prisoners and civilians. To tame war was to treat it as a machine; with just some minor adjustments it would run in a smoother, more civilized manner.

It was all seen as a simple matter of mechanics. Nothing needed to be random anymore. Man could control everything. Even himself. These new concepts of 'systematize' and 'control' inevitably filtered down into the world of athletics.

In 1867, the Marquess of Queensbury rules were introduced into the world of boxing, in an attempt to tame the brutish sport. The National Association of Professional Base Ball Players was formed in the United States in 1871. In that same year, the Rugby Football Union was organized in England. Over the next 25 years, the first tennis match was played at Wimbledon, the Amateur Athletic Association was formed, the International Olympic Committee was formed, the first organized hockey team appeared, and the game of basketball was formalized.

By now, The Kincaid Competition was also in need of reorganization. In 1882, a man from Geneva had won. According to the Rule of Victor's Realm, the competition would have to be held in his hometown the following year. But a problem was immediately apparent—there were no deer in Geneva. Added to this was the fact that, in previous years, a number of fights had broken out over who would control the purse strings for each contest. So The Kincaid Committee was formed. It would administer to the rules, the money and The Book of Kincaid. The Committee would travel from site to site, year to year.

The Committee's first act was to modify the Rule of Victor's Realm. This rule would now refer to the "Champion's Country of Citizenship," not merely to their hometown.

With regard to sport, the creation of governing boards and setting strict guidelines as to what could or could not be done on the field of play were new, but pervasive notions. In 1905, in the United States, 18 students were killed playing in a college football game. A public uproar ensued. The world watched as those brash and violent Americans, who had transfigured the game of rugby to their own liking, now sought to tame their creation. President Roosevelt met with leaders and coaches of college athletics. He demanded that the rules of college football be made more civilized. And they were.

As if in reaction to this attempt to repress the violence of competition in their own country, 43 Americans entered The Kincaid when it returned to England that next year, 1906. Combined with other nationalities, this meant there were well over 100 people paying an entry fee that year. They showed up wearing helmets and shin guards and elbow pads and heavy gloves and other bizarre protective gear of their own invention.

More people paying the entry fee obviously meant more money for the coffers of The Kincaid Committee. But this created another problem. There were too many people in the woods, bumping into one another and scaring off the deer. The contest ended in a "No Take" for the next three years. A change was needed, one that would make people less likely to put their money down but, at the same time, would not entirely discourage people from wanting to participate. The risk needed to be raised, as did the reward for assuming that risk.

To start with, the entry fee was increased; this, it was believed, would force people to consider their potential financial loss and thus hinder many who would have otherwise entered. The prize money was increased too, so as to encourage those who were more serious about actually winning.

But the Committee also wanted to generate more excitement. If too many years in a row ended in a "No Take," the public might begin to assume that it was simply too difficult to catch a deer without using a weapon; interest would wane.

Thus, two new rules were added for the 1910 competition. The contest would now last from dawn of November 10th until the onset of darkness, November

11th. This would give each participant more time within which to catch a deer.

The other new rule would eventually become known as the Second Rule. Since so many people had been wearing a variety of protective gear, it was decided that, regardless of latitude or longitude, nothing was to be worn above the navel, nothing below mid-thigh. So, though there was more time allotted, there was also a greater harshness to be endured. But who, the question was asked, would want to risk running around half-naked through the woods at a northern latitude in November? In response, the Chairman of The Kincaid Committee at the time, Allen Horn, reportedly said, "Those who wish to be coddled should stick with rugby."

The rule changes had the desired effect. Far fewer people were willing to risk their money to run through a frigid forest in nothing but a pair of shorts, without a weapon, in pursuit of a deer. Or, rather, it should be said, far fewer sponsors were willing to put down their money for such an endeavor.

At this point, I should note that The Kincaid Committee does not regulate who sponsors an entrant. A sponsor may be an individual, a group of individuals, a corporation or group of corporations, or even a government. France, Russia, Germany, Japan, China, Brazil, India, Spain and Portugal have all, at one time or another, sponsored an individual. The Kincaid appeals to national pride.

The Champion's place in society is distinct from that of the traditional athletic champion. In the vernacular of those who associate themselves with The Kincaid, the Champion has achieved something only the greatest explorers and adventurers risk, that of 'leaving fire.'

'Leaving fire' is an allegorical as well as a physical description. Those who cross the line in this competition have willingly left the fires of civilization behind. Thus, the

47

champion is seen as a true hero, one who has endured and succeeded at a trial of almost mythological proportions.

This type of enthusiasm might seem, at first glance, to be overdone. It is extremely difficult to run and catch a deer, but surely such a feat, in and of itself, could not excite the collective psyche of a nation. But there is one aspect of the game that has not yet been discussed here. It is the supreme element of the competition: fear."

Russell once again pushed the pause button on the remote. Another large van had entered the parking lot. Like the first van, this one also had the broad scoop of a satellite dish on the roof. More television people. Then a steady stream of cars arrived, 10, 20, 50. This made it difficult for Russell to assess people as they made their way into the hotel. He guessed that most of the arrivals were reporters, sponsors, guests, or friends and family of the runners. He saw Indian, Middle Eastern, Nordic. He simply chose from among the many faces and then went through the catalogue, looking for a match. He found none. According to his list, there were three runners still unaccounted for. It was possible that they had been among the crowd; if so, he had missed them.

Then the parking lot quieted down again. No one else arrived. No one else left.

He paced about the room. He did a series of pushups and sit-ups. He sat back down on the bed. As he munched on a protein bar he had brought in his gym bag, he considered the possibility that everyone had arrived who was going to arrive. Perhaps the Champion and the other runners had gotten by without him seeing them. They could be downstairs at the reception.

He was restless. He felt the urge to go down and watch the reporters and the other runners and their coaches. He wasn't learning anything here. Maybe. But then he realized it wouldn't be apparent until later whether or not what he was doing was of any value. He decided to stick to his plan. He would remain in his room, at that window, until the Champion's press conference, which was scheduled for 4:30 p.m. He picked up the remote control and pushed the play button for the final section on the history of the game:

"The Kincaid has, at its essence, remained unchanged since its inception in 1476," Ian Rushmore continued. "While the rules of the competition have evolved over the centuries, no one, for whatever reason, has ever made any sort of ruling as to what may or may not take place once the contest begins. It is this element that sets The Kincaid apart from all other competitions and, it has been argued, from all other human interactions.

Yes, there are rules that dictate how and when the contest starts, and there are also rules that must be met in order for the game to be completed. But the kernel, the very heart of The Kincaid, has managed to escape all tampering. In between the starting line and the finish line, there are, literally, no rules.

None.

For most of the year, The Book of Kincaid is stored in this glass case that you see here to my left. The Kincaid lineage died out during the latter part of the eighteenth century. The Committee purchased the castle and today uses it for offices from which to administer the annual competition.

The Book is believed to have been made specifically for the first contest in 1476. It consists of two boards of thin oak and an oak spine. The boards have been pierced with three holes. Three narrow pieces of rope pass through the holes and then through the pages, binding the book together. The boards have been covered with stretched deer skin. The tool work on the leather is particularly fine, with raised images of men and trees and leaping deer.

The book has been subjected to much use. As you can see, in places the leather has worn away, revealing the oak boards beneath. All told, a thousand pages, over 500 of which have been written upon.

Recall that Sir James Kincaid met with the Court of Oyer & Terminer in 1485. At that time, the court had attempted to impose a burdensome tax in exchange for permitting the contest to continue. Kincaid went to London and managed to get the Court of Consent to issue the Writ of Kincaid allowing the contest to go on indefinitely. Soon after that meeting, Sir James had these words inscribed on the cover of the book:

Consensus Facit Legem

Translated, this means: Consent Makes the Law.

Presumably, this refers not only to the writ, but also, and ironically, to those who would enter the contest. It is, in a way, a twisting of logic, wherein the words fall back on themselves. The only law between competitors is their consent that there be no laws between them.

When we keep the Book in the glass case, it is opened to the year 1483. In the earliest years of the contest, there is simply a listing of the entrants' name on each page. When people started arriving from neighboring villages to compete, the pages were then divided into two columns, one for names and one for listing the home village. But in 1483, another column was added. Here… you can see…

this third column was apparently an afterthought, for it is very narrow, the line drawn by an unsure hand. The script is small and barely legible. Above this column is a single word, in the Old English spelling: D-e-t-h. Deth.

Death.

As you may remember, a competitor was killed during the contest in 1483. One really needs to use some sort of magnification to make out the cause of death listed in the new column: 'Arowe' (Arrow). And here, in that same column, in 1484, Edward Aryle, of Bishop's Caundle, Dorset: '?', a mark which I feel safe in interpreting to mean "cause of death unknown."

In the years that follow, a number of other fatalities are listed in the book. Typically, the cause of death was attributed to arrows, spears, or knives. A substantial number of fates were also listed as "vnknawain" (unknown). Perhaps this means that the body was never found; or perhaps the individual simply walked away from the contest and returned to the safety of hearth and home.

After Wayland's Rule of no weapons was instituted in 1737, the deaths did not cease. But the cause of death was no longer listed. Instead, a line drawn through the name indicated that that person had died during the competition."

Russell turned to look and saw Ian Rushmore, the narrator, pick up a poker that leaned beside the massive stone fireplace.

"In order to even to begin to comprehend this game, one must imagine a thin line, very thin, as thin as possible. Usually, the line is no more than a trickle of lime...."

Now he dragged the end of the poker across the castle's stone floor.

51

"...or perhaps an impression made by dragging the pointed end of a stick along the ground. The line is nothing sophisticated, merely a means of demarcation."

In an exaggerated motion, he stepped over the imaginary line he had made with the poker.

"Once you step over the line, you are beyond all legal jurisdiction. It is that simple. By taking that one step you are free, in the broadest sense of the word.

Now imagine walking down a darkened alley in an unfamiliar city. You would most likely be frightened. Thieves or murderers could be hiding in the darkness. Your fear would arise from the possible violation of law at your expense. But in The Kincaid, an older and greater fear is aroused: there is no law to be violated.

To some, severing this tether might hold appeal. But it must be remembered that there is never just one competitor. Other strangers are running around out there in those dark woods. They, too, are free, in the broadest sense of the word. The first question to be asked is, of course: "What are they willing to do to you in order to win?" One option each competitor has is to simply stay out of their way. Hide behind a tree, perhaps. But if the goal is to catch a deer and win, then the ultimate question arises: "What are you willing to do to others in order to win?"

Tibor Novak, a Czech who competed in 1936, summed up rather nicely his experience of crossing the line. He said that with just that first step, he could feel the laws falling away. With that one step, he was without restriction. Or protection. A sudden fear overwhelmed him. In that instant, he knew that "absolute freedom is absolute terror."

Once the starting line is crossed, skin color, God, Buddha, dollars, drachmas, pounds, socialism, communism, capitalism and all other distinctions are left

52

behind. The individual is just that, an individual, stripped bare of all affiliation. This opportunity is unique in the human experience. Whether individuals form a group or remain separate, whether they deceive or are honest, aid or abandon, advance or retreat, is of no consequence to the Committee.

Ironically, the Committee exists only as a means to regulate the temporary obliteration of all things regulatory. Control is left to the individual competitor. In other words, between the starting line and the finish line, there is nothing to fall back on, nothing to appeal to, nothing to call in as reinforcement. The individual has no recourse other than himself. Many have claimed that this absolute aloneness, this absolute individualism…this is the true source of terror. To put an end to that fear, and return to the relative safety of the civilized world, all one needs to do is…."

And once again, Ian stepped over the imaginary line had had drawn with the poker.

"…. cross back over the line.

That, ladies and gentlemen, is all there is to it. That is the game known as The Kincaid. Thank you. And good night. And good luck to those who dare to cross the line."

The video had ended.

"To those who dare," Russell whispered and lay back on the bed.

His eyes closed. His mind drifted. He thought back to an evening in July of the previous year. He had just come out of the woods. He was wearing shorts. No shoes, no shirt, just shorts. The heat that night was oppressive, and the weight across his shoulders had grown heavy. Sweat stung his wounds. When he saw the lights of an approaching car, he scampered down into the culvert.

The car slowed down as it passed.

It was a police cruiser. He waited. The car picked up speed and went on its way. Russell moved back up onto the pavement and headed for the center of town.

Moonlight was dulled by summer haze.

He passed the Catholic Church. He was expected at that church in just a few hours for a wedding.

His wedding.

His parents were in favor of the marriage, even though they were Protestant and the ceremony would be Catholic.

But Sarah's parents were opposed. After all, Russell and Sarah were so young. Her folks knew Russell had no intention of going to college. Actually, he had no prospects other than that crazy game in which people got hurt or killed. But her parents were also worried the two of them might elope, so they finally relented and gave reluctant approval to the marriage.

Russell didn't really care about the church service. That ritual was for Sarah. But he did have a ritual of his own that he wanted to perform. Tonight.

He adjusted the weight across his shoulders and continued on into the heart of Turney, Connecticut.

Each streetlight cast a halo in the thick night air. As part of his stealth, he kept close to the storefronts, reducing his visibility.

"Hey you down there! What the heck are you doing?!"

So much for stealth.

It was a man's voice, loud and full of accusation, booming along the empty streets. Russell wasn't sure where it had come from, maybe from the apartments above 'Betaluna,' the bar where the locals and lushes hung out. But he didn't look back. He simply changed his pace from a quick walk to a full run.

The voice sounded again: "What the heck are you doin' with that thing?"

Russell darted left, out of sight, went two blocks, and then turned right onto Locust Avenue. He was worried. The person who had shouted was probably calling the police. He continued running and came to the residential area where Victorian houses were set close together. He was breathing heavily.

He turned left, then right.

The house finally came into view. The porch light was on, but the windows were dark. It was late. Everyone was asleep.

He stepped into the shadows of the alleyway and looked up to the open windows on the second floor. He called out in a tone that was hushed, but urgent.

"Sarah!"

He waited and then called out again. "Sarah!"

The silhouette of a human figure appeared at one of the windows. The female voice was an angry whisper: "You'll wake the dead!"

Oops. Not Sarah. No, this was her mother, Mrs. Wolcott.

She whispered again, this time with demand: "Russell, where on earth have you been?"

"I need to see Sarah!"

The fawn across his shoulders bleated.

Mrs. Wolcott's voice rose well above a whisper. "What in God's name is going on down there?"

Now the fawn let out a high pitched bawling sound as it squirmed against his grasp.

"Dear Lord!" Mrs. Wolcott exclaimed.

The alleyway brightened as a broad shaft of light came from the house behind him. The neighborhood was waking. People were getting out of bed, raising shades, turning on lights, drawing back curtains.

The urgency in Russell's voice grew. "Please get Sarah! Tell her to meet me out front!"

He went to the front of the house and waited anxiously in the darkness beneath the tree. He kept an eye out for dogs and neighbors. And the police.

Sarah came out the front door into the porch light. Through the thin cotton nightgown, her slender body was a silhouette. She looked to her left and to her right.

He watched her in admiring silence. Spirit of child, form of woman. Delicate and lustful, of flashing eyes and quick laughter, Sarah.

"Russell?" she said. "Where the heck are you?"

He stepped away from the tree, into the light.

She looked at him. She half raised her arm, as if to point at him. Or at the fawn. Or at both of them. She let out a gentle whimpering sound.

"Come on!" he said.

"Oh...Russell...!"

"Come on!"

"Where...what...?"

He turned from her. He walked toward the road.

She caught up to him and asked, "The fawn...is it a wedding present?"

"No."

"No?"

"No."

"Then what are...."

"Just come with me."

They crossed the paved street.

She said, "You're bleeding."

"The usual."

One of her slippers came off and she stopped to put it back on. She said, with obvious annoyance, "Wait a minute!"

He stopped and took an impatient breath. He was certain the police were on their way.

The irritation was still in her voice. "You show up at 4 in the morning and just expect me to come along with you to who knows where?"

"Yes," he said. He turned from her and began walking again.

"You disappeared before the rehearsal dinner was even over. Everybody was looking for you. People...."

"I know."

She ran to catch up. "People were pretty upset. It was embarrassing," she said.

"I'm sorry. I was running out of time and I...I had to do this."

"In the chase?"

He nodded. "Can you forgive me?"

"Mr. I-have-to-do-it-now-no-matter-what."

"I said I was sorry."

"I was afraid you had gotten cold feet!"

"In this heat?"

She giggled, and then, as if struggling once more to be firm with him, said, "Russell Bowen...tell me right this minute what you are up to! Where are we going?"

"Not far."

Their pace was quick, and soon they were beyond the streetlights of town.

"Stop for a second. I want to touch it," she said.

They stopped.

The fawn's white belly was pressed against the back of Russell's neck. He held the front legs firmly together in his left hand, the rear legs in his right hand. The fawn's reddish brown coat was mottled with white spots along the back. It held its head upright. The large ears were erect. The brown eyes stared at Sarah.

Russell rubbed his cheek against its flank. "Go ahead. Touch it."

She reached out.

The fawn's ears lay back against its neck. It bleated and squirmed.

Sarah backed away.

"It's okay," he assured her. "Try again."

She reached out again and this time was able to draw her hand along the head several times. "It's...it's spectacular."

"Yes," he said. "Spectacular."

And then they were moving again, side by side.

Crickets chirped. Fireflies sparked. Without warning, Russell went charging down the embankment and up the other side into the woods.

Sarah remained on the road. "Now what?"

"Follow me."

"But I'm not dressed to go into the woods."

"Come on. It will be all right."

She began to delicately negotiate the steep grade of the embankment, but her slippers would not hold and suddenly she was running, arms flailing, the white nightgown flowing, and she let out a cry of laughter as her momentum brought her down one side of the embankment but only part way up the other. She reached out and grabbed onto a sapling to prevent herself from sliding back down. She giggled. "Now I know why they're called slippers!"

Russell moved down the grade to help her. He took a firm footing. But with both hands on the fawn's legs, the best that he could do was to simply lean toward her, dipping one shoulder with the elbow out. Sarah locked her arm around his.

"All right?" he asked.

Sarah's face, the fawn's face and his face were just inches from one another. She looked at him, then at the fawn, then at him again. What was that in her eyes? Elation. Yes, he recalled, that was true elation.

With their arms locked together, and Russell walking backwards, they moved slowly up the steep pitch until they were on level ground. Sarah continued to hold onto his arm as they went a short distance into the forest.

"Far enough," Russell said.

They stopped.

"Kneel," he told her.

"What?" She laughed uneasily and looked around. "Here?"

He said it again. "Kneel."

Her tone suggested reluctant curiosity. "All right," she said.

She crouched down and then leaned forward with her knees pressed against the earth.

"Ready?" he asked.

"For what?"

He knelt down beside her. He leaned forward, easing the fawn off his shoulders onto the ground. Then he released both hands from its legs.

The fawn stood. But it seemed startled by sudden freedom. It just stood there.

Russell smacked his hand against the earth. "Run!" he shouted.

In a single, swift motion, the fawn turned away, lifting its front legs while pushing off with its rear legs.

And was gone, scampering into the vague shadows of the moonlit forest.

"To have and to hold," Russell said. "But none to keep."

He looked over at Sarah. Her gaze was set upon the vanishing fawn. She had both hands to her cheeks. Her mouth was open.

He said, "I do."

She looked at him and nodded. Her tone was solemn. "I do," she said.

He got to his feet. He held out his hand.

She took his hand and stood.

He kissed her.

He said, "Tomorrow, your church."

And the next day a ceremony was indeed held at her church. A tuxedo and a beaded wedding dress; friends and family and flowers; and music, wonderful organ music. Bach trembled beneath everyone's feet. It was glorious, Sarah told him later, absolutely glorious. But, she said, it paled in comparison to the night before when he had come to her with the fawn across his shoulders.

How far away that night seemed now. Back then, it was *someday* when he would run The Kincaid. The future was something merely talked about and dreamed of, something amorphous, a mere shadow. Now, someday was here.

He was startled from his reverie. He sat up on the bed and looked out the window. A van was pulling into the hotel parking lot. A car followed right behind it.

With quiet admonition he said, "Look about!"

The van had a troubled complexion, pock-marked with dents large and small. This was a carriage of rust on four wheels, leaning strongly to one side, as if one shoulder was lower than the other; the windshield was badly cracked and looked like an exploding star. Russell saw wobbling tires and a puff of smoke as it ground to a halt.

The other vehicle was a different species. This car was shiny, with no signs of wear; black, with dark windows; mysterious. It moved swiftly to one of the few remaining parking places. Two men got out. They pulled suitcases from the trunk. Both men had blond hair that was pushed back from their faces by the incessant wind. They both wore long dark overcoats, collars turned up. Their movements were sure, confident. They were chatting and laughing. Russell thought the taller of the two men was definitely here to cross the line. He looked younger than his partner, appearing fit, poised, unperturbed. His movements suggested strength and confidence.

Russell continued to watch the two men as they carried their suitcases across the parking lot. The younger man held the door open as his companion passed into hotel. Then the man, at the very last, just before he entered the hotel, turned, looked up straight at Russell.

And waved.

Russell fell back abruptly on the bed.

Caught. Embarrassed. Humiliated.

"Damn!"

He waited a few moments, and then sat up to peer cautiously between the curtains again. The man who had waved was gone.

Russell looked to the other vehicle, the dented, rusted van. A man had gotten out. From this perspective, he looked huge. He wore a red and black checkered wool jacket. But he was also wearing shorts, which was peculiar, considering the day was so cold and windy. He stood in front of the van, as if studying it. The van certainly could not have traveled very far, not in that condition. And Russell didn't see a suitcase. Which all suggested that the driver lived nearby and probably worked somewhere in the hotel.

Now the large man in the shorts lay down on the ground. Part of his torso disappeared under the vehicle.

Fixing his van.

Russell turned from the window. He read through the list of those who had achieved sponsorship. A Russian was listed: Yuri Kozlov.

He opened the catalogue to the heading "Russia," and went to the listings for the last names beginning with 'K.' He saw the face of the blonde man who had just waved at him from down in the parking lot:

YURI ALEXANDROVICH KOZLOV
Age: 24
Height: 6' 4"
Weight: 208 lbs.
Nationality: Russia (Vladivostok)
Trainer/Coach: Dmitry Ivanovich Federov—Kincaid
Competitor in the 1999 running.
Notes: As of this printing, Kozlov has qualified for the Russian Olympic Team; track and field; decathlon.

Russell whimpered and tossed the catalogue across the room.

Another Olympian. Another professionally trained athlete.

Doubt blossomed, darker than ever before.

What had he gotten himself into? He didn't have a chance against these people. They would demolish him. He should have listened to Sarah and her parents and even to the damn desk clerk downstairs: this *was* insane.

He should pack up his things and....

But he quickly countered, struggling to quell the rising tide of fear.

The other runners were afraid, too. Yes, of course. Everyone was afraid. Doubt and fear were part of the game, just a part of the game.

And besides, it wasn't all about athletic ability. The winner would need to understand the ways of white-tailed deer. There was....

His cellphone rang. He rushed to it.

He was disappointed because it wasn't Sarah.

"Oh...hi, Dan."

Dan Lowry, his trainer.

"Are you alone, Russell?"

"Yes."

"That's not good," Dan said.

"It's fine. Really."

"My apologies again for not being able to be there with you. But with my wife down with pneumonia, I just couldn't..."

"I understand, Dan."

"Talent..." Dan said.

"Dan...not now."

"Talent..." Dan said again, with emphasis.

"All right, all right," Russell said. "Talent does not win."

"Go on," Dan said.

"Intelligence does not win."

"Come on, Russell," Dan shouted. "Your life is on the line here!"

"Intelligence does not win!"

"All right!"

"Anger does not win! Strength does not win!"

Dan's voice was suddenly low and serene. "And so?" he said.

"Composure," Russell said. "Composure wins."

A few moments of silence passed between them.

"You'll do fine," Dan said, at last. "Just don't let them get behind you."

"I'll remember."

"I'll be up at dawn to light the fire."

"Thanks, Dan."

"Look about," Dan commanded, and hung up.

Russell went back to the window. The lights in the parking lot had come on. Typical New England fare: cold, windy, dark. The strange man in the shorts was still lying beneath his van.

Russell looked at the clock. Not quite 4:30 p.m. Go downstairs, he told himself. The reception has probably already started. The Champion must have arrived for his news conference by now.

Russell wanted to see how the Champion did in the spotlight. It would be revealing. But there was one more foreigner to arrive, wasn't there? He looked at the list.

Albert Girard, Canada.

Yes, the Canadian.

Perhaps Russell had missed his arrival. So maybe he should read about him now in the catalogue. No, he thought, he wouldn't break his own rule. He would wait to read about the Canadian until after he actually saw him.

He rolled up the catalogue and stuffed it in his back pocket.

He went out into the hall. When he looked to the left he saw a man at the far end of the hall. The man wore a dark gray suit. He seemed ominously casual, just standing there with his hands clasped in front of him. Security, no doubt. Russell nodded to him, but the man did not return the gesture. Russell stepped away, stopped, turned, and went back to make sure the door to his room was locked.

He went to the elevator, pushed the button and waited. The elevator door opened. No one was inside.

He stepped in, pushed the 'Lobby' button. The door closed. As the elevator began its descent, he took a series of slow, controlled breaths. He thought of Sarah. He thought of that summer night with her and the fawn in the woods and wished that....

The elevator came to a stop. One more deep breath.

"Composure wins," he whispered.

The elevator door opened.

CHAPTER 6

LIKE AN OX

$\mathcal{T}$ he lobby was relatively quiet. Two security men flanked the main entrance, stern in their stance, each wearing an earpiece and dark suit.

Russell went to the front desk and asked the clerk, "Where's the Champion's press conference being held?"

"Cancelled."

"Cancelled?"

The clerk shrugged. "That's all I know," he said.

"How about the reception? Where's that?"

The clerk gave a nod of his head, sideways, to his left. "At the end of the hall."

As Russell stepped away from the front desk, some sort of commotion caught his eye. He turned to look. He was unsure what he was witnessing.

At the hotel entry, two sets of glass doors were separated by a vestibule. At the far set of glass doors, closest to the parking lot, a large man was just entering. But what was odd was the man's approach. Apparently, he was too large to pass through the doorway in normal fashion. In obviously practiced motions that were exact and swift, the man bent sharply at the knees, lowered his head, turned sideways and came shoulder first through the doorway. However, the hat-thief wind continued to hold the door open behind him. He went back, pulled the door closed and turned to approach the second set of glass doors.

Now that Russell had a better view of him, he realized this was the same man who had crawled beneath the rusted, pock marked van in the parking lot. The closer this man came, the larger he seemed. He appeared to be at least a foot taller than the doorway. And a foot wider. When he arrived at the second set of glass doors, he pulled on both doors at once. But only one opened. And yet again he bent his knees, lowered his head, turned sideways and passed through the doorway into the main lobby of the hotel.

"Oh my God...," Russell muttered.

The security guards, previously so ominous and firm in their stance, now seemed somewhat tenuous about their positions. Both had mouths agape. One pressed a hand to his ear piece and spoke in a low tone. The other guard stepped back.

The huge man grunted as he looked around the lobby. The sleeves of his wool jacket were too short, exposing massive forearms. His hairy belly was visible because the hem of his shirt did not reach to his waist. The blue denim shorts had obviously been made from full length pants; cut off by an unskilled hand leaving a wavering hem; strings of fabric dangled against the massive thighs. He stomped his enormous leather boots. He passed a hand over his curly black hair. The dark brown eyes wandered in their sockets before finally settling on the desk clerk.

The clerk was as still as a statue, gawking at the colossus.

As were the security guards.

As was Russell.

For the average person, about ten paces separated the stranger from the front desk. He was there in three. His voice boomed. "Girard," he said. "Al Girard."

The clerk took a step back. "Girard?"

The huge man glared at him. "You need me to spell it for you?"

"Oh...ummm. From Canada. Correct, Mr. Girard?"

"Just check me in, pal."

Russell felt a surge of panic. This behemoth was the competitor from Canada.

Girard picked up a pen at the desk. But instead of signing the register, he snapped his head toward Russell. "What are you looking at?"

Russell did not reply.

The enormous man put down the pen. He moved toward Russell.

"Oh, hell...," Russell thought. And into the shell he went.

Girard stopped in front of him. He stood with his legs apart and his fists pressed against the hips, a monstrous akimbo. He looked down at Russell in intimidating silence.

Anything that Russell might say or do was risky. He might disclose something that could be used against him later. He didn't know what that might be, a word, a gesture, a tic, a smile. So he offered nothing.

"You crossing the line?" the Canadian asked.

Russel did not reply.

The giant moved closer. "I'm talking to you, little man! You running The Kincaid?"

Russell's heart beat quicker. He continued to stare straight ahead, at a point below the Canadian's sternum. He wondered about the height of the man. Seven feet? At least. And his weight? Three hundred pounds. No, more. Four hundred pounds.

Now Girard whispered, "Are you deaf or something?"

Still, Russell gave no reply.

"Hey!" Girard shouted. "You at the desk! Who is this guy?"

The clerk leaned over the front desk and looked toward the two men. "That's Bowen," he said. "The American."

"Bowen, eh?" the giant said. Now he bent down, legs straight, with his hands on his knees, the posture of an adult entering into conversation with a child. He brought his face close to Russell's. "The turtle?" he said. "That's kind of an old and obvious tactic, Bowen."

Russell could now see the dark eyes and the broad, flat nose. He could see the stubble on the cheeks and the protruding jaw. He saw crooked, widely spaced teeth. He smelled garlic and beer.

Russell didn't frown. He didn't grimace or flinch or let his eyes wander. Nothing. He would give this man nothing.

Girard let out a low grunt and brought his face even closer.

Now Russell could feel the air on his cheek as it was exhaled through the man's broad nostrils.

One of Girard's eyes closed and the other peered curiously into Russell's eyes. The enormous man said, "I've cracked tougher shells than yours, pal."

A bead of sweat trickled down from Russell's armpit.

Finally, Girard straightened up. He made a snorting sound, like an ox. He returned to the front desk. He signed the register. "The key," he said.

The clerk obliged.

"The reception?" the giant asked.

"It's in the Nutmeg Room, Mr. Girard. To your right. At the end of the hall."

Girard walked down the hall, thunderous, massive, passing Russell but not looking at him.

When Girard opened the door at the end of the hall, Russell heard sounds of clinking glasses and laughter escape from the reception room. He felt a sudden yearning at those sounds of cheer, sounds of life without fear, of life without threat. He watched the giant man bend sharply at the knees, lower his head, turn sideways in the doorway and then disappear from view as the door closed behind him.

"Whew!" uttered one of the security guards. The other guard let out an uneasy laugh.

"A big boy," said the clerk. "Yes, sirree, that's one helluva big boy."

Russell watched the guards as once again they assumed their silent stance of intimidation. He watched as the clerk returned to his duties.

Their lives seemed so straightforward, so safe. A part of him envied them their distance from the dangerous events about to unfold; and yet another part of him was eager for that danger. He turned from the clerk and the security guards and followed after the colossal man named Girard.

CHAPTER 7

ALWAYS THE SAME

*T*ables of drinks and hors d'oeuvres lined the perimeter of the Nutmeg Room. Several hundred people stood about, eating, drinking, talking. Chairs had been set in arcing rows before the stage. On the stage, a podium was flanked by a long table and more chairs.

As Russell moved about, he sensed anticipation and excitement. He heard Italian, French, Greek, German and a host of other languages, some of which he could not identify. People wore all manner of clothing, from tuxedos and gowns to blue jeans and T-shirts. He recognized several movie stars and politicians.

Waiters and waitresses came and went, trays of food and drinks held high. Here and there, people of various nationalities stood in front of cameras and bright lights, conducting television interviews; others stood alone in front of a video camera, engaged in a reporter's soliloquy.

Laughter rose and fell, ice cubes clinked against glass.

And there, unmistakable, was the only skyscraper in the city, Girard, massive, towering above the crowd, grabbing handfuls of food from a tray held high by a waitress. Russell saw it as an oddly amusing sight, one that was full of risk. The enormous man might live to regret that appetite.

Russell would play it safe. He would not eat a thing.

The Kincaid was one of the most heavily wagered upon events in the world, right up there with the Super

Bowl of American football and the World Cup of soccer. Millions of people bet on the outcome of this game. Office workers, factory workers, friends and family, big time gamblers and small time bookies, from Moscow to London and Tokyo to Mumbai, from one dollar bets to astronomical sums, just for fun or for tremendous risk, the wagering was known to be feverish. Billions of dollars were at stake. There was much to be won, much to be lost. Russell was well aware that there were people who would do whatever they could to predict or influence the final results.

He had read just about every word ever written about the game. He had read some of the books twice. The most informative source had been Malinowski's *Death Guards the Prize*. Malinowski had not personally written the book because he couldn't lift a pen or press a single letter on a keyboard. He ended up as a quadriplegic during the 1949 running when one of the other competitors pushed him off a rocky ledge. Ten people had been expected to run that year, but only seven crossed the line. A runner from Austria and another from Brazil were drugged at the reception; something had been put in their drinks. The runner from Hungary was poisoned later at the contestant's dinner. None of these people died, but neither were they in any condition to run the following morning.

In another book, *Forest of Fear*, about the 1962 competition, Russell read how a runner from Ireland had returned to his room after the contestant's dinner and found two thugs waiting for him. They shattered his knees with a baseball bat.

This competition began long before the line was crossed. So Russell wouldn't eat anything other than what he had brought in his gym bag. He wouldn't even drink the water unless he got it from the tap himself. And he would keep the door to his room locked at all times, so no one could tamper with his food supply.

He made his way through the crowd. He moved without destination.

Until he saw the deer.

Despite the room's large size, the warmth emanating from the fireplace offered an immediate sense of comfort. Floor to ceiling shelves on either side were lined with leather-bound books. Here and there were trophies, some silver, some gold, some in the shape of deer, others in the shape of winner's cups. The fireplace was tall and wide, a gaping mouth of burning logs.

The mantle and surround were of darkly stained oak. On the mantle were more trophies. Above the mantle, the stuffed head of a white-tailed deer stared blankly out over the room. In most ways it was typical of the species, judging by the shape of the ears and the antler configuration. But in one striking way, it was not typical of the species. This deer was white. Pure white.

Russell stood on the hearthstone in front of the fire. He stared up at the unusual sight.

"The ghost deer," said a voice behind him.

Russell turned. He recognized the man as the Chairman of The Kincaid Committee, who had narrated the video about the history of the game. "Ian Rushmore," he said.

"And you are Mr. Bowen, I believe," Ian said. His English accent was strong. "The Connecticut Yankee with 'good feet,' yes?"

They shook hands. "Pleased to meet you," said Russell.

Ian motioned with his drink toward the head of the white deer. "What do you suppose? Did the taxidermist just make it look like a ghost deer?"

"Perhaps. Maybe it's an albino or piebald that has been doctored," Russell said. "Or it could even be a normal deer that's been bleached somehow." He shrugged. "But a ghost deer? Around here? One percent chance. A rare creature, and if...."

"Indeed," Ian said, and suddenly looked devastatingly somber. His mild, affable countenance had given way to something far more stern and direct.

"Mr. Bowen," he said, "come this time of the year, I am a man of countless obligations. Harried is the word, actually. I do not get much time to stand around and chat. But one of my obligations is to introduce myself to the runners at the reception, before everything gets started. I've already spoken briefly to the others. You are the last.

I should tell you I am fluent in five languages, and am able to get around rather awkwardly in three others. But if I have to use a dictionary, or even a translator, I make a point of telling every runner the same thing." He paused, as if for effect.

Russell played along. "And what is it that you tell them?"

"If you're not afraid, you're not paying attention."

As forthright as the Chairman seemed to be, Russell was not about to reveal anything to him or anyone else about his fear level, one way or the other. So he simply said, "Thank you." And left it at that.

"What? Oh. Yes, I see." Ian said, and smiled. "Very well, then. Sorry to be so dramatic about it all. It's just that, after 18 years of doing this, and seeing how young many of the runners are, I feel obliged to warn them.

So many have crossed the line with no concept of the dangers that...."

A woman's voice, shrill and close to Russell's right ear, intervened. "Ian! You simply must come meet my new friend."

Russell now felt a jostling from his right as the woman nudged him aside and took his place in front of Ian.

"Really, Ian," she said, "do come meet him. Absolutely charming. Rather entertaining, with oodles of money. In cryptocurrencies, he says. But I rather suspect that he's actually some sort of thief. A civilized scoundrel. He's with the group that sponsored that handsome chap from Russia. I told him that we...." She turned to look at Russell, as if noticing him for the first time. "Oh, dear, am I interrupting something?"

"Ms. Isabel Milligrew," Ian said, "Meet Mr. Russell Bowen."

"Oh...," she said, suddenly deflated. "The American?" Her left elbow was now cupped in her right hand; she made a motion with her left hand, swirling the ice in her glass.

The way she looked at Russell reminded him of the sponsors he had met with last summer. They had poked and prodded. Some threw stones at him to test his reflexes. They looked in his mouth, like horse traders. They timed him in sprints and longer distances. One even held the lit end of a cigar against the sole of his foot, testing the thickness of the calluses. They quizzed him intensely on the habits and physiology of the northern white-tailed deer, *Odocoileus virginianus borealis*.

They had studied Russell literally from head to toe, and this Milligrew woman was assessing him in a similar, but silent fashion. She was as the gambler before the race, studying the horses in the paddock. And judging by the look on her face, she didn't like what she saw. Her grimace suggested distaste. Or pity. Russell wasn't sure which.

"Yes," she said. "Well…, I think I'll leave my money on the Canadian." She turned back to Ian and tugged on his arm. "Come along, dear, and meet my fascinating friend."

Ian nodded to Russell, and winked. "Must be off."

As Ian and the woman moved away into the crowd, Russell heard her saying, "That's the American? My heavens, Ian, it's like sending a lamb to slaughter. He won't…."

And then, mercifully, he could no longer hear her.

Russell moved on through the crowd. At one point he squeezed between the backs of two people and found himself before a small table set against the bookshelves. Alone on the table was The Kincaid trophy, a silver sculpture of a scene at the edge of a forest, set on a burnished wooden platform.

An identical trophy had been manufactured by the same London silversmith company for over three centuries, one for every year of the running since the reign of King George II. Stamped across the front of the base were the maker's hallmarks, flanked by two words 'Semper Eadem,' Latin for 'Always the same.' Perhaps these words were the maker's claim of consistent quality of craftsmanship through the centuries, or perhaps the words referred to the predicament represented by the piece itself.

On the trophy's oval platform, a tall, spreading tree stood among smaller trees and dense shrubs of undergrowth. A stag with a broad rack of antlers was out in the open, in front of the large tree; the deer's tail was raised and the right front hoof was held up off the ground. The deer faced a man. The man was also out in the open, among rocks on the hillside as if, perhaps, he had just stepped out from the undergrowth by the large tree. He was clad only in a loincloth. His posture was one of caveman stealth, hunched, knees bent and arms slightly raised from his sides as he faced the buck. He carried no weapon.

Russell had coveted this trophy since he was very young. He didn't just want to possess it; he wanted to win it. This had been the object of his passion. Over the years, he had seen innumerable pictures of the trophy, from every possible angle.

He admired the craftsmanship. The work was intricate, delicate, done entirely in sterling silver and....

Suddenly, he felt the presence of someone close, uncomfortably close. He looked to his left. He recognized the man at once.

Mishima Nakamura, the Japanese baseball player. Just inches away.

Nakamura was short and slender, with straight, thick black hair. He did not smile. He did not speak. He pointed at Russell and shook his head. Then he pointed at himself and nodded. He held his hand out toward the trophy and pointed at himself once more.

Russell made no comment, but he understood. Nakamura was saying that he, not Russell, would win the trophy.

Now Nakamura reached out to the trophy and touched the human figure facing the deer. Then he touched a finger to his own chest. He gave a single firm nod. He looked at Russell and smirked.

So the man facing the deer was Nakamura.

Russell nodded.

Time to come out of the shell, at least for a moment. Time to play the game.

The core of the competition, the absolute essence, was right there in the trophy's design, but was not visible from the front. Russell reached for the trophy and turned it around. Now a clever but subtle detail could be seen. Hiding among the exquisitely crafted shrubs was a third figure, a man in the act of throwing a spear. The object of his aim could not be determined. The deer and the other man were both in the line of fire.

"You don't need to speak English to understand that," Russell said.

Nakamura stared at the trophy. His victorious smirk disappeared. His thin lips tightened.

"The first rule," Russell said. "You forgot the first rule."

Now Nakamura's hands were clenched into fists. His body shook. He raised glaring eyes to Russell.

"You lose," Russell said.

Nakamura's right hand shot out, stopped just shy of Russell's throat and was then drawn back.

The speed and accuracy of the thrust had been startling. Russell did his best to hide his astonishment. He also resisted an instinctive urge to drive his knee into Nakamura's groin.

The little man could have killed him or, at the very least, crushed his windpipe. Russell kept his eyes focused on his opponent's eyes. He worked hard to subdue his ire and indignation. And fear. The object now was to maintain a placid, unaffected air. But he was ready to pounce. He would make Nakamura regret doing anything like that again.

The two men stared at each other in tense silence.

Russell gauged Nakamura to be a tempest in a teacup. The man's rage was obvious. But there was something else, something that sparked or perhaps accompanied the furor. Russell could sense it but could not name it. Nakamura wasn't angry solely at having been embarrassed by this incident at the trophy table. He had arrived loud and angry in the parking lot. He had kicked the car, twice. He had kicked over the suitcases before entering the hotel. And now, this. But, at the moment, Russell could identify only the rage. All else about the diminutive man seemed indecipherable.

Nakamura, still having uttered nothing, abruptly turned and walked away.

Russell let out a sigh of relief. He clenched his hands into fists, relaxed them, clenched them again, relaxed them. "Anger," he muttered as he turned away from the trophy table. "Anger does not...."

A voice called out: "Attention! May I have your attention, please!"

Russell recognized the voice as that of Ian Rushmore.

Ian was at the podium up on the stage. His smile was a suggestion, not a response. Again he called out above the din of the crowd: "Everyone! Please, listen up!"

The room gradually fell silent.

Ian continued: "If you would all kindly take a seat, we can begin."

CHAPTER 8

CONSENT

$\mathcal{T}$ wo men tossed an enormous log onto the fire. Sparks rose and disappeared up the chimney.

Most of the people in the Nutmeg Room had seated themselves. However, reporters stood by the bookshelves, some with video cameras, some with still-cameras, others scribbling in notebooks or typing on laptop computers. Russell had also chosen to remain standing, by the fireplace. He wanted to see, and from here he had an unobstructed view of the proceedings.

The giant, Girard, was not far away. He had pushed together two chairs and then sat, occupying both chairs at once.

Ian was up on the stage, still standing at the podium. Behind him, six people sat facing the crowd. All wore bright orange vests.

Ian raised his arms. "Welcome everyone."

As he continued to speak, there as a low murmur from the seated crowd as interpreters translated.

"To begin with," he said, "about last year's Champion. As I'm sure most of you are aware, he did not appear at the press conference. Actually, he won't be coming at all. He has injured his ankle and is unable to run."

"He chickened out, you mean," Girard called.

Ian gave a slight bow. "And for the editorial, we thank you, Monsieur Girard."

The giant raised a hand in acknowledgment. "Hey, any time, pal."

Russell pulled the rolled up catalogue from his rear pocket. He turned to the listing for Canada and read:

ALBERT GIRARD
Age: 29
Height: 7' 4"
Weight: 413 lbs.
Nationality: Canada (Ouelt)
Trainer/Coach: None
Notes: Occupation - logger

He looked over at Girard. The man was monstrous, unnatural, a freak. Each hand was bigger than Russell's head.

Ian was saying, "...our first ever female contestant, Adriana Ortiz."

Ortiz, the marathon runner from Mexico, was seated in the front row. She stood and turned to face the group.

Russell immediately focused his attention on her. The first word that popped into his head: firm. Limber but sturdy; certainly not the emaciated look of most distance runners. The white sleeveless dress revealed her arms to be defined, muscular. She had an elegant, delicately shaped head. A smile, but faint. Her dark brown eyes were certain, unperturbed. She gave away very little.

Ian said, "Ms. Ortiz finished fourth overall in the Olympic marathon this past summer in Rio. Since then she has been training just south of here, in Pachaug State Forest."

The crowd applauded.

Ortiz bowed, turned, bowed again to Ian, and then sat back down.

A turtle in her own right, Russell thought. She was playing it smart, revealing little that might be used against her later. Such a beautiful, strong, sexy woman. Her presence here was perplexing.

"Russell Bowen," Ian announced and pointed at Russell.

People turned in their seats to look at Russell. Camera bulbs flashed. Whispers rose.

Being the focus of so much attention was uncomfortable, but Russell managed to keep his discomfort from showing. He did not wave or smile or bow. With his hands clasped in front of him, he stood perfectly still, his eyes set on no one particular person in the crowd. He did his best to appear impassive and unconcerned with what was taking place around him.

"Mr. Bowen is a native of Connecticut," Ian said. "He has been training in the southwestern part of the state. Other than that, we know very little about him. Except that he claims to have good feet."

Laughter was followed by mild applause.

"Next," Ian said. "Albert Girard."

The giant stood.

A murmur of surprise passed through the group.

Girard tried in vain to make the shirt-tail reach the waistline of his ragged shorts. His exposed belly protruded.

Camera bulbs flashed.

The huge man growled, "Don't call me Albert."

Cautious laughter arose from some of the people. Most, however, continued to gawk in silence.

"How would you have me address you?" Ian inquired.

"Al."

"Very well, Al Girard," Ian said as he rummaged through his papers. "I don't seem to have any information about your training."

"Training?" the giant said and tugged indignantly at the waist of his ragged shorts. "I've been working, pal. Logging. My parents, uncles and aunts, brothers and sisters, cousins, they all pitched in to help me pay the entry fee." He pointed at Ian. "And you know why they did that?"

"Yes," Ian said simply.

Girard drew his head back. "Oh?"

"Because you will win, that's why."

The giant smiled. "And then pay them all back."

"Of course you're going to win, Mr. Girard," Ian said. "Why else would you be here?"

Laughter passed through the group.

Girard narrowed his eyes suspiciously at Ian. "Are you..."

"Thank you, Mr. Girard," Ian said. "You may sit down."

"I'm not finished yet, pal. I...."

"But you are finished, Mr. Girard," Ian said in a pleasant, but firm tone. "We are moving on. Please, do sit down."

Girard looked around briefly at the group. Then, without further argument, he sat back down on his two chairs.

Ian said, "Yuri Kozlov, from Russia."

A blonde man stood up. He wore a dark suit with a blood red tie.

Russell recognized him as the man who had waved to him from down in the parking lot. The other

Olympian, a decathlete. He looked no older than 18. Probably very strong, with exceptional endurance.

Kozlov was blushing. He bowed in every direction, each bow a jerky, eager motion. His blond hair flopped.

Ian said, "Mr. Kozlov won the bronze medal in the decathlon at the Olympics last summer in Rio. Since then, he has been training in Foster, Rhode Island, which is just east of here."

The crowd applauded. Some cheered and whistled.

Russell studied him. Kozlov could not be what he appeared to be. He was too good looking, too strong, too sweet, too…. much. Maybe he was like a Golden Retriever; on this side of the line, gentle, shy, almost timid; but being set free in the woods tended to provoke regression to primordial imperatives. Perhaps his harmless and docile manner was not guile, but neither was it the complete story. Perhaps.

The Russian continued to bow and nod and blush.

"Thank you, Mr. Kozlov," Ian said at last.

The Russian sat down.

"And our final entrant," Ian said, "Mishima Nakamura."

The diminutive man rose and turned to face the crowd.

Wiry and quick, Russell thought. Very quick.

Nakamura pointed at Russell and glared.

Russell felt uneasy, but saw nothing new in Nakamura. The man was positively fierce; he hid nothing. He was a wolf in wolf's clothing. But the aura of some unnamed facet remained; Nakamura was determined, stubborn, full of rage, and…and….

"Mr. Nakamura plays baseball for the Yomiuri Giants in Japan," Ian said. "He left the Giants early in the past summer in order to train just north of here, in southern Massachusetts."

Among the flashing camera bulbs, Nakamura continued to point at Russell until finally a hand appeared on Nakamura's shoulder and tugged at him. He sat back down.

That was it. Five runners. Russell wished there were more than five, so as to keep the deer moving. Out of all, only Ortiz seemed questionable; too delicate and feminine. Running marathons on track and pavement was indeed taxing, but it was tame compared to running barefoot through the New England woods in November, chasing while being chased. Still, there was something enigmatic about her.

"I realize," Ian Rushmore said, "that, by now, those of you in the running must be well acquainted with the rules of this game. Even so, one of my responsibilities is to ensure that no one crosses the line who has not been made fully aware of what it is they are about to embark upon. Of the few rules that we do have, some need further explanation.

Though the first rule really needs no explaining, neither can its' import be overly emphasized. It is fairly straightforward. But in the many years I've been associated with this game, I've been disturbed by the number of novices who take the first rule as advice rather than edict. I assure you...no, I warn you...that the first rule is indeed a *mandate*."

He paused, casting a serious gaze over the group. An uncomfortable period of silence elapsed before he at last said, "Look about."

Heads nodded; a murmur of discussion arose among the group.

Ian continued. "The second rule is as follows: you will wear nothing above the navel, nothing below mid-thigh. Mid-thigh is recognized at that point measuring half way between the center of the greater trochanter and the center of the patella. Simply put, halfway between the knee and what most refer to as their hip bone. We offer some leniency with regard to this rule, but not much. Contact lenses are permitted. Eyeglasses, because of the protection they afford, are not permitted. No hats, no headbands. No kerchiefs. Also, no belts. Go naked, if you choose. Protection of the genitals is permitted. But no jock straps are to be worn. We try to limit those things that might be used for purposes other than clothing, such as a belt, sash, things with straps and so forth.

Now along this same line, we have the issue of scents. The use of scents is permitted. Raccoon urine, fox urine, doe in estrus urine, buck in rut urine…whatever it is that hunters use these days to attract their prey…be my guest. But please, if you intend to use one of these scents, we ask that you wait until after dinner to do so."

More laughter arose.

Out of the corner of his eye, Russell noticed that Girard had turned to look at him.

"You going to put on some turtle piss, Bowen?" he called, and then delicately touched behind each ear, like a woman dabbing on perfume.

Russell couldn't restrain a smile.

Ian was saying, "…doubt as to the acceptability of what you intend to wear? Bring it forward this evening. Once we arrive at the starting line, there will be no discussion. And while we're on the subject…" and now he held up a piece of dark clothing.

Members of the media drew in close.

Camera flashed.

People pointed. Voices were raised.

"Obviously..." Ian said, loudly, and then waited for the room to quiet before continuing. "Obviously, this piece of clothing has generated some heated discussion. As you all know by now, Adriana Ortiz sought and received dispensation with regard to the second rule. She asked that she be able to cover her...her...upper chest area. The decision was left to the contestants. Including the Champion's vote, the results were five to one in her favor. Ms. Ortiz has graciously agreed that, since she received special consideration, she would submit the clothing for inspection." He held the clothing up high. "Anyone?"

Russell didn't care what Ortiz or anyone else wore. But this was an opportunity: clothing speaks.

He made his way down the aisle.

All eyes were on him.

He looked at Ian. "May I?"

Ian stepped forward and handed him the clothing.

Russell turned the garment over in his hands. It was a type of sleeveless, one-piece race suit. The fabric looked familiar. He was then stunned to see on the back, in block white letters: 'KALYPSO'.

But she wouldn't have....

Keep looking, he told himself, just keep looking.

He found no buttons. No zippers. No straps. But how did she get into it? She probably just stepped in through the mostly open back. All in all, it was an intelligent design. Sleek. Nothing to get snagged. Thick padding at the genital area. Instead of being deeply cut at the hips like a typical bathing suit, it came down like shorts to hug the thighs. Smart. This reduced the possibility of a stick or branch getting caught, while adding warmth and protection. Was there a pocket on the rear of the right thigh? No. He tried the other one. Yes; on the rear left thigh was a slit, no flap. Very good. He had learned a lot about Ortiz. She was left-handed. And she would chase.

Suddenly, the piece of clothing was gone.

He looked up.

Nakamura had yanked the garment from Russell's hands and was now tugging at it, looking inside, inspecting it.

Russell stared at him. This bonsai had outgrown its pot. He felt the urge to pummel Nakamura. Instead, he simply looked at Ian. "Thank you," he said. Then he turned and walked away. After only a few steps he felt something soft hit him on the back of his neck.

Gasps arose from the crowd.

Russell didn't need to turn around. He knew what had happened. Nakamura had thrown Ortiz's garment at him. He didn't break stride, just kept right on, smiling all the way. By the time he had returned to his spot by the fire, something was going on at the front of the room. Nakamura had apparently retrieved Ortiz's garment and was now shaking it at Rushmore while speaking harshly to him.

Ian looked to the people in the seats. "Since most of you do not understand Japanese, I will translate. Mr. Nakamura is annoyed. His complaint is, in part, about what he believes women are doing to the traditional structure of society. I told him that his comments on such things were irrelevant to the issue at hand.

He has also complained about Ms. Ortiz's clothing. He says it is unfair. It violates the second rule. It gives Ms. Ortiz the advantage of added warmth and protection. I told him that his objection has been noted, but that he has been out-voted on the issue. I also reminded him that there is still time to withdraw if he so chooses. His sponsors will receive a full refund of the entry fee. I also warned him this offer is only valid until three o'clock tomorrow morning. After that, there will be no refund. He indicates he has no intention of backing out."

Nakamura and he spoke to each other again in Japanese. The tone was clear. Nakamura was furious.

Russell watched, along with the rest of the crowd.

Nakamura now stared at Ian in silence. He abruptly tossed the clothing at him, hitting him in the face with it, and then stormed back to his seat.

Cameras flashed. A murmur of surprise and unease passed through the group.

"Yes…well…," Ian said. "Let's move on to the third rule, shall we? The third rule: you will take nothing with you. No weapon. No compass. No food. No drink. No…, well, as it says: nothing. The forest will be at your disposal. Make a spear. Make a bow and arrow. But there will be a brisk search of your person before you cross the line. You will have nothing in your possession when you cross."

Cross the line. Russell had heard and used the phrase thousands of times. And now, for the first time, the phrase sounded ominous. He sensed darkness and fear. He had to struggle just to remain still.

Cross the line…cross the line….

Ian rummaged through papers as he said, "Those, ladies and gentlemen are the rules for the start. Tomorrow morning, at the Charge, we will review the rules for completion.

Now, about the early morning...." He turned, proffering a hand to the six people sitting behind him. "Our committee members will act as reeves," he said. "There will be more than just these six, many more." He turned to once again face the audience. "Reeve is an old English word. Long ago, a reeve was a type of policeman in the shires of England. Shire reeve. From it, the word 'sheriff' was derived. Consider it to mean that these people have a certain amount of authority. Think of them as ushers or guides. There will be the usual commotion in the morning; darkness and confusion. If you become lost, or have a question, or are in need of anything else, look for an orange vest. We will all be wearing one."

He looked down at his notes. He ran his hand through his hair. "I plan to begin the Charge at 4:45 a.m. tomorrow. Dawn is at 5:01 a.m. Sunrise, 6:31 a.m. The temperature at five o'clock tomorrow morning is predicted to be...are you ready for this? When you cross the line, the temperature will be about 0 degrees Celsius. That's 32 degrees Fahrenheit."

Gasps arose. Teeth chattered. People shook their heads and shivered and laughed.

"The good news?" Ian said cheerfully. "It should warm up close to 45 degrees Fahrenheit during the day, which translates to just over 7 degrees Celsius. The weather forecast is clear and sunny. A beautiful autumn day in New England. But a cold front will approach during the latter part of the afternoon. Possible rain by sunset, which is at 4:31 p.m.

Dark descends at 6:04 p.m. After dark, the temperature is expected to drop dramatically. The rain will turn to sleet and then to snow. Four to six inches of snow are predicted to fall tomorrow night. Wind will gust out of the northeast at 35 to 40 knots. In this part of the world, this kind of storm is referred to as a nor'easter. Powerful. And rather early for such a substantial snowstorm. But, there you have it."

The information stimulated more conversation and more gasps from the group.

"The game will end at dawn on the eleventh," Ian said, "which occurs at 5:03 a.m. My advice? Get this thing completed before the snow falls tomorrow night."

Now there were murmurs of agreement and nodding of heads.

Ian raised his voice. "Here it is. Listen well...." He waited until the group quieted down. But even so, a few of the translators were still speaking. Ian continued to wait. Then, there was absolute silence. All eyes were on Ian as he raised his fist high and then brought it down hard against the wooden podium, once, twice, three times. And each time the sound reverberated throughout the enormous room.

Boom!

Boom!

Boom!

"That," Ian said, "is the sound of First Notice. At 3:00 o'clock tomorrow morning, each contestant will hear three knocks on their door. No one will call out to you. No one will wait for a reply from you. Three knocks. This is what we call First Notice. The French, being French, have come up with their own term for this moment. They refer to it as 'La premiere terreur." Translation? First terror. If you fully understand the implications of crossing the line, the sound of First Notice should indeed strike the fear of God in you. I hope it does. If it does not, I suggest you go back to bed and forget about the contest."

He waited as the nervous laughter rippled through the group.

"If you hear those three knocks on your door, you are in. And your sponsor's money is ours. After that point, no refunds will be given to any sponsor for any reason. Before 3:00 o'clock tomorrow morning you may withdraw at any time, but only by speaking to me in person. No texts, emails, or calls on the phone. People here at the hotel know how to contact me. Simply call down to the front desk and ask to get in touch with me. Again, you must come to me to withdraw. I hope that is clear." He nodded. "Very well, everyone. First Notice is at 3:00 a.m. You will then have 15 minutes to board the bus. No more, no less. The bus will leave from the front of the hotel promptly at 3:15 a.m. Contestants and interpreters only. Members of the press, bystanders, friends, family and sponsors will need to make their own arrangements for transportation." He paused. "Any questions?"

There were none.

"Then we'll close out with the Covenant." He pointed to the five small stacks of papers set beside an enormous book on the table to his right. "I trust that each runner has read the sample Covenant in the catalogue. There is one here for each of you, in your native tongue.

One of the last sentences in it is of the utmost importance. It reads as follows: '*I understand that I have the right to legal counsel before I sign this document.*' If you do wish to consult with an attorney before signing, see me. Arrangements will be made for you. In order for you to board the bus tomorrow, you must have the

Covenant with you and it must be signed, dated, and witnessed. No Covenant, no run. Clear?"

"Clear!" Girard returned loudly. "Can we wrap this thing up, pal? I'm hungry."

Some of the resulting laughter sounded like ridicule, some sounded like actual amusement.

"In good time, Mr. Girard," Ian replied, calmly. "First, the Book. Contestants, please come up front and sign this wondrous, historical book. Then pick up your copy of the Covenant and wait at the far end of the table."

Russell went to the front of the room. He stood behind Adriana Ortiz as she signed the book. He wanted to think of her as just another runner. But her delightful shape prevented him from doing so. He looked away.

Ortiz moved on. Russell stepped forward.

He was startled to be standing by the actual book. *The Book of Kincaid*. A thousand pages. And over five hundred pages used, one per year. It was splendid. So much history. He looked at the front cover and saw the words:

Consensus Facit Legem

"Consent makes the law," he whispered.

He flipped through some of the pages, through year after year. Incredible. All those people had signed their names or made their mark. Hundreds and hundreds of years of people... people who once laughed and cried and ate their food and loved and feared and lit their fires...just like him. And just like him, they had wanted to win the prize. And now they were all dead. It was so mysterious. Wondrous. So many pages and so many names. He had never felt so mortal. He had....

"Please sign, Mr. Bowen," Ian said.

Russell flipped back to the appropriate page. He picked up the pen. He read what had been written at the top of the page:

Year of the Running: 2020
Place of the Running: Burwick, Connecticut, U.S.A.

We of this contest are of no laws between us, neither in benefit nor in burden, except those of God, of Conscience, and of Nature.

He signed in the first column:
Russell Bowen
In the second column, for hometown, he wrote:
Turney, Connecticut, USA
He moved to his right. The Covenants were laid out on the table, white papers evenly stacked. He read the first line of the second stack:

'I, Russell Bowen....'

He picked up his stack and went to stand in front of Ortiz. She gave him a quick smile. Russell bowed slightly, shook her hand and then stood beside her.

She had barely looked at him. And her handshake was quick, neither weak nor strong. She was being clever. Keeping to herself, all the way.

The others signed in.

Girard shook hands with Ortiz, saying, "Nice to meet you, honey." He then moved to stand in front of Russell.

Russell was prepared to have his hand crushed until he fell to his knees and howled in pain. But the giant's handshake was surprisingly limp, even weaker than Ortiz's had been.

Girard smiled, revealing teeth that went every which way. He winked. "I can play the turtle, too, pal." He took his place next to Russell.

Kozlov came next. The Golden Retriever. His hair flopped as he bobbed up and down. He smiled incessantly as he shook hands with Russell.

"Honor to me," Kozlov said. "Honor to me."

His handshake was strong. And endless. The man was definitely a charmer. Either awkward or cunning.

Nakamura shook hands with no one, looked at no one. After signing, he went directly to the end of the line, next to Kozlov.

"Ladies and gentlemen," Ian announced. "Our entrants for the year 2020 running of The Kincaid."

The applause was loud. People stood and cheered. More cameras flashed.

"Let me reiterate," Ian said loudly as he once again faced the line of contestants. He raised his arms for quiet. "Before we go into dinner, let me reiterate: First Notice is at 3:00 a.m. I recommend you set your alarm clocks and/or have someone from the front provide a wakeup call. And remember: no Covenant, no run." He looked at his wristwatch. "Nine hours, 27 minutes until First Notice."

CHAPTER 9

CIVILITY

𝒯o his right sat the Russian, Kozlov. Kozlov and his translator seemed quite at ease, talking as they ate. Next to them sat Nakamura and his translator. To the left was Ortiz's translator, then Ortiz, and next to her, Girard. At the opposite end of the table from Russell was the Champion's seat, which was empty.

The dining room was crowded and noisy. At a table to his left, Russell saw Richard Beck sitting by Ian Rushmore. Beck was the senior Senator from the State of Connecticut. His head of wavy, silver hair was easily recognizable. With a silver tongue to match, or so it was said. He had fought hard for the game when State courts ruled that it couldn't take place within the State of Connecticut due to its inherent violence. Senator Beck made it into a constitutional issue: Freedom of Assembly. The case ended up in the Federal Court, which ruled, rather obtusely, that no violation of law had yet taken place, nor did there appear to be any intent to break the law. Thus the State had no standing to intervene. The game could proceed. This angered a lot of people.

The Senator had then angered even more people when he said that The Kincaid represented the American ideal because it made cultural heritage a meaningless notion. This game stripped the individual of culture and tossed him into the woods. Just like that. "What could be more exciting or demanding?" the Senator wanted to know. "And what could be more

American?" The game failed to acknowledge any difference between people. Cultural diversity became trivial and irrelevant. But the Senator's comments were considered politically incorrect and served to aggravate the situation. Several groups protested the court ruling, to no avail. So it was little wonder that Senator Beck was now beaming as a cameraman stopped in front of his table. Beck had won a significant political victory. And for him, this must have been a type of victory party.

Russell felt someone tap his arm. He turned.

"No eat?" Kozlov asked, straining at English.

Russell shook his head. "No, I'm not eating." He lifted his plate of food and offered it to the Russian.

Kozlov nodded with enthusiasm as he accepted the plate. The blond hair flopped. "Yes. Yes. Thanking you. Many times."

Russell smiled and nodded.

Kozlov put down his knife. He extended a hand to Russell. "God luck."

Russell could not restrain a smile.

Kozlov was charming. Maybe his English was as weak as it seemed. Or maybe there was some sort of Russian phrase that had a similar meaning to both 'God be with you' and 'Good luck.'

Or maybe he was testing Russell somehow. This game did strange things to people. Every nuance was a possibility of intent, strategy, character. It was the interpretation that was frustrating. Who ever knew what anyone else was really thinking?

And yet it was pretty simple. Kozlov was, no doubt, determined to win. He was probably under tremendous pressure from the Russian government to win in the name of national pride and justify the investment they had made in his training. And if Russell got in his way, Kozlov would probably try to kill him.

He shook Kozlov's hand and said, "Good luck."

And it was then, as they shook hands and smiled at one another that Russell saw it. That glint in the eye, an ever so brief but telling glint in....

The table shook.

Silverware jumped.

Water glasses toppled.

Girard had pounded his fist on the table.

The room was immediately silent. Waiters and waitresses stopped in their tracks.

Girard stared at Nakamura's translator and roared, "What did he just say?"

The translator shook his head, as if refusing to comply with Girard's demand.

The giant stood. His chair fell over backwards. His face was red. While looking across the table at the translator, he pointed at the baseball player, Nakamura. "*What* did he say?"

All eyes but Russell's were on the huge man. There was no need to watch Girard. The giant was so obvious as to be transparent. Russell watched the others.

Ortiz acted as though this was all just a part of normal dinner conversation. She continued chewing her food, glanced up at Girard, nodded, maybe even smiled a little. Unperturbed, that was the word for her. But her translator had jumped up pretty quickly and moved away from the table. Kozlov's translator had done the same. They stood behind their chairs, napkins in hand, ready to bolt.

But little Nakamura had stood and, with his waist pressed to the table, was leaning toward the giant, glaring.

Nobody's strategy was more obvious than that of Girard. There was no need to provoke him. So what was it that Nakamura wanted? This was more than just teasing. This was something ruthless, cruel.

"What did he say, goddamn it?!" the giant shouted.

The translator replied in a faint voice, "Mr. Nakamura say, 'Big body, little brain.'"

From somewhere in the otherwise silent dining room came a single snort of restrained laughter.

Girard extended his arm across the table. Nakamura simply leaned back, avoiding the massive reach. The giant moved as if he would come around the table. "I'm gonna break your smartass puny...."

Ian Rushmore stood, napkin in hand. "Please, please, please...!"

The giant stopped.

"Mr. Girard and Mr. Nakamura," Ian said sternly, "I demand civility before the line. Both of you, please sit down."

Civility before the line, Russell thought. That's a good one. But where is the line, exactly?

Girard waved a hand in Ian's direction. "Yeah. Okay, okay."

Nakamura's smile was both sly and vicious.

The giant pointed at him again. "But I'm gonna get you, pal."

People reseated themselves. A buzz of conversation filled the room. Waiters and waitresses resumed their duties.

Nakamura sat down.

Girard reset his chair and, while still standing, put his hand on the elegant, lovely head of Ortiz. He said, "Didn't mean to scare you, honey."

Ortiz dabbed her napkin to her mouth. She stood and faced the immense man.

He smiled down at her.

It was swift, exact, coming up from down low, her knee into his groin.

Girard dropped to the floor at once. His mouth opened and his eyes closed. A retching sound came from deep in his throat. One hand clutched at the table, while the other hand was set protectively between his thighs.

A woman screamed. Other people gasped.

Ortiz spoke. The words jerked and rolled. "Not me touch!" she said. She sat back down. She placed her napkin in her lap, calmly picked up her knife and fork, and resumed eating.

Girard now lay on his back on the floor. He rolled from side to side with both hands between his thighs, groaning.

People rose from their seats and came to his aid.

Russell had seen enough. He stood, gave a quick bow to those still seated at the table, and left the room. He went back up to the second floor.

It was time to study.

The security guard was not in the hallway.

Russell put his ear to the door of his room. He didn't hear anything.

He put his hand on the doorknob and gently turned.

The door opened, just a crack. It was not locked. But he was certain he had locked it before heading downstairs.

Someone had been in his room. Or maybe was still in there.

He kicked the door and jumped back as it banged against the wall.

CHAPTER 10

ALL WEARS AWAY

She was standing by the window. The curtains were open. On the sill sat a bottle of wine, and a glass, partially filled. She whipped around to face him, obviously startled.

"Jeez Louise, you scared the daylights out of me!"

"Sarah? But I thought...."

"As if I wasn't scared enough already!"

"But...how did you get in here?"

"Not easily," she said.

He shut the door. "There's supposed to be a guard out in the hall."

"I don't know about that," she said. "But they're frisking people at the front door."

"You...."

"I told them that I was Ms. Russell Bowen. Showed them my ID. They let me in. Hey, aren't you glad that I came?"

He was unsure. And let her know it. "Should I be?"

She said, "I had to come."

"And I see you brought wine. You didn't happen to bring any bread and cheese, too, did you?"

"In the suitcase," she said.

He went over to her suitcase. Clothes. Shoes. Make up. A loaf of bread and a small block of hard cheese for her.

And for him, she had packed sushi rolls, avocados, and an enormous stir-fry of tofu, chicken breast, egg whites, tofu, vegetables and white rice.

"It's still hot," she said. "I even brought a bowl and a fork."

"You're the best wife ever," he said. He filled the bowl, sat down and began eating. "And by the way, you look lovely."

She cocked her head. "Are you making a pass at me, mister?"

"No."

She came over to him. She took hold of his hand and pressed it to her breast. "Are you sure?"

"Sarah...."

"Arrrgh. I figured as much." She let go of his hand and moved away. "This whole thing is so frustrating," she whined. She inhaled and exhaled deeply, through her nostrils. "And terrifying. Russell, aren't you terrified?"

"Of course I am."

"You say it so calmly."

"It's to be expected, a crucial part of the game."

"It's surreal," she said. "All those media people down in the parking lot and in the lobby. So many cops and security guards...."

"I have to say, I'm surprised to see you here. I thought you were boycotting because you didn't want anything to do with this anymore."

"I know that's what I said," she muttered. She began pacing back and forth in front of him. "But after you left this morning, I realized that I might never see you alive again. Whoa! There was a moment. What to do? What exactly am I meant to do? Should I pack up my things and walk away? That would certainly make a statement about how I feel. But walk away to what? Righteous solitude? No, thank you. Should I stay with you and grin and bear it because, as you keep reminding me, I knew what I was getting into when I married you?" She stopped pacing. She faced him and shrugged. "So much for choice," she said.

"Sarah...."

"But actually, you're right, as much as I hate to admit it," she went on. "It's true, I knew you were going to run, and yet I still committed with you to a marriage and a mortgage. I knew full well that when you ran you might get seriously injured or killed while your insurance was in default. Your health, your life, our house, our life together...everything. Everything at risk. Everything that matters! But hey, I knew what I was getting into, right?"

"Sarah, I'm sorry, but I just can't deal with this. Not now. I have to prepare...."

"You're right," she said again, with emphasis. "You're right about all of it, Russell Bowen. And so what? So what if I knew what I was getting into? After we got married, I started seeing things differently. I saw this game for what it really is. I began to worry about what might happen to you. I began to worry about you, and the money and the mortgage. You just keep telling me I can't claim that I didn't know."

"Because you *did* know."

"Yes, Russell, you're right! You're right, right, right! I'll say it again: So what? Being right is no excuse."

He let out a disparaging laugh. "Did you hear what you just said?"

"The question is: Did *you* hear what I just said?"

"I think that you...."

"You think being right justifies leaving me behind to fend for myself."

"We've been through this so many times," he sighed. "This is about a commitment I made. And following through on it."

"Commitment, schmomittment," she said. She began pacing again, then stopped and faced him again. "It was only this morning that I realized we're coming at this from different angles."

He stood up from the chair. "Sarah...."

"I'm not committed to you. I'm committed to *us*."

He held his hands out toward her, palms up. "Stop," he said. "I really can't discuss this anymore. Not now. I can't. I only have a few hours before...."

But she did not stop. "Yes, yes, you have to prepare for winning. Well, I don't care about winning. No, I take that back. I do care about winning: I'm sick of it. I'm sick of hearing about it. I'm sick of the 'sacrifice to win.' I'm sick of the 'drive to win' and the 'winning attitude.' It's everywhere. Win! Win! Win! Nothing else matters, it's all about winning. It's on my box of cereal in the morning and on my TV at night. It even sleeps with me. It's a contamination."

She paused and when she spoke again her tone had softened. "Oh...Russell...I just want you to come back home to me, safe and sound, win or lose, that's all."

She turned to the window, with her back to him. "There. That's what I really came here to say. To say it out loud and make sure you knew."

He stood, put his arms around her. "And I love you for it."

She stroked his hand. "Thank you."

He turned away. "Okay," he said. "Now, I have to get to work."

She picked up her wine glass from the sill, saying, "You know, I've read all the same books that you have read about this game, Russell." She looked at his reflection in the window. "I've studied the tactics and strategies with you. I've read the catalogues. True, I don't know the plants and birds and deer like you do. But I have a pretty good idea of what the game itself is all about. Treachery, that's what it's about." She turned to face him. "Don't... betray anything out there, Russell. Do you understand what I mean?"

"I know what I'm doing, Sarah."

A look of sorrow crossed her face. She raised her glass, in the gesture of making a toast. "All wears away but arrogance," she said. She looked at him. "Isn't that what the poet said?"

"It's not arrogance," Russell said.

"You're about to enter a contest where people try to kill one another. And you say you know what you're doing? Of all...."

"Sarah, maybe it would be best for you to go back home."

"No," she said, pleading. "Please!"

"I have to concentrate. I can't afford to be distracted...."

"I've had my say," she said. "I'll shut up now, I promise." She pantomimed zipping her lips. "I brought my suitcase because I want to stay the night. I won't bother you anymore. Really, I'm finished. I want to spend the night with you, and in the morning I will watch you cross the line. Then I'll going home. I'll fret in the privacy of my own house, thank you very much."

She moved close to him. "When I get home I will light the fire," she said, "and I will keep it burning until you come back home safely to me. Okay?"

He nodded.

She stood on tiptoes and kissed him.

"I do love you, Russell Bowen," she said, and then sat down on the edge of the bed. "Now I'll leave you alone. You want to study, right?"

"Yes."

"The behemoth from Canada?"

"Yes. Girard. What about him?"

"He'll lag."

He smiled at her. "Is that so?"

"But you probably figured that out the first time you saw him," she said. She flinched when someone out in the hall shouted:

"Russell Bowen!"

"Who...?"

The booming voice sounded again. "Where are you, Bowen?"

Now there were several knocks on the door.

"You in there, Bowen?"

Russell went to the door. "Who is it?"

"Hartley! Lemme in!"

Russell opened the door.

A short, chunky man pressed by him into the room. "Here's our boy," he said. He wore a dark suit. The blue tie was considerably off center. His narrow face was flushed. "Hell," he said. "Took us all day to get to this God forsaken place. Where the heck are we?" He looked at Sarah and then at Russell. "We missed the reception. Arrived late for the contestant's dinner. And where's Bowen? Nobody knows. Now I find you up in your room with a woman? And a bottle of wine? The night before?"

"That's no woman," Russell said, and winked at her. "Sarah, meet Jake Hartley, one of my sponsors. Who is apparently drunk."

Sarah nodded to the man, but he continued to focus his attention on Russell.

"Yeah, I had a few tasty beverages. And I don't give a rat's ass who she is, she shouldn't be in here. Where's Lowry?"

"Dan couldn't make it," Russell said. "His wife is very sick."

"Oh, sorry to hear that," Jake Hartley said. "Well, then, why aren't you down with the rest of them at the festivities?"

"Because I'm up here talking to you," Russell said.

Hartley scratched his head and frowned. "All right, all right. Look, we've put up two hundred and fifty grand for your entry fee, Bowen. That buys us the right to make sure you're okay and ready to go. Are you okay and ready to go?"

"Yes."

"No one has tried to poison you or break your legs?"

"Not yet."

"No dope or drinking?"

"Not yet."

Jake pointed at him. "Well, make sure you don't. There's a lot at stake here."

He looked at Sarah. "What is it about this guy? We see his picture in the catalogue. What kind of weirdo uses 'good feet' as his resume? We just had to check him out. Some other sponsor beats us to it. Kalypso Industries. Huge conglomerate from Greece. Clothing, mostly. They see a tie-in with hunting apparel. They offer to pay his entry fee. And what does Bowen do? He turns them down. 'Not up to my standards', he says. Okay, now we really have to check this guy out. And we do. Check him out from head to toe. Not very impressive to look at. Seems like a nice guy though. Well, you know what they say about nice guys. Not a chance, we thought. Not a chance.

But then we saw him run. This guy runs like the wind. Like the wind through bramble and briar. Flaked a stone with ease, like a regular Neanderthal. Made a spear. And at a distance of forty feet put it through the tire of our rented car. Jesus! That pissed me off! Try explaining something like that to a rental car company. Amazing thing is, the spear isn't even his style.

And tough? I held a lit cigar to the bottom of his foot. Stunk. But he didn't flinch. 'Good feet' is right. I even tried to punch him in the face when he wasn't expecting it. Caught my fist in mid-air and twisted my arm until I was on my knees, begging for mercy." He looked at Russell. "Something else about you, Bowen. Don't know what it is. Wily? Aloof? What is it? Dunno. But we put our money down."

"Are you done?" Russell asked.

"The odds are against you, Bowen. Literally. The colossal Canuck is the favorite. Who's going to get around him? That monster! Jesus! What'd he do, crawl out of a myth? After him, the odds are on the Russian, then the Jap. Word on the street is that Nakamura is in deep to the Japanese mob. Gambling losses. Real trouble. He owes a boatload of people a boatload of money. Then the woman. And then there's you, dead last. Last, Bowen. But, then again, high odds mean more money for us when you win. Ha! And you *are* going to win, aren't you, Bowen?"

"Yes, Jake, I'm going to win."

"And what about this three in the morning crap? First Notice? You back out after that and we don't get a refund, no matter what. Is that true?"

"That's how it works."

Hartley stepped close to Russell. When he spoke again, a cold sobriety had replaced the bouncing, jovial tone. "You back out after First Notice, for whatever reason…. some very angry people are going to…. Well, I don't need to explain it to you, do I, boy?"

There was almost no space between the two men, and yet Russell managed to move closer to Jake. "Time for you to go," he said.

"As long as we understand what's what," Jake said, and winked. "See you at the starting line!" He went to the door. He pointed at Sarah. "No messing around." He opened the door and on his way out said, "And lock this freakin' door behind me."

Russell closed and locked the door.

"You know some of the most charming people," Sarah said.

CHAPTER 11

WITNESS

O n the desk in front of him, Russell had the catalogue, the Covenant, a pad of paper and a pen. He started with the Covenant. It began with the words, *"We of this contest are of no laws between us...."* But then it went on. And on. And on. Not in English, but in legalese. The main subject of the Covenant was liability during the competition. But the document did not simply state that Russell was accountable for his own well-being once he crossed the line. Rather, an attempt had been made to name *all* those who were *not* liable for his well-being, which, in truth and in theory, was everyone else in the world. Due to this legal process of elimination, the original 15th century Covenant had grown from a few lines to more than thirty pages. Russell struggled with the small print of the first few pages and then went right to the last page:

"...that should any physical, emotional, spiritual or mental harm come to me by act of animal, act of man or act of God, due to accidental or intentional causes; due to man-made or natural hazards, mentioned or otherwise, I understand that I will have no means of redress, neither legal nor otherwise for said injury, neither from the Committee nor from any of its members; nor from any other competitor; nor from the estate of said competitor; nor from any owner of the property upon which the competition is held; nor from any lien holder of said property; nor from any lessee of any part or parcel of said property; nor from any owner or lessee of any machine on said property; nor from any trust or other entity, nor from any member of said trust or other entity that may hold title to said property; nor from any owner, lien holder, lessee, trust or other entity of land abutting, adjacent to, contiguous with, or entirely separate from said property; nor from any governmental (federal, state or local) agency, nor from any member of those agencies either in the country of my origin, country of my citizenship, or country wherein The Kincaid Competition is held, to include all dominions, protectorates, colonies and extensions of said countries. I further understand that this agreement applies, in understanding and in practice, to any and all representatives or groups of representatives, relatives, by blood, marriage or otherwise, heirs, descendants, associates, professional or otherwise, of said individuals, groups or entities listed above.

I understand that upon crossing the line on the tenth day of November, 2020, I thereby willfully surrender all rights, including but not limited to: those rights which may have been earned by duty, effort or circumstance; awarded to me or bestowed upon me at birth by race, creed, or nationality; bequeathed to me by man or God in the country of my origin, country of my citizenship, or country wherein The Kincaid Competition is to be held.

Furthermore, I understand that I surrender these rights only in relation to and only in conjunction with the other competitors of The Kincaid Competition, and only for the duration of said competition, within those bounds proscribed by said competition; and in doing so both they and I will have no laws between us, neither those laws of my country of origin, my country of citizenship, or the laws of the country wherein The Kincaid competition is held, neither in benefit nor in burden, except those of God, of Conscience and of Nature, until I and\or they cross back over said line, or 5:59 p.m. EST on the eleventh day of November, 2020, whichever comes first.

I understand that I will have no means of appeal, legal or otherwise, for any agreements, nor for any consequences of said agreements, stated or implied, that have been set forth in this document, neither in the country of my origin, country of my citizenship or country wherein The Kincaid Competition is held, to include all dominions, protectorates, colonies and extensions of said countries.

I understand that I have the right to legal counsel before I sign this document.

I have read and understand this document.

I assert that I am of sound mind and body and on this, the tenth of November, 2020, I will cross the above-referenced line in The Kincaid Competition of my own free will and intent.

Signed by me,   Date:

Witness: Date:

He looked over at Sarah. She was lying on the bed, flipping through a trashy magazine she had brought with her. Her glass of wine, bread and cheese were on the bedside table.

"I need you to be a witness," he said.

She came over and watched as he signed and dated the document. He handed her the pen.

She frowned and then shrugged. "Just because you are a witness to insanity doesn't mean you consent to that insanity. Right?"

"Right."

She sighed, signed and then lay back down on the bed.

He set the Covenant aside and pulled the pad of paper close. He made three columns on the paper:

Name | Strategy | Weakness

In the first column he wrote: *Ortiz: The marathoner.*

Fortunately, he had been able to inspect her clothing. He had been able to deduce that she was left-handed, that she would probably keep a flaked stone in the pocket on the rear of the left thigh, and that she would chase.

Next to her name he wrote as the most likely strategy: *Chase.*

Ortiz was elegant, clever, enigmatic. She had played it smart up until the very last. She appeared so calm when introduced at the reception, and paid little heed to Girard when he raged against Nakamura at the dinner table. But Russell recalled what had happened in the parking lot. She had taken her hand off the hat in that terrible wind. Of course the hat blew away. What did she think was going to happen? And then there was the company that had made her clothing: Kalypso.

Russell was familiar with Kalypso Industries. They had come to him with an offer of sponsorship on one condition: that he wear shorts they had manufactured. Russell said he already had shorts. He was told that if he didn't agree to wear their shorts, Kalypso would not sponsor him. He agreed to try the shorts for a practice run.

They were black shorts, snug fitting and, it was claimed, made of some fancy new kind of 'space age material.' As with Ortiz's outfit, KALYPSO had been printed in block letters across the back. Russell was astounded to see that the shorts not only had a zipper but a flap as well. Both were dangerous. Anything extraneous increased the chances of snagging something. For example, if a branch got caught on the zipper flap as he was running, the branch could pierce his abdomen. Or worse.

Russell said no, he did not even want to try the shorts. But they insisted and told him, if needed, there was plenty of time to redesign the shorts. They would make another pair without a zipper or flap in time for the competition. Just try the shorts, they said, to see how the material holds up.

Well, the material didn't hold up. After about three hours of running through the woods, briars and branches had torn the shorts in at least four places. He gave the shorts back to them. "No deal," he said. And walked away.

Apparently, Kalypso had approached Ortiz with the same offer. This was probably how she was able to achieve sponsorship so early. After handling her outfit, Russell was positive that it had been made of the same material as the shorts he had tried. But Ortiz wouldn't dare wear clothing that she herself hadn't tested. Or would she?

Once again, he recalled the hat. She had taken her hand off the hat in that fierce wind. What did that say about her? Up until the incident with Girard at dinner, she had seemed demure, sophisticated and mysterious. Up until then, she had done well to conceal herself. Cautious. She could have let Girard's touching her pass without incident. She could have just continued eating her dinner. But she didn't. Had she been completely in control, or completely out of control? There was something inconsistent about her.

So what was her weakness? As he saw it, weakness was simply a strength overburdened. He considered the three most obvious signals: The choice of clothing from Kalypso. Taking her hand off the hat. Kneeing Girard.

Under the last column he wrote as potential weakness for Ortiz: *Negligent.*

No, that wasn't it.

He crossed out 'Negligent.' and wrote: '*Reckless.*'

Yes, that seemed more fitting. At times, she acted rashly, without consideration for consequence. Okay, good. Ortiz was, at times, reckless.

Next.

He wrote: *Al Girard.*

The giant was self-evident. Sarah had only read about him in the catalogue and she figured him out. His dimensions would determine his strategy.

Beside Girard's named he wrote, as his probable strategy: *Lag.*

The giant wouldn't run. He was too large to carry his own weight over a long distance though the woods of New England. He would lag behind. He would let others do the work. The giant wouldn't chase. He couldn't chase. He would wait at the finish line. He would be the last obstacle for anyone who might come in with a deer. He would block their path, take the deer from them and then cross the line in victory. A simple but effective strategy. Obvious. But even an obvious strategy was not necessarily one that was easily defeated.

The catalogue indicated Girard worked in the logging industry. He spent his days with fallen trees and chainsaws. There was no doubt he was strong. Girard was clever to offer Russell such a limp handshake at the reception. Now Russell could only guess at his strength. But the odds were good that the giant could crush a man's skull with one hand. So avoid the grasp. Stay away from him. But could the huge man endure? Lagging was tough. Lagging required that you spend a lot of time in one place.

Russell considered the van Girard had arrived in. That contraption didn't look like it could have made it all the way down from Canada. But it had. And what was the first thing the giant did? He crawled underneath it. Yes, he took care of it. And what about when he made his way through the door to the hotel? The wind held the door open behind him. And he actually went back to close the door. Then, at the reception, he had mentioned that he was going to pay back all the family members who pitched in to help him pay the entry fee. The giant was a man of duty and obligation.

But was he fully aware of what he was in for? Maybe. If a weakness was merely a strength overburdened, and his strength was duty then.... hmmm... a sentry at his post for too long was bound to eventually lose the ability to focus, and become distracted from his duty. Easily deceived, swindled or beguiled. Well, Girard had certainly been beguiled by Ortiz at dinner. Then again, probably everyone had been beguiled by Ortiz.

So if duty is your only focus, then you are easily deceived. How did that make sense? It made sense only when the strength was overburdened. Under stress, the giant's attention was easily diverted. Did that make sense? What was another word for distractible?

He didn't know what to write.

Beside Girard's name, as possible weakness he wrote: *Distraction*.

Next he wrote: *Yuri Kozlov.*

The Russian. What was he going to do? Charm the deer into surrender? Let's see...won the bronze medal at the Olympics. Decathlete. What do they do in a decathlon? Ten things. But which ten things? Hammer throw. Pole vault. Long jump. Javelin. That's it! The javelin was thrown more for distance than accuracy, but Kozlov could have practiced to refine his aim. Absolutely. He would probably fashion some kind of javelin, a lance or spear.

To the right of Kozlov's name he wrote as the likely strategy: *Spear.*

What else did he know about Kozlov? The Russian was very relaxed when Russell first saw him out in the parking lot. Laughing, talking, unaffected. And astute. He knew to look about. In the parking lot, he was the only one who noticed Russell spying on him from above. He had looked up, smiled and waved.

At the reception he presented himself as being overly excited, hesitant and shy. And yet at the dinner table, when they shook hands, just before the giant pounded his fist on the table...what was that? Was it his imagination or had he actually seen something revealed in the glint of the Russian's eye? Was it all a ruse? It had happened so fast, but maybe he was not the unassuming, charming person that he presented to the world. He was hiding something. It was there, in that one look. But what was his weakness? Russell didn't see one. Kozlov seemed to have it all. An Olympian, big, smart, calm...Kozlov was trouble. Absolutely. But everybody has a weakness.

Beside Kozlov's name he wrote, as possible weakness: "*?*"

He wrote: *Mishima Nakamura.*

A baseball player. So, he could run, swing a bat, throw....

Throw!

Beside Nakamura's name he wrote, as possible strategy: *Stones.*

Nakamura was rabid. From the moment Russell first saw him in the parking lot, kicking the car. Pointing and glaring at Russell at the reception. Throwing Ortiz's clothing at him. And then at Rushmore. Taunting the giant at the dinner table. He was actually leaning across the table toward Girard. The little guy was daring and fearless. His weakness? Anger. No. It wasn't just anger; it was something else. What? He still couldn't put his finger on it. He was....

Even though he knew that was not quite it, as a weakness for Nakamura he wrote: *Anger.*

As a matter of fact, this little exercise seemed to have failed completely. He had thought this part would be so easy. Just observe and record. But none of this seemed to fit as tightly as he needed it to fit. He didn't take any of it as fact. These were tendencies and possibilities, nothing more. Everything he saw these people do and heard them say offered a hint about how they would approach the chase. Only time would tell if his interpretations were accurate or not. For now, he would just let it all settle in his mind. The information might offer something to be acted upon. Or against. It might rise to his conscious mind during a time of need. He had gathered the data and stored it. If needed, he could retrieve it at will.

Names written on paper. It was surreal. These were the names of people who, in a few hours, might try to kill him. Anything to win.

"Russell…"

He looked over at Sarah. She was sitting up on the bed. He wondered what had happened. She looked like she was about to cry.

"I'm really scared," she said. And burst into tears.

He went to her and held her.

He felt her body shudder. He felt her shoulders rise and fall as she stuttered for breath. He felt her tears against his face.

"So scared," she whispered.

He didn't attempt to reassure her or tell her that there was no need to be afraid. He didn't even try to distract her from her fear. He just held her. He continued to hold her until she stopped crying.

Then, without speaking, she climbed under the blankets with her clothes on and lay there in silence until she fell asleep.

He leaned down and kissed her gently on her cheek. Then he turned from her and once again deliberated on the word to best describe Nakamura.

CHAPTER 12

TIME

*H*e awoke. He had fallen asleep on top of the blankets. He got out of bed and looked at the clock.

12:30 a.m.

Only a few more hours until First Notice. Three knocks on the door. After that, Russell and his sponsors were all in. Until that point, he could go find Ian Rushmore and back out. He and Sarah could go home.

He felt a hollow in his gut, yet he wasn't hungry.

He set the alarm for 2:15 a.m.

He looked at his list.

Kozlov. If the Russian was so much in control of the situation, then…what? The dictum states: your greatest strength is your greatest weakness. So if control was Kozlov's greatest strength, loss of control was probably his weakness.

He crossed out the "*?*" by Kozlov's name and replaced it with: *Frenzy.*

It was a guess. Or maybe it was a hope. Kozlov had to have some area of weakness.

How about Nakamura? Anger? No. Still didn't ring true. Russell remembered a possible strategy that he had not yet considered: the tyrant. There had been a tyrant back in the early seventies when The Kincaid had been run in India, for the chital, the species of deer found in India. One competitor had hunted down and killed all five other runners before he even thought about the deer. Because that's what a tyrant does first, eliminates all competition. But he was so tired after disposing of the others that he didn't have the energy to chase the deer. It turned out to be a waste. That game resulted in a No Take. Every strategy has its weakness.

Perhaps Nakamura was going to play the tyrant. That would fit his personality.

Russell turned off the light. He got back into bed, fell asleep but woke again later. Once more, he went to his list.

He crossed out the word anger by Nakamura's name and replaced it with: *Desperate.*

That fit. Nakamura wasn't just angry. He was desperate. Desperate men take desperate measures. So…might he still play the tyrant and immediately come after Russell in the cold and dark? Yes, Nakamura might do just that.

Russell went back to bed. He slept for a little while. He dreamed of deer. Hundreds of deer running through the woods, bounding and leaping with the white flags of their tails raised high. And he was chasing them. It was glorious. He felt free. Suddenly he sensed a presence behind him and he was afraid. Something was behind him, drawing closer. He turned his head to look.

Just then, the alarm went off. It was 2:15 a.m.

He got up. He took an ice cold shower to get his blood flowing. Then he turned the temperature dial, trying to ease the tension by letting hot water beat down on the back of his neck. He looked down at his callused feet.

"Platypus feet," Sarah had said. Indeed, they were distorted.

He looked at the scars on his calves, thighs, abdomen and arms. He pushed his fingers against the broad scar on the upper part of his chest. From running in the woods. And scars from Lowry, his severe and demanding trainer. Marks of the teacher.

He stepped out of the shower. He wiped the steam from the mirror. He ran his electric shaver over his skull until the hair was no more than a shadow across his head.

He leaned close to the mirror, and peered into his eyes.

He saw fear.

When he came out of the bathroom, Sarah was standing at the window, with her back to him.

She turned to him. She said, "Did you change your mind and decide to join Marine Corps?"

He passed his hand over his head. "Just figured...."

"I know," she said. "Nothing to get snagged." She smiled and then pressed her lips together. Her eyes were tearing up. As she walked by him, she said, "I'd better take my shower now."

He dressed. He reached into his bag and pulled out a banana, some dried fruit, and a wrapped bagel with peanut butter. He ate it all, washing it down with a sports drink spiked with honey. He left the energy bars for later.

Then he sat in the chair. He did not look at his list again.

Leaving fire.

He and the others would soon be leaving fire.

Into the cold, lawless dark.

He turned his head toward the bathroom door. He could hear Sarah. She was talking to herself in there. Nervous energy, no doubt. A form of frenzy. He could not help her. There was no solace for those left behind.

There was nothing he could do for her now. Except walk away from the game. He looked at the clock.

2:55 a.m.

There was still time. He could run down the hall to Ian Rushmore's room and tell him that he was backing out. Was all the money in the world worth risk losing what he....

Sarah came out of the bathroom followed by a trail of billowing steam. She was in mid-sentence: "...all those wonderful little sayings you have. 'The threat is from within.' 'Lose your fear, lose your rear.'"

She dried herself off with the towel as she kept talking. "Some of them are really very good. 'Life beckons, death pursues.' Remember? Oh, and this one: 'The poet considers. The warrior strikes.' I like that one. And 'After prolonged fear comes loss of poise.'"

He stared at her naked body. She was lovely. He wanted to touch her.

She said, "...and, oh, yes. 'Those in the chase must perish, yet the chase endures.' I...."

"Sarah...."

"Okay, okay, I'll shut up," she said, but then continued, "But I don't remember ever feeling so...."

A loud, heavy knock sounded on the door, followed by a second, followed by a third.

And then silence.

She stared at Russell. Her eyes were wide. She held the towel clenched beneath her chin.

He stood.

"Time," he said.

CHAPTER 13

THE TRUE PRIVILEGE

*R*ussell put on his down parka. He carried his gym bag in one hand, the Covenant in the other. He exited the elevator, passed the front desk and then stopped between the guards at the glass entry doors.

He couldn't tell if it was a man or a woman standing out by the waiting bus. The collar of their coat had been drawn up, and a woolen cap had been pulled down to the eyebrows. The coat was bulky under the bright orange vest. The figure stomped heavy boots and clapped gloved hands.

Russell recalled the term Ian Rushmore had used. That person out there was a reeve. Russell could see their breath as it rose, indolently, up and away. The ferocious wind of the day before was gone. Now the air was calm. And cold. Very cold.

A spasm of fear passed through him. Yes, over the years he had trained on countless mornings of snow and ice. Yes, he had even conditioned himself to rise at two or three in the morning to go for a run in the woods. But at this particular moment, he fully realized that the days of training and conditioning were done. There would be no more practice.

Today he would run for his life.

He muttered a calming, "Shhh."

"Need help with something?" the guard to his left asked.

Russell shook his head. He zipped his parka all the way up to the chin. He went out the door. The cold bit into him at once.

He handed the signed Covenant to the bundled reeve. The reeve fumbled with the papers, then nodded and grunted. The bus door opened and Russell went up the steps.

Another orange-vested man was seated at the wheel. He had a clipboard on his lap, pen in his hand. He nodded. "Russell Bowen," he said.

Russell nodded, and moved to the rear of the bus. He sat by the window. Moments later, he heard the door open.

Adriana Ortiz and her translator boarded the bus. She didn't look at Russell. She chose a seat near the middle of the bus.

Careless and chase, Russell thought. No, not careless. Reckless. That was it. Reckless and chase. But she didn't seem careless or reckless right now. More like subdued. Reclusive.

He heard the door open again.

Yuri Kozlov and his translator came aboard. They were both smiling and red-cheeked, chattering in Russian to each other. Kozlov nodded at Russell and said, "God morning."

Russell nodded back.

Kozlov seemed totally relaxed. The blond, floppy hair was gone. He had shaved his head, too.

The words for Kozlov? Spear and frenzy. A good guess. Maybe.

Once again the door opened.

"Make way for the big man," Girard said as he came up the stairs. He bumped his head. "Crap!" he shouted. He thrust the heel of his hand against the ceiling and left a permanent impression in the metal. He then moved to sit directly behind Ortiz. He rubbed his head.

Russell could hear Girard's breathing. It sounded mildly labored, as though the man had just completed some type of strenuous activity. Which he had indeed done, that of getting his huge frame from his room to the bus. So Russell was reassured. There was no way Girard could run for any distance. Russell also took what he had just witnessed as yet another warning: stay at least an arm's length away from Girard. The man was incredibly strong. And that arm was long.

But the quick and somewhat humorous incident also piqued Russell's curiosity. Someone of Girard's size always had to be watching out for low ceilings, narrow passageways and so forth. Being on guard against that kind of thing had to be a part of his everyday life. Yet Girard had still bumped his head. The man had been so eager to board the bus that he forgot the limits of his physical dimensions. Despite his enormous size, the Canadian was fitting nicely into one little word: distraction.

Ian Rushmore boarded. He appeared pale and drawn. He looked around the bus. "The other reeves are already at the starting line," he said. "So, we're waiting on Nakamura. But not to worry, we will leave at exactly 3:15, as promised, no matter what."

They waited in silence in the cold bus.

Ian looked at his watch.

Nakamura was acting like the boxer who stays longer than necessary in the locker room while his opponent waits for him in the ring. Build the tension. Do anything to be in control. Mr. Desperation.

Russell heard a tap on the window. He turned to look.

127

Sarah was out there, waving at him. Her hair was still wet from her shower.

He lowered the window. He stood and reached a hand out toward her.

She took his hand and squeezed it. "Luck," she said. "And look about."

"Yes." He withdrew his hand and sat back down.

She touched her hair. "Yikes—Ice!" she said. "My hair...it's freezing!"

"Go get in the car."

"Look for me at the starting line! Otherwise I'll see you again at home."

"We'll sit by the fire."

Her shoulders lowered. "Oh...yes.... I love you Russell Bowen"

"Back at you," said Russell.

She waved and then ran off.

He turned and wiped the condensation from the rear window so as to watch her. But the parking lot was a maze of car lights and people moving about, and he could not tell which one was Sarah. Exhaust fumes rose. The line of cars stretched out onto the road for as far as he could see. The people back there were bystanders, waiting to be led to the secret site.

He heard the door open again. He turned toward the front of the bus.

Nakamura had finally arrived, accompanied by his translator. Nakamura walked slowly along the aisle, head held high, eyes straight ahead. He, too, had shaved his head. He stopped and focused his attention on Russell. He grimaced as he drew his index finger across his throat.

The man frightened Russell to the core. Because Russell understood: the desperate are without mercy.

Nakamura waved a dismissive hand at him, and then sat.

The reeve who had been waiting by the bus door boarded. The door closed. The wheels turned.

Russell watched out the window as they traveled. He saw darkened houses, their occupants asleep, still in the ease of unknowing. Warmth of blanket, comfort of pillow, nearness of lover; asleep, oblivious to this machine carrying people toward a harshness from which none would return whole, and from which some might not return at all. He understood for the first time, knew it to his core: sleep is the true privilege. He suddenly yearned to be in bed. With Sarah beside him.

He turned to look out the back window. The line of car lights looked like an eerie serpent in the darkness, rolling with the hills, winding with the road, endless.

Bystanders were a strange breed. There was so little for a spectator to see during The Kincaid Competition. But bystanders liked to be near the game, or so it was said. They liked to light their fires and sit and talk and laugh while nearby, just across the line, out in the darkened woods, others were in the terror of the chase.

Eventually, the bus made a sharp right turn, uphill. It groaned and strained and continued uphill. The vehicle wobbled, bounced and tossed its passengers from side to side.

A house came into view. Lights glimmered in the windows.

The bus stopped.

Ian Rushmore stood and faced the group. "Please go into the house through the kitchen door," he said. "Coffee, tea and snacks are available inside. Then go into the front room for the Charge."

Nakamura rushed to be the first one off the bus after Ian.

Russell felt no hurry. He waited until everyone else had left before he stood, moved forward and then went down the steps. A spotlight on the gable end of the house cast long shadows on the earth, shadows of vehicles moving, people walking, breath rising.

He shivered in the cold.

Reeves with flashlights directed the steady stream of vehicles that had followed behind the bus.

Horns honked. People cheered. A pickup truck with Canadian plates passed by with people standing in the open bed of the back. They held cans and bottles of beer and were singing: "*En guarde pour Girard! En guarde pour Girard!*"

Fancy cars went by. Large trucks loaded with firewood went by.

Russell walked on. He entered the house. The building was old. He saw exposed beams, posts and ceiling joists, and a massive fireplace in which logs were burning.

The giant had already hunkered down on the stone hearth. He cradled a steaming cup in his hands. The others stood about, sipping hot drinks, eating muffins.

Firelight flickered.

The room was silent.

Girard turned his head. His eyes narrowed, almost squinting as he looked at Russell. He spoke. The tone was low and gentle, yet somehow conveyed an unmistakable asperity: "Your last day, Bowen."

CHAPTER 14

THE CHARGE

$\mathcal{T}$hey were all gathered for the Charge in the front room of the old house. There was a fireplace in there as well. Chairs faced the fire. On the mantel above the fireplace was a blackboard, upon which a map had been roughly drawn.

After closing the door to the kitchen, Ian Rushmore went and stood in front of the fire, facing the group. "We'd better get started," he said. He looked at his watch. "Not much time left. Quiet down, please."

The room fell silent.

Ian said, "We begin the Charge."

A low murmur rose as the translations began.

"Actually," Ian said, "I should start by telling you that yesterday I gave you some information that has proven inaccurate. I told you it would be around 32 degrees this morning. It isn't. According to the thermometer, it's only 27 degrees Fahrenheit out there. I believe this translates to about -3 Celsius."

Girard, having found the chairs too small and the ceiling too low, had simply sat down on the floor with his back against the wall. "Minus three?" he said. "And us in nothing but shorts?"

Ian smiled. "You may go naked if you wish, Mr. Girard."

The others laughed.

The giant sipped his coffee and shook his head. "*C'est pas vrai.*"

Ian looked to the others. "Mr. Girard has just used French to express shock and disbelief." Then, once again looking at the giant, he said, "You sound serious, Mr. Girard. Are you having second thoughts?"

Girard stared blankly at his cup. He shrugged.

Rushmore prodded. "You knew that the competition is always held on this date, regardless of longitude or latitude?"

"Yeah, I knew."

"You knew we would cross at dawn?"

"Well, sort of."

"I don't understand, Mr. Girard. Either you knew or you didn't."

"Well...what you said yesterday about sunrise not happening for so long after dawn...." The giant looked around hesitantly at the rest of the group. He said, quickly, "I figured dawn and sunrise were the same thing."

"A common error, Mr. Girard," Ian said. "Dawn is first, then sunrise. I'm afraid you will have to find your own means of warmth until the sun rises. Do whatever you need to in order to survive, Mr. Girard. Whatever you have to do."

"But...."

Ian said, with sudden impatience, "It is too late now to withdraw without losing your entry fee, Mr. Girard. But do you wish to withdraw?"

Girard's response was equally brusque. "Hey, calm down, pal."

"You...."

"Why the hell don't we just wait a few hours for it to warm up? That's all I'm saying."

Ian nodded. "Yes, indeed," he said. "That sounds quite reasonable. Perhaps we should also hand out boots and sweaters. And guns. That's reasonable, too, don't you think?"

"Don't be a wise guy."

"I'm sorry for the misunderstanding, Mr. Girard," Ian said. "Truly. But we *will* cross at dawn. As we have for centuries." He looked at his watch. "So, I will ask you one last time. Do you wish to withdraw?"

On the giant's face, Russell saw concern verging on fear. Girard had probably intended to just stand by the finish line in the warmth of the sun, steal the deer from someone else and then go home with the prize money. What could be easier? Now he was realizing it might not be quite so simple. He would have to stand and wait in the cold, almost naked. And wait. And wait. Lagging deadened the senses. It would require incredible stamina. He would have to hold his position all day and even into the night, perhaps even for another entire day. One mistake, just one moment of daydreaming, and someone could run right by to the finish line. True, someone of Girard's size and strength would be difficult to circumvent. But only if he was alert to the approach.

Also, his feet were probably soft. He wouldn't be able to move about much even if he wanted to. Russell remembered what it was like when he first started training, before he had forced calluses to develop on his soles and between the toes. A true tenderfoot. Stepping on the smallest twig or acorn or pebble was excruciating. And it prevented him from focusing his attention on anything else.

Maybe the giant had spent a lot of time in the woods cutting timber, and maybe he did have a better understanding of the forest than most people. But that wouldn't be enough today. Strip a man down, and his relationship to the forest changed, no matter how much time he had spent there.

It seemed as if Girard was just beginning to realize what he was in for. But surely he had heard the stories. Everyone had heard the stories. Until the sun rose, the cold would be brutal. In previous contests, many had been hurt, even killed, not by the cold itself, but by their attempts to stay warm. Running around or jumping up and down in the dark woods was dangerous. Slip on a rock and break an ankle or leg; or take a low hanging branch in the eye; or tumble down a mountainside. Perils were everywhere. And while concentrating on getting warm or worrying about your feet, there was an even greater threat: the other competitors.

The room was silent while Girard seemed to seriously consider whether or not he would continue.

Ian prodded. "So...?"

Girard said, with obvious reluctance, "I'm still in."

"Very well," Ian said. He faced the entire group. "Now, as I'm sure you are all aware, I'm permitted to tell you a number of things: the weather, a basic description of what constitutes in bounds and out of bounds, and the history of man's interference on the land in question."

He raised a hand and pointed. "Right out here, right outside this house, there are about 80 acres of level field. Plenty of room for the bystanders. It's not a plateau.... it's more like a... what's the word...a terrace. It's like a terrace, with the land descending to one side, but rising up from the other.

About a hundred yards from this building is a stone wall. It stands about waist high. There is a gap in the stone wall, an opening large enough to drive a farm tractor through. That gap in the stone wall is your start and finish line."

He pointed to the blackboard. "Our map. Crude, but it will suffice. Here is the house in which you now sit, at the base of Mashentuck Mountain. And here is the start and finish line."

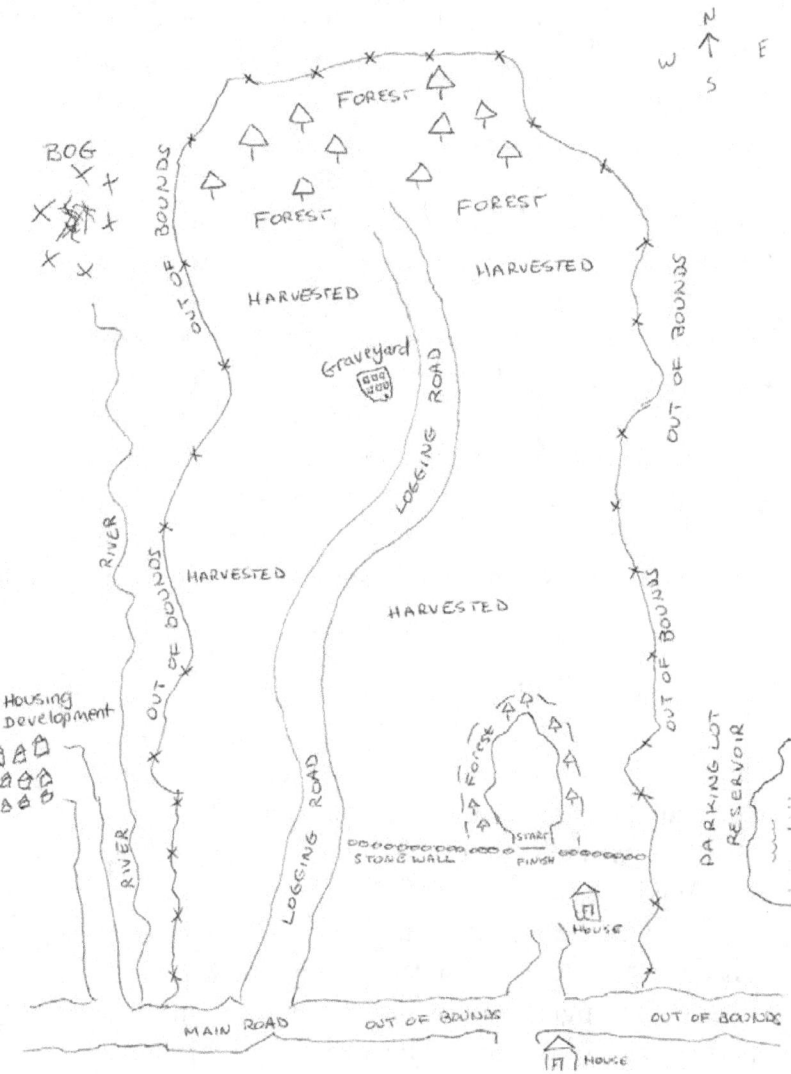

He turned to face the group, cleared his throat and said, "Now, please listen closely. It doesn't matter if you walk or run over that line, fall, slip, stumble, jump, or fly, are shoved, or faint—once you cross that line, you are IN the game. And then it doesn't matter if you walk or run over that line, fall, slip, stumble, jump, or fly, are shoved, or faint—when you cross that line for a second time, you are OUT of the competition. Cross once to begin, once to end. Does everyone understand?"

No one spoke.

"I'll take your silence as being indicative of comprehension." He turned back to the map and pointed. "Beyond the starting line...here...there's a short trail that the present owners have made. It loops around and comes right back down toward the house from the west. And beyond that trail, there are approximately 1,800 acres of undeveloped land, of which about 600 acres were harvested for timber two years ago. So be aware. A certain portion of this mountain has numerous stumps and discards lying about, with uneven and sometimes unstable terrain. Now...."

Nakamura's translator stood and bowed. "Please explain this word, *discards*."

"Yes, of course," Ian said. "Mr. Girard, since you are a logger by profession, perhaps you would be willing to explain about discards to the group."

Girard grunted. "Why would I do anything to help these lunkheads?"

"Very well," Ian stated. He looked to Nakamura's translator. "For the sake of consistency and fairness, I will say it in English rather than Japanese. Then, your interpreters can take over. However, if there is still a lack of clarity, I will do it in each language.

When loggers cut down a tree, sometimes they don't want or need the entire tree. They just want the main trunk of the tree. They cut the branches from the trunk. They cut off the top of the tree. That which they leave behind, the debris, is referred to as 'discards.' Sometimes discards are stacked in piles, and sometimes they are left scattered about." He looked to Girard. "How was that for an explanation?"

The giant did not respond, neither by word nor expression. He sipped his drink.

Ian waited while the translators finished. Then he pointed to the map on the blackboard and continued: "Once again, this house sits near the base of Mashentuck Mountain. Up the mountain from here is north. The windows in this room face west. In that direction is the logger's road, which runs north south, somewhat parallel to the driveway. Further to the west," and he pointed to the left side of the map, "the mountain drops off steeply. Very steeply. At the bottom there is a river and at this river's northern end, bog. Your attention please! The bounds to the west are the river and bog. Even further west is a residential area, a new housing development. Actually, some of the houses are still in the process of being built over there. So if you should find yourself in that development, be forewarned. You are out of bounds. As long as you stay within the bounds I'm describing, you are on private property. You may move out of bounds if you like, but must realize that you will then be subject to the laws of the State, as well as to the potential objections of those upon whose land you trespass. In other words, the Covenant is null and void when you are out of bounds.

Also be aware that, despite all the publicity surrounding this event, some people may not know anything about The Kincaid. A scantily clad person running through someone's yard in autumnal New England will not be something the local populace is accustomed to seeing, and their reaction may well be unpredictable."

Laughter rose as the translations were finished.

"To the east, Mashentuck Mountain falls off more gradually to land belonging to the town. You will see a stone wall and many 'No Trespassing' signs. Attention! Bounds to the east: stone wall.

There is a small mountain stream, about here," and he pointed to a line, serpentine, right of center of the blackboard. "This feeds a body of water that once functioned as a reservoir... about here," and now pointed to a wobbly edged circle. "This entire area is a park. People swim there in the summer months, skate in the winter. It is closed to the public at all other times, including now.

To the east of the reservoir, the land rises again, to Cook Hill. There is a new development of houses up there as well. Here, again, people may have no idea why you are running near their property.

Now, to the north, the mountain drops off fairly steeply to a road, then farmland. Barbed wire fences and pastures and plowed fields. Attention! Bounds to the north: road.

To the south, where our bus pulled into the driveway, there is one house across the road and then much forest and bog before you will come to a river. Attention!" He paused, looked around, then said: "Bounds to the south: road.

Now, should you, for whatever reason, come back down this way, back toward the finish line, but are not done, do not cross through that gap in the wall. You must go around it. Jump over the wall at some other place. If you do cross the line, you are done with the competition. Out. Caput. Finis. Over.

I will say it again: that line is to be crossed twice, and twice only. Once to start, once to finish. Do not cross it a second time, from any direction, without first being certain you are done.

So, these are the bounds." He pointed again to each landmark on the blackboard as he spoke: "River, bog and housing development to the west; land of the water company to the east; road to the north, road to the south." He looked to the group. "Clear?"

"Clear!" the giant bellowed.

"Very well," Ian said. "Now, the earliest deeds in Burwick date from 1708, the year it was incorporated. But there were people living on this land before then. And some of them were living up here, on this mountain. There is a small graveyard right about here," and he drew a small square near the center of the blackboard. "The Walker's, the people from whom we leased this land, and who, by the way, are now comfortably enjoying a visit to the Virgin Islands, at our expense...."

There were ooo's and ahh's of envy from the group.

"The Walker's ancestors are buried up here. Loggers left trees standing around this graveyard, so it is like a small island in the middle of the harvested area," and he pointed to the appropriate marking on the map, "right about here. This house, the house we are in right now, is the only house remaining on the mountain. The others either burned or rotted away;

some were even hauled off the mountain by teams of oxen in the early nineteenth century. I tell you all this to warn you that there are some old cellar holes with fieldstone foundations out there. There are also dug water wells. Take care not to fall into one of them."

Ian waited until the translators finished.

"Any questions?"

None were raised.

"Now then, a final review of some key rules. Once you change your clothes, you will not be permitted physical contact with anyone not involved with the competition. Do not stop to talk to anyone on your way to the starting line. And if you happen to see your long lost brother, resist the urge to shake hands or hug or whatever. Just the act of a handshake will arouse suspicion. Has a weapon been passed? Don't force a decision on my part, because I'm warning you now, I will err on the side of fairness to the other competitors. Keep to yourself, in all respects. This includes, but is not limited to, receiving assistance of any kind from anyone but a reeve or another competitor. You may not, for instance, take a glass of water from a friend who happens to come up into the woods or meets you on the periphery. If you fall and are injured within view of someone not involved in the competition and they come to your aid, you *will be* disqualified.

Now, if someone shouts instructions of some sort...well, we frown on this sort of thing, but it would not disqualify you. We cannot control every action of bystanders. But, in brief, no aid and comfort. There is to be no physical contact unless you are done.

Now, as to the rules of completion. The victor is the first person to cross the line with the deer. The deer can be dead or alive, gutted or no. There are three possibilities here:

First, there is *sole possession*, whereby an individual crosses the line with a deer and is declared the victor.

Second, there is *communal possession*, whereby a deer is brought across the line by two or more people displaying obvious intentional cooperation in the task; in this instance, the prize is to be divided equally among the competitors involved.

Then there is *aggravated possession*; this occurs when it is obvious to the judges that two or more people are fighting for possession as the deer is brought across the line. Be aware that no prize will be awarded in the case of aggravated possession. In short, there can be no room for argument. Possession must be indisputable.

Remember, the rule states that the winner or winners must exhibit 'complete and continuous possession' as they are crossing the line.

A deer may be caught by any means available. If you should find a loaded shotgun under a rock in the woods, so be it. It is yours to use. If you want, you may fashion a means of dragging the deer across the finish line. Make a cart, complete with wheels if you like. But as I just said, you must demonstrate complete and continuous possession. An angry buck chasing you across the line will not secure victory. You must somehow indicate control of the deer. Even riding a deer across the line is legal. This actually did happen once, years ago, and the judges argued about it. The notion of possession was in question. Was the man being carried or the deer being guided? In the end, victory was awarded. So, if you can ride 'em, ride' em, cowboy."

Nervous laughter ensued.

"Of course, it does not matter who catches the deer. The only thing that matters is who crosses the line with it. There will be at least three of us at the finish line at all times. This will ensure a majority vote on any controversial finish.

As stated, you will be crossing the starting line with nothing but what you wear. Once you have changed your clothes, do not converse with your translator or spouse or coach or trainer. You may only speak to me, a reeve, or to each other. No one else. The competition, for all intents and purposes, will have officially begun and you, until the end of day tomorrow, are separate from the larger group by means of your intent.

It is a tradition, gentlemen... lady and gentlemen... that once you don your garb, you, by agreement and intent, are separate from the common man. You will have entered into an historical and honorable contract. You will each be a potential champion, and as a means of expressing the group's honor and understanding for your aim and abilities, you will, for that brief period between dressing and crossing the line, be deserving of a certain detachment from the rest of us. The Committee hopes that you will treat this tradition with the respect it deserves."

He paused. "Any questions?"

There were none.

"We will subject you to a body search. You have all probably heard about the contestant who shoved a capsule of curare up his rectum with the obvious intent of extricating it later for the purposes of rubbing the poison on a spear or arrow tip. The capsule burst before he could remove it from his person. So... don't. Just don't. Anything you take with you is illegal. But once you first cross that line, all is fair. I hope this is clear.

As I indicated last night, scents are allowed. If you want to smear your body with doe urine, or elephant urine, or whatever it is hunters are using these days, be my guest. But it must be done on this side of the line. You may not take the container with you."

There was a buzz of conversation as Ian shuffled through his papers.

"All right, then," Ian continued. "You will have just over 35 hours. From dawn this morning until dark tomorrow. Tomorrow, dark descends at...." He looked down at his papers. "Dark descends tomorrow at 5:59 p.m. If, by that time, no one has crossed the line with a deer, or to put it more succinctly, if, by that time there is no clear winner, the competition shall be deemed a 'No Take.' A tie. A draw.

We will judge time by my watch," and he held his wrist up for all to see. "It is accurate within seconds of the true time. Any objections?"

There were none.

Ian crouched down and opened a black case at his feet. When he stood erect again, he was holding a brass horn.

"This is our victory horn," he said. "It once belonged to the English composer Henry Purcell. It has been in our possession since 1695, the year of his death. As you can see, it is not like the modern day trumpet. It's more like a bugle. There are no valves. Control of pitch is done with the lips. To play Bach would take much practice. But to sound victory is not difficult.

If you are in the woods and you hear this horn sound, you have lost. Only the victor blows this horn. Believe me, the sound of this instrument carries a long way. If it sounds, you will most likely hear it. I suppose a cannon shot would be more effective, but this horn has been a part of the tradition for hundreds of years.

If the competition ends as a 'No Take,' the horn is not sounded. So, if you don't hear the horn but you are still out there at the onset of dark tomorrow, you might as well come in. The competition is over.

But, please, please, understand. Trust no one until you cross back over the line. Perhaps someone has lost track of time. Or perhaps they didn't hear the horn and you did. Because...well, trust no one, in bounds or out, until you cross back over." He held the horn high for all to see. "Questions?"

Once again, there were no questions.

Ian put the horn back into its case. "Remember what I said about the weather. On top of that, we're expecting rain, sleet and snow, and it will turn deadly cold tonight. Prepare for the worst. Should you get lost or hurt and be unable to make it back to the finish line, hold on. Do your best just to survive. We will have medics on duty here. If you do not return shortly after dark tomorrow, we will come looking for you. Understand? We will not disband until all are accounted for.

Okay then. I have walked this land many times. To put it mildly, it is a rather inhospitable piece of earth. It is rough. Very rough. I am not permitted to tell you the number of deer I saw, or their sex. But I can tell you only that there are indeed deer up there. I have seen them. Not many, but enough for our purposes."

An excited and inquisitive buzz passed through the group.

"Now, if there are no questions," Ian went on, "we will finish the Charge."

He waited. There were no questions.

"Okay, then," Ian said. "We finish the Charge with what is known as Second Notice." With clipboard in his hands, he moved to stand in front of Russell and read,

"'We of this contest are of no laws between us, neither in benefit nor in burden, except those of God, of Conscience and of Nature.' Do you understand?"

"I understand," Russell answered.

Ian continued, "'I understand that within those bounds described to me, once I cross the line, I, in relation to and in conjunction with only those who cross the line with me, will no longer be protected by nor subject to the laws of my country of birth, my country of citizenship, or the laws of this country. I further understand that I have the right to legal counsel before I sign this document.' If you understand what I have just said, please answer by saying, 'I understand'."

Russell nodded and said, "I understand."

He handed Russell the clipboard. "Sign, please, Mr. Bowen."

Russell signed.

Ian then proceeded to do the same for Girard in English, Kozlov in Russian, Nakamura in Japanese, and finally Ortiz in Spanish.

Ian went back to stand in front of the fireplace. "All right. One competitor will cross the line every minute until all have gone." He took a silver bowl off the mantle and held it up for all to see. "There are five slips of paper in this bowl. Each is numbered, one through five. The number you choose will determine your place in the order of crossing the line. For instance, if your piece of paper has a three written on it, then you will be the third person to cross the line. Fair enough?" He waited.

No one spoke.

"All right then. When I call your name, come up, reach into the bowl and take one piece of paper. This time we will go in the order of entry. Ms. Ortiz was the first to submit her entry fee. Adriana Ortiz, please come up and choose from the bowl." He held the bowl high as Ortiz reached in and pulled out a piece of paper. She looked at it and frowned.

Ian said, "Show it to me, please, Ms. Ortiz."

She did so.

Ian nodded. "Ms. Ortiz will be first to cross the line."

She went back to her seat.

"Russell Bowen."

Russell went and reached into the bowl and pulled out the first piece of paper that his fingers touched. He unfolded it. "Five." He showed it to Ian.

"Mr. Bowen will be the last to cross the line."

He went back to his seat. Last? Last was a terrible position. Everyone else would already be out there. Any or all of them could just wait in the dark and then pounce on him as he crossed the starting line. Last was the most vulnerable position, the most dangerous position. His stomach roiled. His throat was dry.

Girard picked '2' from the bowl.

Kozlov picked '3.'

"Mr. Nakamura," Ian said.

His translator, stood and bowed. "Mishima says that there is only one number left. He knows it must be '4.'"

"And?" Ian asked.

"He says no sense to bother."

Ian shook his head. "It doesn't work that way. He is required to choose. It's part of the competition."

Nakamura and his translator exchanged words in Japanese and then the translator looked to Ian. "Mishima says that he will not come up there. He knows his number."

Ian sighed. "Please tell Mr. Nakamura that if he doesn't come up here and take the piece of paper out of this bowl, he will be disqualified."

The translator and Nakamura again spoke in Japanese. Nakamura sat silently with his arms folded across his chest.

Ortiz stood and spoke in Spanish to Ian.

Ian put his hand to his mouth, as if trying to hide his smile. Then he was laughing.

Ortiz sat back down.

Ian stifled his laughter. "Yes, well...," He shook his head. "I suppose in the name of fairness I must translate what she said. Ms. Ortiz said...," He cleared his throat. "She said Nakamura should be given an enema so that the rest of us might get some relief."

The giant laughed and clapped his hands.

Ian then translated into Russian.

Kozlov smiled cautiously as he looked over at Nakamura.

Russell watched Ortiz. Why did she want to aggravate Nakamura? Maybe just to make him mad. Because? Anger does not win. Maybe. She seemed as calm as could be. Very relaxed. Just the slightest smile. But provoking Nakamura was risky; it would only make him vindictive against her. Perhaps she was using psychological warfare. Nakamura and the giant had had their little run-in at the dinner table. Nakamura and Russell had had a confrontation at the trophy table. And now this, with Ortiz. She has helped divide Nakamura's rage. Maybe she was using his own anger to wear him down. Adding fuel to the fire. Could be very smart of her after all. Nakamura now had a personal gripe against everyone except the Russian. The clever Russian.

In a swift and abrupt motion, Nakamura stood. He stomped to the front of the room. He reached into the bowl, handed the piece of paper to Ian without looking at it, and then returned to his seat.

Ian said, "Mr. Nakamura has chosen '4.'" He put the bowl back on the mantle. "So the order will be: Ortiz, Girard, Kozlov, Nakamura, Bowen. Anyone unclear as to their position?"

No one spoke.

"Now," Ian said, "you will go upstairs to change. Once you go up there, all coaches, trainers and interpreters will kindly leave the house and join the bystanders outside. A female reeve awaits Ortiz upstairs, a male reeve for the rest of you. Once you have changed, come down the stairs, take a right, and enter the kitchen from the other doorway. Once everyone has gathered in there, Final Notice will be given."

He clapped his hands once, loudly, a startling and unexpected sound that caused everyone in the room to jump. He had their full attention as he whispered: "Look about."

Then, in his normal tone of voice he said, "In the order drawn by lots, then. Adriana Ortiz."

Ortiz stood.

Ian said, "If you will go upstairs and change we will get started."

Her translator interpreted for her. She bent down and kissed him on the cheek. Then she picked up her bag and moved through group with grace and silent dignity, head held high.

Russell listened intently. He could barely hear the stairs respond to Ortiz's ascending weight. Light on her feet. And swift. A goddess of the hunt.

The room was silent.

Russell stared at the fire.

These were difficult moments. Waiting. There was no amount of training that could prevent the apprehension he now felt, so he just let it happen. He didn't attempt to deny it or repress it. This was the time when the climber at the base of the mountain finishes readying the gear and looks to the peak. This was the time of the boxer approaching the ring. A certain collapse must be permitted. The rational mind must relinquish some of its domain. Instinct must be given its rightful berth. This was an inner shifting, tumultuous and profound. These were the last moments of warmth and protection. And law. These were the last moments in civilization.

Voices came from upstairs.

All heads turned as Ortiz could be heard coming down the stairs. Russell caught a glimpse of her as she entered the front hall and went the other way toward the kitchen. The female reeve followed quickly after her.

Ian said, "Mr. Girard. You're next."

The giant rose, but only part way. With knees deeply bent and head lowered, he passed sideways through the doorway.

Russell listened as he went up the stairs.

The giant's step was predictable. Heavy, not with any expression of confidence, but simply lumbering and solid. The stairs creaked.

Russell looked out the window. Cars were still arriving in a steady stream. Beams from the headlights bounced through the darkness as the vehicles came up the rutted drive.

The room was again silent.

With every passing moment, the tension in him grew. He considered that in just a few minutes the others could, if they so chose, come after him with sticks and stones or their bare hands.

And kill him.

The Charge had gone smoothly. There had been no incidents other than Nakamura's hissy fit over drawing a number. Because of the rules, so pervasive and yet so subtle as to have gone unnoticed, so far no one had tried to kill anyone. And yet it was more than the fear of consequence that kept everyone in line. The group had acted in subconscious accordance with the rules. This happened every day, all over the world. This was how humanity survived humanity. Whether in obedience or disobedience, an association with the basic rules was complete, always, for everyone. Russell was struck by the simplicity of it all. He and the others had been born into law and grown into law. The law had always been there, like a parent, guiding, scolding, protecting. But in a few minutes, by taking one step across an imaginary line, that relationship would fall away. By taking one step, all laws of all nations would dissolve.

It was unfathomable. How was anyone to prepare?

A part of him wanted someone, anyone, to come in and say that the game had been called off. Everyone go back to bed! The Kincaid has been cancelled!

But he knew that wasn't going to happen. They were going to cross the line. They were going to step into the remote past, back to the mystery of time before the rule. There would be no safeguard, no stop-gap, no police. The only authority would be that of tooth and nail. They were going back, back in time, leaving fire, going reverting to origin, back to where science could only guess and religion could only mythologize. This game was a regression to the primitive, a blatant rejection of history. This game was a dismissal of progress, regardless of definition. Once they crossed the line they would, except for a pair of shorts, bear no evidence of culture. They would be human only in posture. There....

Russell caught himself. He was face to face with the beast. And the beast was loss of control.

He passed his tongue over his dry lips. He wrung his hands.

The stairs moaned. Girard appeared momentarily at the base of the stairs before disappearing into the front hall so as to go back toward the kitchen.

"Mr. Kozlov," Ian announced.

Kozlov stood. As he went toward the stairs he stopped in front of Russell. He didn't say a word. He smiled.

Russell did not smile in return.

Kozlov was, physically, human perfection. Tall, slender and broad shouldered. Handsome. And a true Olympian. He had still shown no weakness, no quirk or eccentricity. It was strange, but Russell both hoped and feared that the Russian's weakness was endurance. But not physical endurance. No, Kozlov could probably outlast all of them physically.

Kozlov moved swiftly to the stairs.

Light-footed, like Ortiz. The stairs barely gave notice of his weight. Even so, Russell could tell by the sound that Kozlov was taking two stairs with each step.

Kozlov, the smiling Russian. The charming Golden Retriever. Man of the mask. Kozlov was hiding something. Russell could smell it.

Once again Russell turned to the window. He saw the flames in the fireplace reflected in the panes of glass. This tension he was feeling could be debilitating if left unchecked. There was a point at which the tension became more of a strain and less of an advantage. It could grow until it suddenly cast him into a frenzy. And frenzy was intelligence overwhelmed by rage.

On the other side of the line, people were capable of doing what they would never consider doing on this side of the line. Especially once a deer was caught. He didn't understand exactly how the message was conveyed, but somehow, like an electrical current passing through the forest, competitors seemed to know when a deer had been caught. And everyone would try to converge on the one who had the prize. Intent then escalated, or de-escalated, to primal proportions. Someone had the prize, the Golden Bough, and it was up for grabs until it was brought across the line. Perhaps this would be when Kozlov's endurance would fail. Perhaps this would be when the smiling Russian would show his true colors. He wouldn't be saying 'God luck' then. In the frenzy.

Russell had experienced mild frenzy, many times.

Late for an appointment! Hurry! Coffee spilled and toast burned! Hurry!

Control slipped away, mistakes were made, tempers lost.

But in The Kincaid, temper could be lost to its very origins.

Hurry! Hurry!

becomes

Kill! Kill!

Tempers lost.

Most people went to the grave without ever experiencing true frenzy. Electric lights and traffic signs and policemen and all the other trappings of civilization reduced the likelihood of such an encounter. But it still happened. People knew of it. They read their newspapers and watched the nightly news on TV. Oh, yes, they knew. They had guard dogs and locks on their doors.

True frenzy was a threat to the unprepared because it combined extreme rage and extreme frustration to produce extreme power. A frenzied competitor could become crazed enough to rip out another's eyes or bite off their ear or break their neck. But frenzy used much energy and left those under its influence open to attack. In most sports, there was a referee to step in and subdue the rage, to retain order, to enforce the rules. The Kincaid had no need of a referee, because there were no rules to adjudicate. Frenzy roamed free.

During the chase, the forest offered constant objections to intent. The contestants were trying to catch a wild animal with their bare hands. Their bodies were exposed to thorns, rocks, branches and bitterly cold temperatures. Cuts, bruises, and scrapes collected on their bodies all day long. Irritation escalated into anger. The contestants tired. Frustration increased. Anger slipped to rage. There is not much distance between rage and frenzy. The Kincaid could do this to people, especially if someone has a deer across their shoulders and is headed for the finish line.

Russell took a deep breath, and exhaled slowly. Calm down, he told himself. Calm down. Talent does not win. Strength does not win. Intelligence does not win. Anger does not win.

Composure wins.

There was no other game that compared to this— not American football, not ice hockey, not rugby, not boxing. A boxer can lose his first bout, learn from it and use the experience to his advantage in his next fight. A sprinter can lose and run again. Not so with The Kincaid.

Lose and you're done.

No sponsor would be likely to invest in you again.

If you survive, that is.

It was unfair. How could anyone possibly prepare?

His lips moved in silent admonition: The threat is from within. From within.

He thought of his trainer Dan Lowry throwing spears and stones at him. He recalled how Lowry had punched him and chased him while he carried a sandbag across his shoulders. Trying to imitate the competition. But Russell had known Lowry wouldn't kill him. Not intentionally anyway. It was as close as they could get to duplicating The Kincaid. But deep down he knew. He knew it was just practice.

As Lowry had told him, many times, war is the premise of all games. From chess to poker, from golf to volleyball, they were all the offspring of war. And the mother of war? The primeval enterprise: survival.

In other words, The Kincaid.

Catch the beast and bring it back to the fire.

Or die.

No one in command. No rules of engagement. Murder? No. There is no such thing as murder in The Kincaid. Murder is a term of law.

Russell forced himself to think about something else. Sarah. Her face, her eyes, her smile, the smooth curves of her body. Oh yes. Something other than the competition. Something other than the threat. Something to live for.

He wanted a drink of water. His throat was parched.

Now, reflected in the window glass, he saw Nakamura stand even before Kozlov had come back down the stairs.

He turned to look at Nakamura.

The man stood rigidly, staring at Ian.

The world was full of people like Nakamura. Obnoxious, persistent, and talented. If he was on your team, he inspired respect and encouragement. If he was on the opposing team, he inspired hate and revenge. He was the dream of all coaches, the player who would do anything to win. *Anything*. Nakamura would scramble, kick, bite, and sacrifice; he would push the rules to their very limit. And now there would be no rules for him to push.

Kozlov came down the stairs and went to the kitchen.

Ian looked to Mishima. "Mr. Nakamura."

Russell listened as Nakamura climbed the stairs.

Nakamura's step was heavy, despite his size, heavy with notice of determination and assurance.

Russell pulled two high protein energy bars from his gym bag and began eating them. Otherwise, there was nothing left to do...but wait. He stared blankly at the fire.

He tapped his foot. He stood, stretched and yawned.

He paced.

Eventually, Ian spoke. "This part is difficult," he said.

"Yes," Russell replied.

Now Nakamura could be heard coming down the stairs and then heading for the kitchen.

Russell's stomach had never felt so hollow.

He grabbed his bag and went upstairs.

CHAPTER 15

MUNDANE AND PROFOUND

A reeve waited for Russell at the top of the stairs. The reeve smiled and proffered a hand toward a room. "In here," he said.

Russell went in and closed the door. He was in a bathroom. He opened the curtains on the window, but because of the reflected glare he could not see through the glass. He shut off the light. Now he could see outside. He was at the gable end of the house. The outside spotlight was somewhere above the window, pointing down and away from where he stood. Across the lawn he could just see the gap in the stone wall that Ian had mentioned; the starting line. Far to the right and left of the starting line he saw row upon row of vehicles parked in the field. For as far as he could see, fires dotted the landscape. The bystanders had wasted no time. Some stood around fire pits that had been dug in the earth. People had set up barbecue grills and camping stoves. Others milled about. Concession stalls had been erected, as had wooden bleachers. Cars and trucks were still arriving. He could hear music blaring. An ambulance was parked ominously behind one set of bleachers.

He closed the curtains, turned from the window and switched the light back on. He cupped his hands and then drank deeply from the sink faucet. He splashed ice cold water on his face. Then he undressed and removed the shorts from the bag.

Sarah had made the shorts out of deersin-kin. The irony was not lost on him. Use the beast to catch the beast. He had tried other designs, all store-bought, but they had proved unsatisfactory. Some had necessitated a jock strap. No, no straps allowed. Regular shorts had loops and pockets and zippers. Nope, no good. Bathing trunks were never tight enough at the thigh, nor were they strong enough. Bicyclist's shorts did not hold up against the thorns. Gym shorts were too loose; smaller sizes were constrictive.

Sarah made four attempts before she came up with what he wanted. These deerskin shorts were smooth and supple, but tough. Only a knife could cut them. Inside there was a flap over a pouch at the crotch. The pouch was to hold the plastic cup that protected the genitals. The flap was designed to prevent the cup from coming out of place.

At the rear of the right thigh, on the outside of the shorts, just below the buttocks, was a pocket, a slit, without a flap. This was where he could store a flaked stone, out of the way and yet easily reachable. The shorts were tight at the thigh, somewhat loose in the crotch and then tight again at the waist. No loops, no buttons, no belt, no zippers, and no other pockets. To urinate he had to pull the shorts down. They were difficult to take off and put on. He had to struggle to get them over his hips. The only other drawback was that the deerskin sometimes made him sweat where it met flesh. Otherwise, they were ideal. Nothing extraneous to get snagged. Branches and thorns offered no threat. Genitals, which Sarah referred to as "the family jewels," were protected.

He rummaged through the bag until he found the plastic cup. He slipped it into the lining provided for it in the shorts. He coated his thighs and hips and crotch with talcum powder. He began putting on the shorts and then stopped. He opened the door and waddled out with the shorts around his calves. "Search before I put these things all the way on," he said.

The reeve crouched down. He pulled at the plastic cup, peered in, then ran his hand against the pouch.

"Turn around," he said.

Russell did so.

"Bend over."

He bent over, allowing the reeve to insure that nothing had been hidden between his buttocks.

"All set, Mr. Bowen."

Russell pulled the shorts up, struggling to get them to slide over the powder on his hips. He went into the bathroom, stuffed his clothes into the bag, then stepped back into the hallway.

"Over there," the reeve said, indicating the gathering of gym bags of the other contestants on the landing.

He tossed his bag among the other four. He remained there, unnerved by a consideration that he considered both mundane and profound: some of those bags might never be retrieved by their owners.

"Mr. Bowen…" the reeve said.

Russell turned away, and went down the steep steps toward the kitchen for Final Notice.

CHAPTER 16

GO!

*B*efore Russell reached the bottom of the stairs, he could smell it. The odor was strong, pungent, unmistakable.

The monstrous figure of shoeless, bare-chested Girard was in the center of the kitchen. He stood with his chin to his chest. His knees were bent. The back of his neck was actually pressed against the ceiling between two joists of the old building. It was as if the man was standing in a dollhouse.

A reeve was crouched in front of him with a pair of scissors.

Russell asked, "What's going on?"

"Mr. Nakamura complained that Mr. Girard was in violation of the Second Rule," the reeve said. "You know: nothing above the navel, nothing below mid-thigh. I measured. Mr. Nakamura was correct. Usually, a half an inch or so over length is acceptable. But Mr. Girard's shorts were almost two inches over length. We're just trimming them back a little."

Russell studied the shorts. They were the same shorts the giant had worn the day before: cut-off blue jeans. The top button strained to duty against the pressure of his enormous, hairy gut. The flap covering the fly wavered, revealing here and there a glint of the metal zipper. There was no belt, but the loops were still intact, as were the pockets.

Surely, Russell thought, only someone who was going to lag would dare choose such clothing.

Girard's chin was so far forward that his voice box was affected. He sounded as though he was strangling as he yelled, "Hurry up!"

From outside came noises of the crowd, shouts, laughter, and the sound of car engines as bystanders continued to arrive.

Russell winced, momentarily pinched his nostrils closed, then waved a hand in front of his face.

Ian asked, "You recognize that odor, Mr. Bowen?"

"Doe-in-estrus urine," he said, and made a gagging sound.

Ian laughed. "Yes, very good, Mr. Bowen. Ahhh...the unforgettable aroma of urine collected from a white-tailed female in heat. Mr. Girard saw fit to slather it on, head to toe. Several bottles of it, apparently."

"It'll lure them in," Girard growled. "Right into my open arms."

Russell stepped to the left, away from the Canadian. He looked to the other contestants who had also given Girard a wide berth. They stood shoulder to shoulder on the hearth in front of the fire. Three warriors awaiting battle. Each had their hands behind them and legs apart, like soldiers in the stance of ease.

Nakamura and Kozlov wore similar shorts, dark colored, tight fitting, with no visible loops or straps or buttons. Cycling or running compression shorts? Or custom made? Russell wasn't sure.

Ortiz's clothing hugged her thin, muscular frame, accentuating small breasts and narrow hips.

Ian Rushmore was now at the kitchen counter, studying pages on a clipboard.

Russell leaned against the doorjamb. Immediately to his left was the door to the outside. He watched the reeve finish trimming the giant's shorts.

"Okay," the reeve said.

The giant immediately knelt down on the wood plank floor. He rubbed the back of his neck.

"All set to continue, Mr. Girard?"

Girard nodded and waved a hand at him.

"Very well," Ian said, and took a clipboard off the counter. "Everyone! Pay attention!" He passed slowly in front of those who stood on the hearth, then passed by Russell, then Girard. He looked at each person in silent address. He moved to the middle of the room.

He said, "This is your final opportunity to withdraw from this competition that most people consider absolutely insane." He held an extended finger by the side of his head, and twirled in the universal sign of mad, loco, demented. Then he translated his warning into each competitor's native language, and they responded in kind.

"Hell, yes we understand," Girard. "We've already been through this a million times. Let's just get on with it."

This was the last admonition. Ian was trying to deter them from crossing the line. This was more than a man simply trying to alter their course of action. It was as if civilization itself was reaching out to them, and Russell sensed a yearning to comply. Yet he also recognized that what was taking place in that room was the essential hypocrisy of the civilized world.

Civilization was always cautious about anyone who would leave the fire, yet it continually pushed people to do so. It encouraged people to sail uncharted seas in search of new lands. It incited people to climb the highest peak. It catapulted people into outer space. It was a duplicitous creature, pulling back with one hand while pushing forward with the other.

And the Chairman was making a final attempt to pull them back.

Now Ian looked at the five of them and said in a solemn tone, "Okay then. Final Notice." He put the clipboard down on the counter, folded his arms across his chest and stared at the floor in silence.

Russell wondered: Will any of us come to our senses? Will any of us step forward and admit that this whole thing is totally crazy?

His knees felt weak. He wanted to cross the line, just cross the line and begin. At the same time, he wanted to curl up into a fetal position and weep.

He went over next to Ortiz and crouched down in front of the fire. The warmth was soothing. He held his hands out close to the flames.

He could still back out. He could find Sarah and go home. It was tempting. They could deal with Jake Hartley and the other sponsors. He would pay them back the money. Somehow.

His heart was racing. He tapped his chest, lightly, with one finger.

"From within," he muttered.

Looking out was looking in.

He went back to stand by the door.

He didn't look at the others. He looked at Ian, who was still staring at the floor. Ian was giving everyone the chance to do what Russell had just done: doubt.

Finally, Ian looked up. He said, "Very well," and looked at his watch. "It's just a few minutes before five."

He put on his heavy coat. Then he walked across the room, said, "See you at the line," opened the door and went outside.

The reeve remained in the far corner of the room.

No one spoke.

The door to the outside opened. Russell could feel the cold air on his naked legs and torso. The reeve at the door did not come into the house. He simply called out, "Whenever you're ready!" And then pulled the door shut.

The reeve in the far corner of the room pointed at Adriana and nodded. "Ortiz," he said.

She and the reeve came over by the door.

Russell backed away.

The reeve looked at his watch.

It's going to happen, Russell thought. No one is going to stop us. Not even ourselves.

The reeve put his hand on the doorknob. "Ready...set..." He opened the door and shouted, "Go!"

Ortiz went out. "*Victoria!*" she cried.

The reeve shut the door. "Girard, you're next."

The giant rose from his crouched position and came with knees deeply bent to the door. He glanced over at Russell with a look of both hesitation and inquisitiveness.

Russell nodded, not to reassure, simply to acknowledge, but the giant had already turned his face forward again.

They waited. No one said anything. Outside, it had grown strangely quiet.

Then a roar came from the crowd, cheering and shouting.

Ortiz had crossed the line.

Nakamura stared straight ahead. As did Kozlov.

The reeve studied his watch.

They waited.

A minute passed.

Then, "Ready! Set!" and the reeve pulled the door open again. "Go!"

Girard stopped on the threshold.

The reeve reached out, gave the giant a push forward and then shut the door.

Girard could be heard shouting and swearing.

The reeve said, "Kozlov."

Kozlov took long strides to the door. He did not look at Russell.

Outside, it was quiet again. Silence.

Now the crowd cheered again.

Girard had crossed the line.

The reeve focused on his watch. "Ready! Set!" and the reeve pulled on the door. "Go!"

Kozlov went out.

The reeve shut the door. "Nakamura," he said, again looking at his watch.

Nakamura moved to the door. Quick, expressionless, exact.

They waited. It was quiet outside. The fire hissed.

Now the crowd cheered.

Kozlov had gone.

The reeve studied his watch. "Ready! Set!" He pulled the door open. "Go!"

Nakamura didn't move. He looked at the reeve.

The reeve nodded firmly and waved a hand. "Go! Go!"

Nakamura went out.

The reeve shut the door.

Russell did a few pushups and then began running in place. He heard the crowd cheer.

Nakamura was in the woods.

"All right, Mr. Bowen," the reeve said.

Russell stepped forward, silently reassuring himself. In a few moments the queasiness in his stomach would be gone. Reluctance would be replaced by determination. In a few moments all the training and practicing and experience would be called to purpose. Just across the line.

"Ready! Set!" and the reeve pulled on the doorknob. "Go!"

CHAPTER 17

COLLECTIVE MEMORY

*R*ussell could not feel the cold through the thick calluses on his feet. Nor did the frost rigid leaves and blades of grass between his toes cause any discomfort. But the rest of his exposed flesh stung. The cold was as a bitter swarm, and his skin responded with sudden vulnerability: raw, exposed, desperate for the sanctuary of warmth.

He ran.

To his left and to his right were enormous bonfires, and as he passed them he slowed his pace so as to absorb some of their soothing heat. Beyond them, ropes and stanchions formed a narrow aisle.

He ran on.

He saw faces, young and old, male and female. Some people just stared, but most were shouting, cheering him on.

"Go! Go! Go!"

Their shouts were deafening.

They waved flags and pennants and handkerchiefs. Cameras flashed. Lights glared.

"Go! Go! Go!"

He thought he saw a glimpse of Hartley. He glanced to either side, searching for Sarah, but could not find her. It was too crowded, too hectic, too loud.

Too cold.

Up ahead, Ian Rushmore was standing at the gap in the stone wall. He was waving, urging Russell toward him.

Russell went to him and stopped. He ran in place. On the ground in front of him was a thin white streak of lime. This was the starting line, and this was the finish line.

He looked up. He took his bearings.

The sky to the east showed only a hint of dawn breaking. The stars in the western sky were bright. He followed the arm of the Big Dipper toward the North Star. Eventually he would need another sighting, some sort of landmark, just in case when he returned there was cloud cover and the stars were not visible.

Ian looked at his watch.

Now the crowd quieted down.

Russell inhaled and exhaled rapidly, again and again, increasing his heart rate. The cold air was jagged against his lungs. Each breath was shallow. He couldn't breathe deeply enough.

Ian raised a hand and then suddenly brought it down.

Russell crossed the line.

The crowd let out a collective, rowdy cheer.

With that first step, the hunter-warrior rose up in him, roaring in his blood, thrusting him forward into the darkened forest. He shouted, a peculiar and haunting vocalization, a cry from the abyss. Eons had broken through to the surface. Ages of history, of prehistory, all manner of time, all manner of the chase, the endless chase, back, somewhere back to the source of all things vestigial, it had all boiled up in him with that first step across the line. It rushed from his lungs and to his throat and out of his mouth so as to announce itself. At no other time could he have made such a sound. It could only be brought forth by this act, this willful act of crossing the line.

The cheering and shouting of the crowd stopped at once when he cried out. He did not look back nor feel any sort of self-consciousness. The people in the crowd may have been startled by the sound but, regardless of their culture or language, the sound had not been alien to them. He knew the cause of their sudden silence. They may have been in the comfort of coats and hats and socks and boots. They may have had fire and hot drinks. But he sensed they had been startled into silence because they realized their wonder at those who entered the cold, dark forest in quest of the beast had, after all, not been wonder, but the stirring of some entombed and collective memory.

CHAPTER 18

THE WOLF TREE

$\mathcal{S}$ hortly beyond the starting line, Russell saw low hanging hemlock boughs that reached all the way to the ground. He parted them as he would part two curtains, lowered his head and found himself in near complete darkness.

He stopped advancing but ran in place. He let his eyes adjust to the diminished light. He rubbed his arms.

He glanced behind him, then to his left, straight ahead, to his right, then forward again. This constituted 'looking about,'—the first rule. Anything that had ever lived in a burrow or a den or a nest or a cave; anything that ever swam or had ever flown or had ever crawled or walked or slithered, all had learned the rule: look about. Nature's imperative is to encroach, so look about. His intent was to do this repeatedly for as long as he was out there.

He jumped up and down. Then, as he was doing some push-ups, he heard something. He looked to his right and saw darkness rushing toward him.

He stood and tried to run but his feet slipped on leaves and pine needles. He fell. He lay on the ground, looking up.

Though he could discern few details in the darkness, he was certain of the identity. Out here in the dark forest, Girard was even more of an imposing figure than he had been in the small house. He was gargantuan.

He came toward Russell with both arms extended above his head. He was not carrying a rock. It was more of a boulder.

"No!" Russell cried as he rolled away. "Stop!"

Girard continued to advance.

Russell shouted, "Stop! You need me, you moron!"

Now Girard stopped advancing, and cocked his head. "Huh?"

"You'll lessen your chances," Russell said. "Without me, you'll have a much harder time winning!"

There was no war without an enemy, yet the chance of victory diminished without a certain amount of cooperation from that enemy. For now, it was a necessary tension of opposing forces: Russell and Girard needed one another.

The tendency of the white-tailed deer was to bed down, then move and browse, bed down again, then move and browse, in an almost ambling coverage of its territory. When frightened, deer ran fast, incredibly fast. After only two strides they could be moving at full speed, about 40 miles per hour. The source of this power came from the thrust provided by their deceptively thin rear legs. Those legs were incredibly strong. Which was why deer had little difficulty jumping over a seven-foot fence. There was little else to rival a deer for leaping ability and acceleration.

But they couldn't run long distances. They tired quickly. So, for now, Russell wanted as many competitors as possible out there to keep the forest alive with disturbance. Don't let the deer bed down. Keep them moving. Wear them out. The competition, and thus the entire forest, funneled down to that one small gap in the stone wall at the finish line. Girard was needed to slow things down should someone other than Russell approach the line with a deer. Without the giant there, someone could cross the line unopposed. And Girard needed Russell to be out there so as to increase the chances of a deer being brought in.

"Listen!" Russell said. "Everything in the forest will catch a whiff of that deer scent you slathered on. But your human scent will ride along with it. Understand? The deer won't be fooled! They'll avoid you. That's why you need the rest of us, to scare the deer towards the finish line, where you'll be waiting."

"You think you're so smart," Girard said, but tossed the rock aside, and then hopped up and down while thrashing his arms about. "Zut! I'm freezing to death!"

Russell scrambled to his feet and ran off.

He continued along the path that had been made by the owners of the property. The path led uphill, which was just what he wanted. He stopped, did several pushups, then he was on his feet again, running.

He already knew his assumption. He had based it on what Ian had described during the Charge.

The deer had superior senses. Their depth perception was suspect, but they could detect a slight motion at a great distance, day or night, like a cat. Their hearing was as acute as that of a dog. But smell was the strongest sense a deer possessed. Depending on wind conditions, they could pick up a scent from as far away as half a mile. If possible, they tended to move into the wind so that the scent of anything coming toward them would arrive on the moving air and thus provide advanced warning.

But moving into the wind meant their own scent was being carried away from them. Vulnerability lay to the rear. A predator could pick up the scent and follow. As a result, deer frequently stopped and looked about. In their natural habitat, they were high strung, extremely cautious creatures. They were always on guard. And constantly taking messages from the air.

At night, the air cooled and settled into the lowlands. Russell figured that was where the deer would be now, down where the scent of any predator would be brought to them on the falling air. When the morning air warmed, it would rise. The deer would move with it, heading uphill to where the rising air would carry the scent of any approaching threat.

But, when it came to deer behavior, there were tendencies, but few rules. Their first impetus was safety, regardless of wind conditions. If the white-tailed deer obeyed strict rules, then no hunter would ever leave the forest empty handed.

Russell planned to eventually get to the top of the mountain. He would then move back downhill, zig-zagging laterally across the mountainside with the hope of intercepting the deer as they made their way uphill with the warmer air currents.

But his immediate goal was warmth.

At this time of year, the sun would rise well south of east. If he stayed in the forest on the lower part of the mountain, it would be a long time before the air warmed enough to make a difference. So he would move north, uphill, and maybe even climb a tree so as to encounter those first rays of sunlight.

The cold was vicious. As he ran, he continually clenched his fingers into a fist and then extended them, again and again, encouraging blood flow to keep them from numbing.

Now the path headed west. He saw that it then turned back, heading south, down to the house and the finish line.

Between the trees he could see the glinting of the bystanders' fires.

Those lucky bastards.

He could build a fire. He had practiced doing it many times using a method called the fire plow, which involved pushing a narrow wooden shaft repeatedly and with great force against a flat broad piece of wood. This removed very small particles from both pieces of wood. Eventually, friction ignited the particles of wood which could then be added to tinder.

But fire was dangerous salvation, a double-edged sword. Not only would building a fire require that he stay in one place, but the light and warmth would attract others, making him an easy target. So, no fire. He would keep moving. He would get ahead of the deer and attain the uphill advantage.

He left the path and was now in deep forest. The trees were old, tall, with thick trunks. White pine, oak, maple and hickory. He held his hands up in front of his face as he ran, protecting his eyes. The low, dead branches of white pine were sharp, rigid spears. They scratched at his arms and sides.

He stopped and looked about.

He sniffed the air.

He listened.

The forest was absolutely silent.

He did a few more push-ups. He leaped up to grab an oak branch and did a series of pull-ups. Then he was running again. Each footfall announced his passage.

Autumn was a difficult time to hunt. Dried leaves underfoot made noise. Prey were easily alerted. One option was to stalk, or still-hunt, by moving very slowly for a little while and then remaining still, moving slowly, and then remaining still again. Or, since deer do not tend to look up, he could remove his scent from ground level by climbing a tree and then wait and hope that a deer might pass beneath him.

Or he could chase.

He saw light ahead. Through the trees, he saw the faint blue and pink of the southeastern sky.

The first birds of morning sounded. Chickadees. Blue jays. And far off, a cardinal.

Whenever he felt that the cold was gaining on him, he stopped. He did more push-ups and rubbed his feet and legs. He looked about.

Sometimes he stopped and just listened. Was he being followed?

Occasionally he moved to his left or right and headed back downhill before turning and heading uphill again, making a slow, gradual loop, essentially traveling over the some of the same terrain twice. This tactic offered him the chance to get behind anyone who might be pursuing him. It used more energy than just heading in a straight line, but it was a necessary precaution.

Looping.

He had learned it from the deer.

The forest ended abruptly.

It was an eerie light, that of dawn mixing with the fading darkness. In front of him lay that part of the property that had been harvested for timber. Though shadows were diminishing, there was little else he could distinguish other than stumps and the spires of saplings. He would not go out there. Not yet. The branches of the logger's discarded tree tops would pose too much danger in such dim light.

He ran in place, thrashing his arms about. He jumped up and down.

Judging by shadow and silhouette, he was in a peninsula of forest that reached out into the harvested area. This was a good landmark. The finish line was due south of this peninsula of trees.

He looked about. Somehow or another, the loggers must have gotten their machinery up here. Ian had shown on the map where they had made a road or path in this general area. But Russell saw no such evidence yet.

Once again, he was running. In order to avoid the cleared land, he moved downhill and west across the mountain and then once again moved north, following along the line of forest where it met harvested land.

He stopped. He rubbed the top of his feet. He jumped up and down.

He ran.

He looped.

Soon, he came to an opening. Finally: the logging road. It was little more than a wide tract of bare earth with occasional tire ruts, but finding it confirmed that his sense of direction was still accurate, despite the adrenaline, the cold and the dim light. He could follow the road uphill. Except he didn't know how far it continued in an uphill direction. If he followed it, he might find that he was confined to it, unable to leave it because of the discards hiding in the darkness. He could get stuck out in the middle of the harvested area until the sun rose. Easy prey for Nakamura. Or Kozlov. Or Ortiz.

So he crossed the logging road and was again in forest. He was more or less traversing the mountain now, heading west.

Again, he ran with his hands held up in front of his eyes. He came to the edge of the mountain and headed due south, uphill. To his left, the mountain dropped off steeply. Though the sky was quite bright now, the shapes and forms down there were indistinct. There were trees, certainly, but it also looked as though there were boulders and sheer rock face. It was deathly steep.

He noticed a rub on a cedar tree. Even in the dim light, it was obvious. It looked as though a huge piece of machinery had scraped against the tree and torn some of the bark away. But a buck had done this to the tree, not a machine.

This was known as a 'signpost rub' — a message left by a male deer. There were probably many such rubs throughout the forest. The buck had done battle with the tree by repeatedly pushing its antlers against the trunk. The bark had been worn away to reveal the lighter colored wood beneath. This wasn't just a visual display. A scent from the forehead gland on the buck's brow had been left on the exposed flesh of the tree.

Usually, the chosen tree was of a particularly odiferous wood, such as cedar or black birch or hickory. With the bark worn away, the odor of the wood was carried through the forest; the buck's scent went with it. This scent relayed information to other deer in the vicinity. As far as Russell knew, many of the messages conveyed by these rubs were still a mystery. Most likely, the conveyance was concerned with the health and dominance status of the buck that had created the rub. For certain, the signpost was a declaration of territory, but not in the traditional sense. It did not indicate sole possession. Males from other territories could cross this line and enter, but only if they were subordinate. Or were willing to fight to prove otherwise.

It was the equivalent of a person purchasing land and building a house. The land would be surveyed. The surveyors would set their pins as notice of demarcation. The choice of area, the amount of land, and the size and style of the house would all serve as signposts. Any passerby could acquire certain information as to the wealth and power of the owner. So too with a signpost rub.

In essence, the buck had completed its survey. The pins had been set. These were his bounds. Other deer passing by could acquire certain information as to the health and power of the owner.

Theory held that the bigger the tree bearing the rub, the larger the buck that had made the rub. Russell crouched down to inspect the ravaged cedar tree. Judging by diameter of this tree, there was a very large beast somewhere on this mountain.

He ran on.

Then, to his right and high up, he saw an enormous white oak, by far the tallest tree around him. This tree stood alone and looked peculiar because all about it had been harvested. The loggers had left this single tree, a valuable, harvestable tree. The sparing of so large a specimen was a traditional sign left by lumberjacks. It was evidence of control over intent, their own particular way of stating that their arrogance was not entire. It was known as a wolf tree; the elder of the forest.

His attention was drawn to the very top of this tree. Steam rose off its moisture laden branches in the first rays of sunlight.

Sunlight.

He left the forest and crossed a short distance of the rough, harvested land. He moved slowly at first, getting a feel for the change in terrain. Thorns ripped at his legs and sides. His shins knocked against the branches reaching up from logger's discards.

Now he stood at the base of the wolf tree. Most of the lower branches looked as though they had been broken off, probably when other trees around them were felled. If he kept his weight close to the massive trunk as he climbed, what remained of the lower branches would hold him. From high up, he would get the benefit of the sun's warmth as well as a good view of the land. Typically, it was not the climbing of a tree that was dangerous, it was the descent. An attacker who saw someone in a tree simply had to wait for them to come back down.

It was a risk. Hell, it was all risk. But the land around this tree was open. He'd be able to see anyone approaching.

He climbed toward the sunlight.

Chickadees were above him. The small black and white birds did not fly away. They moved up the tree as he advanced. They sang the same musical phrase again and again: 'Dee-dee-cheba-dee-dee.'

Russell knew chickadees used a sophisticated signaling system. He had read that tiny birds had subtly different calls for the degree of threat and even the size and movements of predators, in addition to sounds associated with finding food or defending territory. This particular phrase was a warning call, a notice of intruders and trouble. Russell understood the message being conveyed. 'The threat is from below,' they were saying, over and over. 'The threat is from below.'

They stayed well beyond his reach, but did not fly off.

He continued to climb the enormous tree. He felt it on his hands first, then his arms and shoulders and finally on his back and legs. He moaned with pleasure. Exposed to cold air, his flesh readily responded even to the thin warmth of the November sun.

He stopped climbing. He rested on a branch while bracing himself with a hand on another branch, and looked down. He guessed that he was now 40 or 50 feet off the ground. He looked up. There was probably another 30 feet of tree above him.

The chickadees hopped nervously back and forth among the branches. He let his eyes wander over the landscape.

Details were gradually becoming evident as dawn gave way to daylight. He took his bearings. The land in front of him was that which had been harvested. There were no tall trees, just saplings, four or five feet tall, thousands of saplings, many springing up from the stumps of oaks and maples. Here and there, light brown grass grew in clumps. He saw barberry and sumac, winterberry, stout beech trees and stands of mountain laurel. And dotting the landscape everywhere were clumps of multiflora rose and wild raspberry. It grew in widely spaced groups of single looping canes. In other places it stood in thick crowds, entangled with one another, impenetrable. The thorns of both were sharp, large and numerous. The brush presented a fierce objection to passage. And there were rocks, everywhere, large and small. He saw the loggers' discards here and there in dark stacks, and elsewhere just scattered about, their branches reaching up above the grass.

It was a wasteland, a rough, forbidding entanglement of thorns and rocks and of branches stiffened in death. Undergrowth, exposed to the sun when the trees were cut, had surged at the chance for renewal. It was a wasteland of hundreds of acres that a man, a fully clothed man, would have serious difficulty negotiating without being pricked or poked or scratched. Even if he were wearing boots, he would still find it awkward to get a secure foothold.

But it was ideal for deer. The low growth provided an easily attainable food source. And predators could be easily spotted. A deer would have no difficulty moving at full speed over the rocks and through the brush.

He rubbed his legs and arms to encourage circulation. Looking farther east, he saw that the land dropped off gradually, then sharply into a ravine of rocks and piles of discards, then rose up again to a stonewall beyond which there was more forest. Somewhere over there was the town reservoir Ian had mentioned.

Beyond that he could see for miles. In the distance, the land rolled and dipped in a deceptively gentle contour. Mist appeared to be caught in treetops. Most of the trees were bare, but he saw the occasional dull red of oak leaves, some orange of maple, gold of hickory and beech.

To his right, he saw the landmark peninsula of trees that projected out into the wasteland, where he had stood earlier. Now he had another landmark: the wolf tree in which he now rested. The finish line was south and east of the wolf tree.

He stood. He reached for a higher, sturdy branch. He did a series of pull-ups, then faced south, up the mountain. Far up, the wasteland ended and the forest began again. There was a single clump of trees between him and where the forest resumed. Perhaps that was the location of the cemetery Ian had described as an island of trees in the middle of the harvested land.

He turned to face west. The rocky edge of the mountain was in this direction. Somewhere over there, in the valley beyond the edge, was the housing development Ian had described.

Russell had now gained a basic comprehension of the entire layout. He figured the most likely battleground would be the wasteland. The deer would use it to their advantage.

The cold was persistent and stinging. His position in the tree, despite the sun, offered only brief relief. He clenched his fists and then extended the fingers. He rubbed the tops of his feet. He inhaled and exhaled in rapid succession. He rubbed his calves and thighs and arms vigorously.

He considered all the hours he had spent in the walk-in refrigerator at Ricky Dee's Restaurant. Perhaps it had been a waste of time. His nose and fingers burned with cold.

He needed to get running again.

Before he started his climb down the tree, he looked all around once again. Descending the tree would leave him exposed, especially near the bottom. It was all clear until he looked south, up the mountain. Something was moving. He squinted.

The figure was human. The legs and chest were bare. He could determine no other detail.

He remained still, absolutely still. And waited.

Soon he could tell it was Nakamura, trotting downhill along the logging road. Apparently he intended to use the same strategy as Russell, intercepting the deer as they moved with the warmer, rising air.

Or maybe he was looking for Russell.

Russell began his descent of the tree.

As he climbed down, he paused numerous times to be sure that Nakamura was still in view. Then, because of his low position on the tree, he lost sight of him. He hurried toward the bottom as the chickadees continued to dart back and forth above him. At the last, he jumped and landed on the ground with knees bent, back hunched, and arms out from his sides. He looked about, but saw no one. He crossed back over the rough stretch of harvested land. He went into the forest and continued uphill, away from Mishima Nakamura.

CHAPTER 19

CRAFTING THE WEAPON

$\mathcal{T}$he forest was particularly cold because sunlight was not yet at ground level. Russell ran hard, following the trees along the edge of the wasteland. The branches, stones, acorns, and hickory nuts underfoot caused him no pain.

Eventually he headed east, still in forest.

He stopped. He had passed a scrape. He went back a few paces.

A small area of leaf litter on the forest floor had been disturbed in an almost circular pattern. This was a scrape, essentially a message center for deer. The scrape had been made beneath the overhanging bough of a beech tree.

He looked at the branch. A twig on the branch was shriveled. This was a licking branch. The deer had licked it repeatedly. The animal had also rubbed against it with the preorbital glands in front of its eyes. By doing so, it left information with both saliva and secretions from the eye gland.

Beneath the branch, a dominant buck had pawed at the earth. It had then urinated. Urine ran down across the tarsal glands on the inside of its rear legs, carrying a complex medium of scents to the ground.

Russell knew some of the science. He had read that lactones in the urine interacted with lipids on the tarsal glands. The urine then stained the earth with messages. But no one was entirely sure exactly what was being communicated. A doe that went by a scrape might be able to determine the overall health and size and status of the male by smelling the scent left in the dirt. During the rut, when females were in estrus, a doe might then return to the area to seek out the dominant male which had made the scrape; or they would urinate here or nearby as signal to the male to seek them out. Subordinate bucks encountering such a scrape might flee the area.

"Urine to attract a mate?" Sarah had said when he first explained this to her. "That's disgusting!"

"Maybe," he had told her, "but you'd probably have the same reaction to a list of ingredients on some of your fancy perfume bottles."

To him, there was no difference in the tactics. One way or another, odor compelled.

Most likely, there was a line of these scrapes defining territory through the forest. It was a means of communication for the rut, and the upcoming chase of does in estrus. He could, theoretically, simply wait here, as he could have waited at the signpost rub on the cedar tree. The dominant buck would return to inspect or freshen the scrapes and rubs. The buck would do this to reinforce notice of his presence, to make sure no other bucks were encroaching, and to learn of any does in estrus. But Russell would have to remain absolutely still and quiet, downwind of the buck's most likely approach, and probably for a very long time.

It was far too cold to remain so still and quiet indefinitely.

He struggled to pull down the shorts. Steam rose from the flow of urine as it left his body and landed on the scrape where the buck had urinated.

He did this partly in jest, partly in earnest. The deer were unlikely to glean any lasting import from it. He did it for his own benefit. A physical expression of a psychological depth: 'Deer beware! I am here!'

Russell chuckled to himself as he pulled the shorts up, and then ran.

Soon, he arrived at the northern-most part of the harvested land. For whatever reason, the loggers had come no higher up the mountain.

He looked about, and then gathered several stones. He took them over to a tree stump out in the harvested area. He tossed away those that appeared solid and unbreakable. He kept a few that had fissures in them. He then pounded one stone against another at just the right angle on the tree stump. The stones broke apart into flakes. He was not truly proficient at this technique, but would know which piece was the most appropriate when it showed.

He flaked four stones and then pawed through the shards. He chose one. It was wafer thin, narrow at one end, broad and dull at the other. It fit easily in the palm of his hand. He then used a rougher rock against the shard, in a filing motion, sharpening it. He ran a finger along the thinner edge. He was confident. With enough pressure, it could cut a throat.

He stood. He put the sliver of stone in the pocket of his shorts, on the rear right thigh. He practiced removing the stone and putting it back in place, like a cowboy testing the speed of his draw. It was a good fit. He was satisfied.

The sunlight had still not reached him. He looked about and then did another series of push-ups. He ran in place.

Now, everything was set.

He was warm. He knew the lay of the land. He had his weapon. It was time to get started.

He took a deep breath and then began a slow, cautious walk down the logging road.

CHAPTER 20

FIRST FRIGHT

*H*aving once been worn to raw earth by machinery, the logging road now showed evidence of being reclaimed by the forest. Here and there grew oak and maple saplings, no more than waist high, tufts of brown grass, ferns wilted by frost. Ian had indicated that the logging had been finished several years ago, but this road was obviously still a main thoroughfare. Russell saw prints of raccoon and coyote and fox and deer. However, he saw no evidence of Nakamura having walked along this road. But the top layer of ground was still frozen. Nothing would leave fresh tracks until the sun was higher and softened the ground.

He looked about. He crouched down. He roughly gauged the time since the various tracks had been made. This was an inexact science, and not anything he could fully explain. The gradient of wear, though, was somewhat obvious. An older track, having been exposed to the elements, lacked the sharp definition of those more recently made. It was that simple. He wasn't necessarily interested in determining if deer had been here on the 5th or 6th of the month. He was interested in frequency.

The deer prints were numerous, both large and small. The smallest were most likely those of a fawn. Some people claimed they could tell a buck's hoof print from that of a large doe. Russell did not have that ability. A wider stance would indicate a broader beast, but not necessarily a buck. Common sense might dictate that a wider, deeper set of imprints would be that of a buck but, depending on the season, a pregnant doe, carrying the extra weight, would also leave a broader, deeper print.

Some said that in a thin covering of snow, the sex of a deer was more easily determined. A buck, it was said, tended to essentially 'drag its feet,' leaving a lazy, thin trail in the snow between each hoof print; a doe tended to lift off completely and left only the prints themselves. Russell knew from experience that this claim was, at best, only partially accurate. A buck may or may not drag as he walked. Same thing for a doe. As far as Russell was concerned, the sex of a deer could not be confirmed by tracks alone.

As to the size or sex of the deer he would chase, it was a matter of opportunity. A buck, however, would pose a formidable challenge. This was the beginning of the rut, the breeding season. A buck would be at the peak of its strength, and full of fire. It would be crazed, unpredictable and, with a head of antlers, dangerous. Yet, in some ways, a buck was easier prey. Does were known to be smarter and more evasive than males, especially when they had a fawn to protect. But even a gutted doe or buck would be difficult to drag for any distance, so a fawn would obviously be an easier haul.

Regardless, if he were fortunate enough to see any deer, he would, most likely, go after the first one he saw.

His guess was that most of these tracks were more than just a few days old. They had been made a week ago, maybe longer. He ran his fingers over the outer edges. The edges were smooth, worn by wind and rain.

All creatures are victims of territory. He accepted this as a rule. The deer were no exception. White-tailed deer were not migratory creatures. They had no cause to travel great distances, not even in winter. They essentially stayed put, usually confining themselves to an area encompassing about one square mile. During the rut, females might move from territory to territory, seeking out the largest, strongest and healthiest of the males. Bucks too might well cross into territories of other deer. But for the most part, deer stayed in place.

Dispersal of a herd was a long, drawn out process. Yearling bucks and does were sometimes forced from the group, exiled to other groups, creating entirely new groups. Within each domain, hierarchies were well established. So, too, were the routines of everyday life.

Restriction of territory created intense familiarity with landscape. They knew where to find water. They knew the location of food to their liking, as well as its seasonal availability. They knew the safest places to bed down. They did rove about, always on alert, but returned to the same places again and again. In doing so, they made runways through the forest, a network of interconnected paths created by habitual passage.

Russell was confident that because of their limited territory, these deer would soon return to this area even though no recent tracks had been made.

The deer out here were not a suburban nuisance. They did not browse on tulip or exotic lily. A creature walking erect on two legs was something they would not be accustomed to seeing. The deer in this vicinity retained a certain purity. They were still wild. He was fairly sure that at first sight of him, at the slightest scent of him, they would flee. But, then again, a primary rule of behavior was that there were few rules of behavior. Most was mere tendency. Each estimate at tendency was considered a 'point of assumption.' Perhaps the assumption that he had made today was wrong. Perhaps, for whatever reason, the deer would not return to a place only long ago visited. But he must act on some premise. He chose tendency.

He continued on.

Ahead of him, the land dipped abruptly and then rose up again. He went up the hillock and lay down, cautious as to what might be on the other side. He crawled on his belly to the top. He looked. Nakamura was nowhere in sight. He then looked behind him and to either side.

All clear.

He stood. He went down the other side of the hillock, and continued to move slowly downhill, looking about and stopping every now and then to inspect tracks. After about an hour, the sunlight was finally on him. The air was now moving, ever so gently, out of the west, and had warmed up considerably.

At one point he found tracks that were more recent than others he had seen—no more than a day or so old. The deer that had left these tracks had moved along the logging road and then veered off onto a runway. He followed the tracks onto the runway, which was no more than a narrow path through the thick brush. The tracks led him into the forest and then disappeared among the leaf litter.

Just as he turned to go back, he heard a noise. He immediately crouched down in the runway.

The sound, which had come from the logging road, had not been as distinct as the breaking of a twig or the rustling of leaves. But he was certain that something nearby had disturbed the relative quiet.

Then, out of the corner of his eye, he saw something move. The movement had come from uphill to his right, but he didn't turn his head to look. He remained as still as he possibly could.

He waited. He wanted to reach for the flaked stone in his pocket. But if a deer were approaching, even that small movement could scare it away. If it happened to be Kozlov or Nakamura or Ortiz approaching, any movement on his part might draw unwanted attention. So he remained there, in the runway among the brush, hunkered down, his buttocks almost touching the earth. He stared straight ahead. And waited.

The slow moving object came into view.

Now he could see a doe.

His heart beat faster.

She was beautiful. Her winter coat of reddish gray had replaced the reddish brown of summer. For a female, she was quite large, maybe as much as two hundred pounds.

She took several steps and stopped.

A human's field of view was only about 190 degrees. He knew her field of view was over 300 degrees. She could see almost all the way around her. She could discern movement and, perhaps, the shading of what she observed. But as long as he did not move, she would have difficulty distinguishing his form from any other. If he remained still, perfectly still, she could stare right at him and yet, at best, only suspect his presence. He couldn't believe his luck. The breeze was coming toward him, carrying his scent away from her. She wouldn't be able to smell him unless she got very close. Close enough for him to pounce on her.

But now there was more movement to his right.

He remained absolutely motionless, and continued to stare straight ahead.

This second cause of movement came slowly into view.

Now he could see it—a fawn.

He had never seen such a thing.

The fawn was white, with no spots of black or brown, entirely white, pure, pristine white.

A doe and her spectacular fawn were moving up the mountain along the logging road.

Russell was incredulous. He wanted to cry out in amazement. He could barely restrain himself.

The doe looked to her left, down the runway, directly at him.

He held his breath. He did not blink. At so short a distance even the blink of an eye could send her scampering.

The fawn moved just a little ahead of the doe.

He did not have to move his eyes to study it.

The doe was obviously curious and unsure. She had not taken her eyes off him.

He couldn't hold his breath much longer.

He continued to study the fawn. An albino would have had pink eyes. This fawn was definitely not albino. As it aged, its eyes would eventually turn brown, but for now they were blue. Summer sky blue.

This was a ghost deer.

Not a piebald. Not an albino. A true white.

It was eerily beautiful, and startling—something bright white among so many drab reds, grays and browns.

He parted his lips ever so slightly to exhale, and then slowly took in more air. He still did not blink or let his eyes wander. He stared straight ahead as the doe continued watching him.

Fawns were typically born in late spring or early summer. He guessed that, for whatever reason, this fawn must have been born particularly late in the season. It didn't appear to be frail or sickly, but it was unusually small. By this time of year, a fawn should weigh about sixty to seventy pounds or more. His guess was that this fawn weighed no more than forty pounds.

A dazzling, delicate creature.

It lowered its head into the brush.

He continued to watch.

The doe raised her muzzle. The nostrils flared. She was suspicious. She was trying to pick up his scent. Now she raised and lowered her head, then moved it from side to side. She did this repeatedly, all the while keeping her eyes looking in his direction. This head bobbing was, in theory, a tactic designed to draw out anything that appeared strange or untrustworthy. She was trying to get him to move, to reveal himself and thus confirm her suspicions.

But he did not move. He had practiced this statue-like performance by standing in a bog hour after hour while mosquitoes feasted on him. He could remain like this indefinitely.

He couldn't have set it up better himself. This game could all be over in a few minutes. If either the fawn or the doe would come just a little bit closer....

He was only about five strides from them, but that was still too far. With the first step he took, or even just the tensing of his muscles, she would become aware of his presence and bolt.

The doe turned her head. She was now looking back down in the direction from which she had just come. The muscles at her flank twitched.

Something other than Russell had caught her attention.

Her tail went up, tall and white.

It would be logical to assume that nature had made a mistake in giving the deer a tail of this design, a flag of such obvious notice. A predator could not help but see it and then follow. Some believed that, in fact, it served as a message to anything that chased—see, I'm so quick and already so far of ahead that you might as well give up.

Others believed the raised tail was a means of distraction. If a predator moved in on a herd of deer, the herd would scatter and the forest would suddenly come to life with bright flashes of rapidly disappearing white. As if fireworks were to fill the sky, not in succession, but all at once, the human eye would find it difficult to settle on any one display. So, too, the scattering of white deer tails might, for just a moment, cause hesitation or confusion in the predator. Even if for only one step, any delay offered the deer an advantage.

But there was no argument as to the effectiveness or cause of the white tail in this situation. It acted as a silent alarm. The raised tail served as a warning signal to other deer: pay attention!

This doe had raised her tail because she definitely sensed something was amiss. She wanted her fawn to be on alert too. But the fawn was still feeding, its head lowered in the brush. It had not heeded her silent alarm.

Now the doe stomped a front hoof, another signal of vigilance and alarm. She was trying to get the fawn's attention. But the fawn still paid no heed.

Now the doe gave a quick blow, a snort. The abrupt rush of air left her nostrils with a sound like that made when a candle is blown out. But louder. Much louder. This not only cleared the nostrils so that scent could be more easily detected, but also served as a yet another sound of alarm.

At this, the fawn's tail went up. It abruptly lifted its head from the brush and looked to its mother.

And then they were running.

Even though Russell had expected them to take off at some point or another, and even though he had been in a similar situation hundreds of times, they moved so quickly that he was caught entirely off guard. The fawn dashed by him to his right. The doe headed along the runway straight toward him. It was all happening too fast. He had no time to move left or right so as to get out of her way.

She may have recognized his presence, but did not alter her course.

Being hunkered down made it almost impossible for him to move. Any evasive motion that he might take would require him to stretch his legs. And that would take time, precious time.

The doe was moving at close to full speed after only her first stride. She had the downhill momentum. She was going to run right over him.

The best he could do was to fall over backwards in an attempt to lessen the impact.

But, as it turned out, there was no need.

She rose effortlessly into the air. As she soared over him he saw, ever so briefly, the white of her underbelly contrasted against the blue sky.

He gasped in surprise and wonder.

She landed far downhill of him.

He scurried from the runway and lay down low in the brush. He was smiling, smiling through and through. Seeing the underside of a white-tailed deer as it leaped over him was something he had never witnessed before. And the white fawn, the exquisite white fawn.

His heart raced.

From where he now lay, he could still see the fawn and doe. With a simple turn of his head, he could also watch the logging road.

Point of assumption: the deer would not run far.

If, prior to this encounter, the doe and the fawn had simply been meandering up the logging trail, and had sensed no cause for alarm until just now, then his assumption would prove accurate.

A man who woke to an alarming disturbance in the night would be likely to keep perfectly still to listen for further notice of cause. He might sit up in bed and turn on the light, and then wait to see what developed. Or maybe he would get out of bed to investigate. But he would not be likely to react so fearfully as to go out the back door and run away.

Not at first fright.

So, too, for the deer. They would run, but not far. Not at first fright.

He watched as the doe and fawn bounded downhill. They tore through mountain laurel and black raspberry canes. They gracefully leaped over a stack of discards in their path. The pair moved down to the peninsula of forest that jutted into the wasteland where the trees had been harvested. But only the white fawn disappeared into the forest. The doe stopped and remained on the periphery. Her dull gray coat blended in well with her surroundings. She was difficult to see, in part because of her coloring, but more so because she was absolutely motionless. Nothing could move as quickly as a deer, and nothing could remain as still. Had he not seen her stop, he could have easily looked right by her.

She was looking up in his direction. Her tail was still raised.

She was being smart. The white fawn was easy to see. The doe had been sure to get her young one into the woods, away from the open area.

Russell kept watch on her. But he would not chase, not yet.

If he had been the one who had scared her, she would have led her fawn in the opposite direction, away from him. So something else must have frightened her. Perhaps she had heard or smelled something, or maybe she had felt vibrations through her hooves, and that's why she was now stopped. She was investigating at a safe distance. She was waiting to see what developed.

If he were to start chasing her now, he would be between the deer and whatever else was chasing them. Maybe it wasn't a stray dog or coyote on their trail. Maybe it was Nakamura.

He kept his profile as low as possible, flattening himself against the cold, hard ground.

He waited.

The doe held her position.

He heard another noise on the logging trail. It was definitely not a dog or coyote.

He reached back to his pocket for the stone. He slowly removed it and gripped it tightly in his right hand. He turned his head and peered through the brush.

The sound of footfall drew closer.

Kozlov, the Russian, strode into view. He was moving uphill along the logging road. He was not running quickly, but more or less just jogging along. He stopped and crouched down to inspect the ground.

He was so close that Russell could hear him breathing.

Russell's guess about Kozlov had been wrong. The Russian carried no spear.

Kozlov stood and looked about. He scratched his head and then jogged up the logging trail, in the wrong direction.

Russell felt no smugness over the Russian's error. He knew the path was covered with hoof prints. It was difficult to determine how recently they had been made. And it was logical to continue uphill for, typically, the deer would indeed be moving to higher ground with the warming air. It had been a point of assumption for Kozlov. And he had assumed incorrectly.

Russell turned his head.

Where was she? Then he realized that she had not moved. She was in the exact same place, so still and well camouflaged that he had looked right past her. As had the Russian.

He looked back. Kozlov was no longer in sight. He had gone uphill and disappeared over the rise.

Russell stood, slipped the stone back into his pocket, then turned and looked downhill just in time to see the doe vanish into the brush on the fringe of the forest.

He smiled.

Now the chase could begin.

CHAPTER 21

SECOND FRIGHT

*R*ussell sprinted toward the fringe of the forest where the deer had disappeared. But he was moving too quickly. The terrain was rough and dangerous, and there was not yet any need to move so fast. This was going to take time. The objective was not to run as fast as possible so as to catch up to the deer. That would be fruitless. No one could run that quickly.

Persistence was the key.

He would wear down his quarry, if not physically, then mentally. He intended to force the deer to do something they would not typically do. This could only be accomplished by staying after them, by letting them know he was still on their trail. He would use the acuity of their own senses against them. They would learn of his approach long before he knew of their exact location. Eventually, they would sense the pressure, especially if Kozlov, Nakamura or Ortiz also got in on the chase.

Most predators did not persist. The chase was usually concluded, one way or the other, in a short period of time. The deer would not be accustomed to a predator that persisted. So keeping them on the move would eventually confuse them. Their patience and stealth would be replaced by fear, or panic, or even plain curiosity about that which pursued them. Their breaking point would come. It was one of few rules that applied to behavior: after prolonged fear comes loss of poise.

After loss of poise comes mistakes.

So he would persist. But not at this pace. It would be too tiring. He needed to temper his excitement.

He slowed down to a trot. He was now deep in the forest, out of reach of the sun. It was cold. He stopped. His noticed his legs and arms and stomach were bleeding where thorns and branches had ripped his flesh.

For a few moments, he closed his eyes and breathed deeply, gathering composure.

He opened his eyes. He looked about and then began searching. He didn't see any tracks or other immediate signs indicating which way the doe had gone. If he got down on his hands and knees and searched, intensely studied the brush and ground, he knew he would eventually discover signs. But that would take too long. Though there was no great hurry, but neither was there time to dawdle.

The chase must be constant.

Point of assumption: the doe would not have moved back uphill, not yet. She had just been frightened from there by Kozlov. She would most likely have moved straight downhill, south, in the direction of the starting line. Eventually, she would have encountered the commotion of the bystanders and then have gone either east or west.

He chose east, toward the reservoir in the town park.

He was running again, at a sure, steady pace. His eyes moved with quick intent, looking for signs, watching for obstacles. Even so, once he was back in the area where logging had been done, he fell twice. Both times he tripped on discards hidden under tall grass and brush. Some of these discards were large, particularly the severed tree tops. They were, in and of themselves, like fallen trees from which numerous branches projected upward. The first time he scraped his shin. The second time he cut his left arm, badly. The stiff branch of a dead oak almost pierced his left arm when he fell. But he had been lucky. A bit further to the right and it would have pierced his chest.

Russell was up and moving again. He ignored the blood dripping down his arm.

He came to a ravine. The land dropped off quickly and then rose just as steeply on the other side. Discards lay strewn about, dark among the rocks.

And there she was.

He saw the white plume of her tail on the far side of the ravine. She was in the act of leaping over a stone wall, heading into forest again. Her spectacular fawn was right behind her.

He estimated they were a quarter of a mile away, but the wind was at his back. His scent had probably arrived long before they had sighted him.

Now he was in for a real test. Upon hearing a second alarming disturbance in the night, a man might indeed become so fearful as go out the back door and run away.

Second fright.

Now the doe knew that she and her fawn were being chased.

He went down into the ravine and then up the other side. Yellow signs had been nailed to trees on the other side of the stone wall:

NO TRESPASSING

NO Hunting ✦ NO Fishing ✦ NO Camping

Violators Will Be Prosecuted

He climbed over the stone wall.

Out of bounds.

He was in the town park. He understood he was now subject to the laws of the land. The rules of the game no longer applied.

He found the area where the doe and her fawn had landed after they jumped over the wall. Their tracks were deeply pressed among the fallen leaves.

He ran, and quickly lost their trail because there were so many leaves on the ground. But he would not stop. Not now. He must keep moving.

There were many possibilities. She could be heading toward a place that either offered more protection or was simply more familiar. Or she was trying to lose him by moving cross wind, then with the wind, then cross wind, in a zig-zag fashion. Or she might be moving north then west, doubling back on him, moving back into the wind.

Point of assumption: she was doubling back, looping, trying to get behind him.

He did not stop. He reversed direction while still running and headed back toward the ravine, over the wall, and once again in bounds. He would go west, then north and eventually head east. At some point in her loop, if she were indeed trying to get behind him, he would be there to meet her.

He went back up the other side of the ravine, into the sun. Discards and thorns ripped his flesh. Saplings smacked him in the chest and face.

At one point he tried to use one of the stacks of discards as a springboard, thinking he could just leap onto it and more or less bounce on and over it. But his feet slipped down through the branches. He cried out in pain. He was stuck, engulfed to the waist by the stack of stabbing branches. He had to hoist himself up, like a gymnast on parallel bars, then lift his bruised and bleeding legs to one side to get free of the pile.

He looked about.

He ran.

Russell reached the point in the logging trail where he seen Kozlov earlier. Here, on the relatively clear dirt road, he was able to run faster. The logging road traversed the mountain with only a slight downhill pitch. Without notice, without really even consciously deciding, but out of some instinctive reaction, he left the logging trail and headed due east again, downhill through the wasteland.

If his prediction were accurate, the doe and her fawn would be looping, trying to get behind him, and would have begun moving uphill by now.

Straight into his downhill advantage.

He passed through a dense copse of stout beech trees. They grew so closely together that they formed a thicket of intermingling branches. He held his hands protectively close to his eyes as he pushed through them.

He came out of the beech tree stand and there she was, or at least, there was her tail, raised high in retreat, and beside it, the smaller tail of the wondrous white fawn.

His racing heart skipped a beat.

The doe had indeed been looping, trying to get behind him.

She and the fawn were quickly gone from view.

Beneath his feet, he felt the frozen ground had softened with the warmth of the sun. Now he was on a runway, headed south. He saw tracks. There were many. But only two sets glistened with the moisture of having been freshly pressed.

Then, suddenly, there were no more hoof prints.

He stopped and circled back. He saw a broken twig on a sapling black birch tree. The flesh of black birch smelled like wintergreen when freshly exposed to the air. He sniffed. Yes, the break was fresh.

She had left the runway. She was headed east again, back toward the park. He took off in that direction.

Two coyotes rushed from his path. It was immediately apparent that they were as startled as he. One moved to his left, the other to his right. They were a blur of reddish gray as they fled. He had probably disturbed them from their bed somewhere in the brush.

His stride showed no evidence of hesitation. As he moved, he detected signs of the deer, freshly snapped twigs of red maple, freshly disturbed leaves on the ground. He also saw what appeared to be fresh tracks in softened earth.

He looked about frequently. He chased, round and round, back and forth through the wasteland, losing her trail and then picking it up again, over and over again. This doe seemed surprisingly smart. She was using every trick in the book. She moved upwind and then downwind. She doubled back, headed south for an extended period, then moved east and then north yet again.

Much of his body was now streaked with drying blood.

Gauging by the sun's position, he figured he had been pursuing her for well over an hour when, once more, her trail headed west toward the park.

He didn't stop when he reached the end of the wasteland, even though it was easy to see the 'No Trespassing' signs just beyond the crumbling stone wall. He jumped over the wall without breaking stride.

He was out of bounds again, on land belonging to the town. He was able to move much more swiftly here than in the true forest. Away from the periphery, the thick canopy had prevented undergrowth from sprouting on the forest floor. This area was comparatively open.

Pine needles and oak leaves and acorns covered the forest floor. The deer tracks were slight, but unwavering for an extended period. The doe was moving in a straight line. There would be no more looping, no more moving with or against the wind. She had given up on being clever. She was simply going to outrun him.

He picked up the pace.

Nakamura's timing was perfect. As he stepped out from behind the pine tree, he was already swinging his weapon directly at Russell's head.

CHAPTER 22

TASUKETE

*R*ussell had no time to slow down or to change course, or to even raise his hands in self-defense.

Nakamura swung a huge tree branch just like a baseball bat. It smashed against Russell's forehead and broke on impact.

Russell fell back and down onto the forest floor. He felt no pain. Instinct took over. His right hand immediately went for the stone in his pocket. He jumped to his feet.

Nakamura came at him again with what remained of the branch, which was now short and jagged. He lunged at Russell, trying to stab him.

Russell used his left arm to deflect the branch, while with his right hand he brought his sharp stone down across Nakamura's right arm, slicing flesh. Blood appeared at once.

Nakamura made a ferocious, guttural sound. He turned in a quick circle, performing a roundhouse kick, and brought his foot high toward Russell's head.

Russell ducked safely out of the way.

But Nakamura was so quick that Russell didn't even see the next move coming. The short, jagged branch hit his shoulder like a club, close to his neck, not piercing or even scratching the flesh, just a full, crushing blow.

His knees buckled. He fell to the ground. He quickly rolled away from Nakamura and then scrambled to his feet, ready to continue the fight.

But Nakamura was no longer there. He had gone running off through the woods.

Russell's sense of relief was momentary. Because now the pain rushed in. Blood from the wound on his forehead was streaming down into his eyes. His shoulder ached and stung. He went down slowly, then lay back, flat against the cold ground.

Everything was spinning.

His eyes closed.

He heard a red squirrel chattering in the distance.

He opened his eyes. Had he been unconscious? For how long?

He looked up through the trees and tried to gauge the time by the sun's position in the sky. Was it ten in the morning or two in the afternoon? At the moment, he couldn't tell. He couldn't tell east from west or north from south.

His forehead throbbed. When he rose to his knees, the wound opened up, and blood once again streamed down into his eyes. He pushed away leaves and pine needles until he saw dark dirt. He pressed some of the dirt hard against his wound. He could now feel the blood trickling down the side of his face, but at least it no longer ran into his eyes.

He was angry with himself. Inattention had nearly cost him the game, and his life. He had become so caught up in the chase that he had completely forgotten about Girard, Nakamura, Kozlov and Ortiz.

He slowly rose to his feet.

When he started to look about, his anger increased. He realized that looking about had become a perfunctory exercise. He had not been doing it with the intent of protecting himself, but as a routine, to satisfy a personal rule.

He breathed in deeply, slowly, quelling his anger, regaining composure.

He looked about again, not with a quick scan of his surroundings, but with a keen eye for anything out of the ordinary, for anything moving in any direction.

And something did move. He focused his attention on it. Fifty, perhaps 75 yards away, a red leaf was silently fluttering to the forest floor.

Otherwise, all was still.

He began walking, slowly at first, then more briskly. Soon he was running. But his gait was tame and hesitant. He was hampered by fearful vigilance.

The forest had changed. The threat had become real. Nakamura hid behind every tree.

But the farther he ran, the less the pain of his shoulder and forehead bothered him. And the farther he ran, the less fearful he became.

Nakamura had obviously been more interested in the doe than in him. That's why he had run off. Fighting with Russell had been a bothersome necessity. Fighting took time, and would allow the doe and her fawn to gain ground.

But before Nakamura could safely take over the chase, Russell had to be stopped. So Nakamura had hidden behind a tree, and at the appropriate time stepped out to hit Russell with the branch. Fortunately, the branch was pine, a softwood. Nakamura had probably found it on the ground nearby and picked it up as a matter of convenience, without realizing that at its core, it was punk, rotted. It had broken easily. Had the branch been oak, or some other hardwood, it might well have cracked open Russell's skull.

So now, more than likely, Nakamura was not waiting behind a tree for him. He was focused on winning the competition. He was chasing down the doe and her fawn.

With his confidence somewhat renewed, Russell picked up the pace.

He arrived at a clearing. Ahead of him, he saw an area where there was neither tree nor weed but, strangely, a surface of smooth, black tar.

He stopped.

The sight was disorienting. A parking lot.

How strange it was to see something so regimented out here in the forest.

On the roadway leading in and out of the lot, he saw yellow dividing lines. More yellow lines laid out the location of each parking space within the lot. Here and there were metal signs attached to metal posts:

Do not litter
No parking in this area
Not responsible for stolen articles

He moved forward, pushing through the brush at the edge of the forest. Once again, he stopped. To his left, a wooden fence separated the black pavement from a stretch of sand. On the sand, close to the water's edge, stood a tall, white lifeguard's chair.

Russell had a flash of understanding. This was the reservoir beach that Ian Rushmore had mentioned. Russell saw the floating dock out in the water. From either end of the shore, a line of buoys cut an arc in the water toward the dock, creating an enclosed swimming area.

And there, in the shallows, stood the doe.

She was on full alert, with ears erect and tail raised. She stared at Russell.

He crouched down among the brush.

Apparently, she and her fawn had separated. Splitting apart was a desperate but clever tactic. Anything trailing their scent would come to the point where they had separated and be momentarily confused as to which scent to follow. The fawn and doe would have gained distance on whatever was pursuing them, even if for only a few seconds. The doe may have even slowed her pace with the intent of luring the threat toward her and away from her fawn.

Now, here she was, entirely exposed, but not entirely disadvantaged.

But where was Nakamura? Had he caught the fawn? Was he headed to the finish line? Perhaps he was still off in the woods chasing it down. Or maybe he was nearby, in the brush, watching and waiting for Russell to make the next move.

Russell could wait, hoping that Nakamura had not found the fawn. He could just watch the doe. Eventually she would come ashore and then he could follow her or even chase her. Or he could go in search of the fawn right away.

But one thing was certain. He would not go in the water with the intent of taking the doe. The water was probably extremely cold. He would only last a few minutes before hypothermia set in. Plus, the doe would have the advantage out there. Russell knew deer were strong swimmers, and he would not be able to move quickly enough through the water if she tried to strike at him with her hooves.

He couldn't even be sure it was the same doe. But if it were the same doe, what was she doing out there? Had something frightened her into going out there?

Was she trying to lure him into the water and away from her fawn?

He was startled to see a rock fly through the air in front of him. He turned his head to see where it came from and there was Nakamura, charging across the pavement while launching another rock at Russell.

Russell ducked. Even so, the second rock clipped his ear. He stood up from his crouched position and ran, hunched over, his hands held protectively about his head. He cried out when yet another rock hit him, low on his left side.

Nakamura was going to stone him to death.

Russell stopped and turned. His blood burned with anger and hate. He would take care of the little bastard once and for all.

But Nakamura was no longer pursuing. He had headed down toward the water, screaming as he ran: "Ayyiii! Ayyiii!"

Russell moved back to the edge of the forest, gingerly rubbing his left side where the rock had hit him. He looked about. Then, once again, he crouched down low among the brush. And watched.

While still in the water, the doe moved to the left.

Nakamura mirrored her movement on land.

She moved to the right.

Nakamura moved in the same direction.

She turned away and swam out into deeper water.

Nakamura did not follow. He remained on the shore.

Russell could see that Nakamura still had two rocks, each about the size of a baseball, one in each hand.

The doe swam until she reached the line of buoys. She could go no farther. She now moved slowly through the water, her head held high, following the line of buoys, apparently looking for a break that would let her pass. But there was no break. She was trapped. She would have to move back toward the shore, or drown.

Nakamura moved far to the left, apparently giving her the option of moving toward the shallows at the other end of the swimming area.

The doe started heading that way at once.

When she reached a depth where she could once again stand, Nakamura charged toward her along the sandy shore, hand with rock raised high.

The doe seemed startled at his sudden approach. She stopped and stared. Then she was running with obvious difficulty through the water as she again headed for shore.

Nakamura threw as he ran.

The rock soared just over her head.

Now she was in shallow water.

While still running, Nakamura drew back his arm.

The doe was almost free of the water.

Nakamura stopped abruptly, planting his left foot far ahead of his right foot. His arm came forward. He grunted with effort as the rock left his hand. There was no arc to the trajectory; the rock traveled in a straight line through the air.

The rock hit her, just below the ear.

Down she went on the sand at the water's edge.

"Ayyiii!" Nakamura shouted, as once again he was charging toward her.

But she had only been stunned. She lifted her head. She rose to her knees and was just about to stand up when Nakamura, having no more rocks, and apparently seeing that she was about to run away, leapt onto her.

He landed with his chest against her rump. He clawed and clutched at her and pounded her with his fist.

She tried to shake him off, to no avail. She rose up slightly on her hind legs and lunged forward. Nakamura slipped off her. But he was quick. Before he hit the ground he had grabbed her by the tail with both hands.

She thrashed her head about. She raised her rear end, trying to buck him off of her.

One of Nakamura's hands slipped from her tail. The other still clutched tight.

She moved forward, dragging him on his knees along the sand.

He raised his free hand toward her.

But, apparently, he could hold on no longer. His hand slipped from her tail. And just as he let go, she abruptly raised her rear end and kicked back with her hind legs. Both hooves caught him on the jaw, making a dull cracking sound.

Nakamura's head snapped backwards.

The doe was now free of his grasp.

She ran a short distance and stopped. She turned to face Nakamura again.

Nakamura lay motionless on the ground.

The doe approached him in a posture of challenge: tail up, head low, ears back. She stopped. She snorted. She stomped a hoof.

Russell watched, startled by her behavior. He had never seen a deer do anything quite so brazen. She should have run off. Instead, she actually seemed to be challenging Nakamura. It was foolhardy. Nakamura was just going to get up and pounce on her again.

But Nakamura didn't move.

The doe drew closer to him. She rose up high on her hind legs, like a startled horse. Her front hooves pawed the air. As she came back down, she used her right front foreleg in a whip-like manner to club Nakamura on the head with her hoof.

Still, Nakamura did not move. He made no effort to defend himself or get out of the way.

Again the doe rose up on her hind legs and came down, clubbing Nakamura again and again. Then she turned from him and, with her tail raised high, darted along the dark pavement toward the forest.

Russell came from the low shrubbery onto the sand, following after her.

He looked back at Nakamura and saw that he had not gotten up, had not even lifted his head. But he did hear him speak.

In a voice that was strangely weak, a low, pain-filled rasp, Nakamura called out a single word:

"*Tasukete….*"

Russell needed no translation. The word may have been foreign to him, but the tone and the circumstance left no doubt as to the meaning.

Nakamura was calling out for help.

It was obvious that he was seriously injured. Nakamura wouldn't have let the doe club him on the head like that, not if he had been capable of defending himself.

But Russell did not break stride.

He thrust a jubilant fist to the sky.

One down, three to go.

216

CHAPTER 23

DUMBFOUNDING

Russell continued after the doe, and when once again he came to the stone wall, he leaped over it with renewed vigor and determination. He was back in bounds, moving as fast as the rough terrain would allow. He saw the doe, then lost her, saw her again, lost her.

Eventually she and her fawn joined up again. He could see them, far uphill of him, moving due west, moving away from the reservoir, then south and then, yet again, east, back toward the reservoir, doubling back to the town beach.

Then he lost sight of them.

More so, this time he let them get out of view. If he continued, he was confident he would catch sight of them again. But he did not continue. He remained there among the trees, his hands on hips. His chest heaved. Anxiety and confusion suddenly overwhelmed him. He bent over and rested his hands on his knees as he tried to catch his breath. But even as he did this, he kept his eyes on Nakamura.

It was startling to see an almost naked man lying face down, motionless, out here.

Russell looked about and then moved closer to the edge of the forest.

Well over an hour had passed since he had left this area, and yet in that time, Nakamura had not moved. He was lying in the same place, in the same position.

But the doe…she was getting away. She and her fawn would bed down. They'd regain their strength and then they would run and run and….

Even so…here was a helpless human being lying on the ground….

But after being chased for almost an hour, the doe was probably frantic and prone to mistakes, on the verge of losing her poise. Besides, Nakamura was on his own. He had been warned, just as everyone else had been warned. He would have to take care of himself.

"Part of the game," Russell whispered, as once again he looked about.

The Charge, First Notice, Second Notice, Final Notice. The Covenant.

Everyone had all been made aware of the risks, countless times.

Even so….

Russell pulled the stone from his rear pocket. He stepped out from among the trees and moved cautiously toward Nakamura.

Nakamura lay face down. One arm was stretched out in front of him. A few strands of white hair from the doe's tail were still clutched in his hand.

Russell shouted, "Nakamura!"

Nakamura did not move or make any response.

Russell drew closer to him. He gave Nakamura a shove with his foot, and quickly backed away.

No response.

Russell looked about. He was an easy target, out in the open like this.

With his weapon still at the ready, he crouched down and reached out to Nakamura and pulled on his shoulder.

Nakamura rolled toward him, offering no resistance. His eyes were open, but strangely vacant. White bone was exposed where the doe had kicked him in the jaw. There was no other disfigurement, and only a little blood. But his head was at an odd angle.

"Nakamura," Russell said. "Nakamura?"

He put two fingers to Nakamura's throat, feeling for a pulse.

Nothing.

He couldn't believe it. So he pressed his fingers with more emphasis, up by the ear.

Nothing. He tried the jugular. He pressed his ear against the chest. No heartbeat, no sound.

Still nothing.

Russell looked about again. And saw movement. He focused in on it. A human form was disappearing into the brush.

Adriana Ortiz.

So Ortiz was in on the chase now. She was playing it smart. She wasn't going to let anything stop her. She was going to find the doe and win. She continued to run, without even looking in Russell's direction. She would....

He turned back to Nakamura. He shook him once more by the shoulder.

Nakamura's head lolled limply from side to side.

He put the stone back in his pocket and stood.

He looked up at the sky. Thin puffs of cloud moved lazily by. He looked to the forest and saw gray squirrels on the ground, rummaging among the fallen leaves. He heard finches singing and the incessant hammering of a woodpecker.

Life persisted.

It was dumbfounding.

Absolutely dumbfounding.

He looked back down at the pale, limp body at his feet.

Perhaps the blow to the jaw had snapped Nakamura's head back with such force that his neck had broken. That would explain why his head was at such an impossible angle. Or perhaps death had been due to sheer trauma, a fatal shock to the brain as a result of the force of impact.

The contrast was astounding, bewildering. There was no sense to be made of it.

He turned away.

It was foolish to have stopped. Doing so may have cost him the game. Stupid. A waste of time.

"No!" he said, adamantly, and then added, less forcefully, "I don't know...."

He went to the pine trees down at the water's edge, to the right of the swimming area. He broke off some of the boughs and tossed them into a pile. As he did so, something caught his eye. It glinted in the sun.

He drew close to it.

A strand of fishing line was dangling from a branch.

He envisioned a summer child drawing back a fishing rod so as to cast the baited hook into the water, instead snagging the hook on an overhead branch.

He reached up and took hold of the fishing line. He pulled. It would not come free. He wrapped the line around his hand and pulled again, harder. The line dug into his flesh. Finally, the hook came free.

He removed the stone from his rear pocket and used it to sever the hook from the line. The line was monofilament, a single strand of clear nylon. Thin, but strong; about ten feet in length. He inspected it for signs of weakness. He found none. He rolled it into a tight coil. He stuffed the coil inside his shorts, against his buttocks. He had no immediate use for the line, but neither would he pass it up. This was a gift from the land: something with which to bind.

He carried the pine boughs over to Nakamura and draped them over his body.

In life, Nakamura had been coarse, abrasive and mean spirited. Easy to dislike. And to fear. But to have left him there exposed to the elements would have been a violation. A violation of what, exactly, Russell could not say. But he sensed an ancient obligation. It felt right, and just, to cover the dead.

"We will come back to get you," he said.

He walked away, recalling what Sarah had told him: "You're in the wrong game."

He was trotting as he crossed the pavement and moved back into the forest. Then he was running at full speed, oblivious to the scratching and clawing of branch and briar. "Wrong game!" he cried. "Wrong game!"

He stumbled and yet maintained his balance and was still running, now uphill, straining against the grade, dislodging rocks beneath his feet, slipping, pushing on and on, not running toward anything, not running from anything, just running.

Russell leapt over the stone wall and was back in the wasteland, the area harvested by the loggers. He continued at full force over the rough terrain, bounding from stone to stone, still moving uphill in the bright sunlight until he tripped and fell headlong into a stack of oak and pine discards. He was jabbed and cut and he cried out for the pain. He turned over onto his back, his chest heaving, his heart pounding, his eyes wide as he looked up at the sky. He brought his hands to his face. His body shuddered uncontrollably.

The sight of Nakamura clutching at the doe's hide, then slipping back, hanging onto her tail and finally letting go just as she kicked.... He heard the horrible sound of her hooves connecting with Nakamura's jaw.

He was filled with hate for the game, for this stupid, insane game.

The last word Nakamura had spoken echoed in his mind: *"Tasukete...."*

Russell freed himself of the pile of discards. He wiped his eyes.

A sudden yearning for Sarah came over him. He wanted to lay his head on her breasts, to rest there and idle in her tender warmth. He yearned to be absent from all games, from all prizes to be won, from all struggles. He yearned for comfort.

"Tasukete...."

He muttered complaints to himself about his inability to stay focused.

He started slowly moving uphill again. He went through the motions of looking for signs of deer. He noticed the tracks. He saw the freshly broken twigs. But his surveillance was mechanical, without true intent.

"Quit or get back into it," he said.

But he did not quit. Nor did he get back into it. He continued at the same listless pace, with the same lack of focus. He came to the logging road where, earlier that morning, he had seen Kozlov. He decided to follow the road uphill.

He approached an island of trees, a piece of forest untouched by the loggers. Here was the graveyard Ian had described that morning, where the landowner's ancestors lay buried. It was small, about a dozen gravesites enclosed by a waist-high stone wall.

He sat on the wall.

Tombstones leaned. Leaves fell.

In a nearby stand of mountain laurel, chattering chickadees fluttered about. A red squirrel, high in an oak, scolded with chirps and chucks.

Russell felt strangely depleted. His posture was hunched, his shoulders low. He had neither the energy nor the desire to continue. Perhaps he should cross back over the line. Just go down the mountain and tell Ian Rushmore that he was done.

Done.

His thought process was interrupted by two sounds. The rush of air being forced through nostrils, and the pounding of hooves.

Deer!

He sat up straight, suddenly realizing his vulnerability. He was literally a sitting target.

He slipped down off the stone wall, and crouched behind it. He looked about and then slowly raised himself up to peer over the wall.

Between the trees, far off into the wasteland, he saw three does running uphill.

Perhaps they had been browsing nearby, then picked up his scent and run off. But maybe something else had spooked them, something he hadn't seen or heard because he had been so distracted. Ortiz. Was she nearby? Or Kozlov?

He looked about again. He lowered himself against the stone wall.

The black-capped chickadees in the laurel had been making a frantic, bothered noise. Now, he paid attention to them.

Their musical notes confused him. He should have been the cause of their frenetic banter. But he was directly below them, and they were singing about something else.

Their song was a high-pitched, "Seeet-dee! Seeet-dee!" They repeated this phrase, quickly, again and again, conveying the alarm: the threat is from above.

Russell looked to the sky between the leafless branches of ash trees. The presence of a hawk soaring overhead would explain the disturbance these chickadees sensed.

But the sky was empty.

The red squirrel high in the oak tree was still agitated. It announced its annoyance via repeated, loud calls. He saw that the squirrel was not looking down at him or even facing in his direction.

Russell looked about yet again. He saw nothing unusual, nothing out of place.

But he was now certain that it had not been he who had frightened off those deer. The birds, the squirrel, the running deer…the land was alive with alerts.

A chill ran down his spine.

He pulled the stone from his pocket. Clenching it tightly in his right hand, he scampered a short distance across the forest floor, away from the stone wall. Now he could see all around him.

He looked to the sky again, this time taking in a broader account. Still, no hawk. Nothing.

But perhaps some other bird of prey was perched in a tree. So he lowered his vision and let his eyes roam through the tree tops.

He still saw nothing out of the ordinary. Yet back in the laurel bushes over by the graveyard, the chickadees continued their call of alarm. The red squirrel persisted with its furious chatter.

He was baffled. He turned his head slowly, scanning the forest with his line of sight set lower in the trees.

Their eyes met.

CHAPTER 24

PREY NOT PREDATOR

$\mathcal{F}$ ar off to his right, Russell heard crows cawing and blue jays squawking. Obviously, some sort of disturbance was taking place down there. And it was drawing closer.

But he kept his eyes on Kozlov.

The Russian stood ten or fifteen feet above the ground on a tree branch overhanging the logging road. With his left hand, he held onto the branch above him, while with his right hand he held a spear at the ready, resting across his shoulder. The spear had been shaved sharply to the light colored heartwood at one end. It was so straight that Russell figured it was made of ash; not as heavy as oak or maple, but rigid, with more weight and strength than pine.

So Russell's assessment had been right.

The Russian had chosen to use a spear after all. He also seemed to think that the logging road was the most likely place for deer to pass. Indeed, no more than twenty feet from where Kozlov stood, a runway opened out from the opposite side of the logging road. Deer might well show up there.

By climbing the tree, Kozlov had removed his scent from ground level. Any deer that happened to draw close would be unaware of his presence until it was too late. There was stealth in his tactic. But there was risk as well because, technically, he had removed himself from the chase. Perhaps from that position he could see what was taking place downhill, and maybe an entire herd of deer were moving up in his direction.

But he had only one throw, and if no deer happened to pass within range, he would be out of luck. Or, if he threw and missed, he would also be out of luck; he would need to climb down out of the tree, retrieve his spear and start all over again. The strategy Kozlov had chosen was one of wait and hope. It took up time, valuable time. And, in a way, he was now trapped. He wouldn't risk climbing down the tree, not while Russell was nearby.

The frantic sounds of the crows and blue jays grew louder.

Something was approaching.

Still, Kozlov and Russell stared at one another.

Russell saw both hesitation and resistance in the Russian's face. It was as if he were saying that he knew he was trapped, but Russell had not better come any closer.

Russell had no intention of doing so. He didn't need to. The advantage was his. He was out of the range of any spear throw, and Kozlov was at least temporarily out of the chase.

He had Kozlov right where he wanted him.

Russell used his foot to clear away leaves until he saw a rock that seemed suited to his needs. He held the rock up high for Kozlov to see, and shook it at him, sending a message he was confident would transcend any language barrier: don't even *think* about coming down out of that tree.

Kozlov looked away, toward the ever approaching raucous sounds of the birds.

Russell moved to the very edge of the island of trees. He was now behind a white pine, only one step from the logging road.

Still, he watched Kozlov.

Gone was any consideration of Nakamura. Gone were thoughts of crossing over the line in defeat.

He was back in the chase.

From downhill, the cawing and squawking of the birds grew louder and louder. In the branches of the nearby oak, the red chattering squirrel darted back and forth.

Now, from across the logging road, Russell heard leaves rustling and branches breaking.

Something large was moving around over there. And it was coming closer.

Kozlov could obviously see something. He had drawn back the spear.

Russell heard an unmistakable sound: the rapid pounding of hooves.

Kozlov threw the spear.

The long, slender shaft of wood soared, straight and even.

Russell turned his head, following the flight of the spear with his eyes.

On the other side of the logging road, the doe and the white fawn came running out of the brush. The spear stuck in the earth just behind the fawn, and was still vibrating with the impact when Ortiz appeared. Her face was distorted by an expression of intense concentration and effort. She sidestepped the spear. She did not stop. She gave no evidence of hesitation, did not even turn her head. She ran.

She was no more than thirty feet behind the fawn.

Her clothing, once the object of so much concern, had not held up. It had separated into two tattered pieces; both top and bottom were torn and shredded. Blood was visible on her exposed midriff. Her arms and legs were streaked with red. Her powerful thighs shuddered with each stride.

Russell looked back at Kozlov.

Kozlov was climbing down out of the tree. He was forcing Russell's hand.

Russell could fight it out with him, here and now. Not only was that a risk, it would allow Ortiz and the deer to get away. Another option was to follow Ortiz; but that would put Kozlov behind him, which was also a risk.

Time to choose.

Russell stepped out from behind the tree. He took off along the logging road, racing after Ortiz, the doe, and the white fawn.

They all headed uphill.

Russell ran at full speed, yet gained no distance on Ortiz. He wouldn't be able to keep up this pace for long, not at this rate.

They moved laterally across the mountainside. They moved uphill and then downhill. Russell glanced behind him. Kozlov was nowhere in sight.

Ortiz, the doe and her fawn went up over a rise and for a few moments were out of view. When he reached the top of the hillock, he saw that the logging road wound downhill rather steeply. At a stand of mountain laurel, far down the mountain, the logging road split. In one direction, the road went straight down, south, toward the base of the mountain. In the other direction, it headed back uphill toward the wolf tree, the lone, massive tree in the wasteland.

With its evergreen leaves, the laurel down there was distinctive. The individual bushes huddled close together to form a wide, dense, tangled stand.

To the west, beyond the mountain laurel, there was wasteland and then forest. Russell figured the doe was headed in that direction, to the shelter of the forest, away from the openness of the wasteland.

He jumped over stones and shrubs as he ran. The earth, having dried in the sun, rose up in puffs of dust beneath each footfall.

The doe and fawn had pulled away from Ortiz.

Russell ran harder, almost out of control on the downhill grade. He saw the doe stop and turn to face Ortiz. The doe was going to stand and defend her fawn.

Ortiz drew closer.

But the doe took off again and was quickly alongside the fawn. They both left the logging trail and then, side by side, leapt over the stand of mountain laurel and continued up the grade on the other side, up through the wasteland toward the forest.

Ortiz followed close behind. She vaulted the shorter bushes of mountain laurel like a hurdler, her left leg out to the side and yet pulled close to her, her back arched as her left hand reached toward her straightened right leg.

And was gone.

Russell was so startled that he stopped running.

She had completely disappeared.

He looked about.

Kozlov was nowhere to be seen. And neither was Ortiz.

But where had she gone?

Russell continued running down toward the mountain laurel and then stopped. When he bent over, hands on knees, to catch his breath, he heard anguished moaning.

The stand of evergreen shrubbery had prevented him from seeing the cellar hole where, apparently, a house had once stood; all that remained now was the foundation, the walls of which had been made of fieldstone, large rocks stacked on top of one another. Wild rose grew against the walls. Here and there, ferns grew out of the dirt floor. He saw birch and maple saplings. He also saw scattered bones.

Ortiz lay on her side close to the far wall. She sat up. She held onto her right arm with her left hand. Her mouth was bloodied. She rocked gently back and forth.

He turned his head and could see that the doe had stopped far up the grade, at the edge of the forest. She was looking back down at him. The fawn was nowhere to be seen.

He again looked at Ortiz.

She was trying to stand, but couldn't. She toppled over. Not only did her arm appear to be injured, so did one of her legs.

He realized she was trapped down there. That cellar hole had to be six or seven feet deep. With both an injured arm and leg, she couldn't climb out. She would have to wait over 24 hours before a search party would even begin to look for her. Tonight, the temperature was going to plummet. The nor'easter was expected to dump a half foot of snow, accompanied by swirling winds; a blizzard. Without cover or means to build a fire, she could freeze to death down there.

He looked to the doe and then back at Ortiz.

We of this game are of no laws between us....

First Notice, Second Notice, Final Notice. The Covenant.

He had chosen. She had chosen. And she had been true to her reckless character in that she had literally failed to look before she leaped.

Anyway, she would probably eventually figure a way out of that cellar hole, particularly when the temperature dropped and the snow started to fall. That would spark a creative fire in her. Then she would endure whatever pain was necessary in order to climb up out of there.

Or die.

He looked about.

"*Roto!*" Ortiz yelled out. She pointed to her leg, near the ankle. She nodded. "Malo! Bad," she called again.

He was wasting time.

Yet again he looked to the doe.

Now Ortiz called out, "Por favor, ayudame! Ayudame!"

The doe was well out of his throwing range. It was useless to even try. Even so, he picked up a stone and threw it in her direction.

"Por favor!" Ortiz called.

The doe continued to stare at Russell. Her tail remained limp, indicating she sensed no threat from him.

He picked up another stone and threw it uselessly toward the doe; he picked up another and threw, and another, and another. His movements were frantic, uncoordinated, like a child having a tantrum. He reached for yet another stone on the ground, missed, but followed through on the motion anyway and ended up tossing a handful of dust into the air.

The doe now moved slowly into the shelter of the forest.

"Goddamn it!" he shouted. "I can't ...you...."

He fell to his knees, half laughing, half crying.

He fell forward, now on his hands and knees. He pressed his forehead to the ground, muttering and swearing.

He raised his head. He looked at Ortiz down in the cellar hole.

Her expression suggested both pain and confusion.

She was trapped, and badly injured. And here he was, acting like a lunatic. Of course she was concerned.

He smiled at her, trying to ease her fear. "Me," he said, and pointed at his chest. "Me argue with me. Understand?"

She stared at him in silence.

"No?" he said. "No. Me neither."

He got to his feet. He shook his head.

"Win! Win! Win!" he shouted.

He kicked the earth.

Then, holding onto the trunk of one of the bigger laurel bushes, he eased himself down into the cellar hole. He moved toward her.

She pushed with her elbows and one foot against the ground, trying to back away from him.

"Me," he said, and once more pointed at his chest. "No hurt you," he said, and pointed at her.

"Malo," she whimpered. "Bad." She grimaced.

Her right arm was bent at an unnatural angle, just above the wrist.

He imagined her jumping over the laurel bushes and suddenly realizing the drop beneath her; she had probably put out her right hand in an attempt to break her fall.

Her wincing revealed bloodied teeth. Her jaw was freshly scraped. She made a choking sound and then spit red onto the dirt floor. A fragment of tooth was stuck to her swollen lip.

He pointed at her, then at himself and finally in the direction of the laurel. "Me help you."

She said something he didn't understand, and then lay back with a long, slow moan.

He took notice of the bones that were scattered around. Multiple ribs, legs, skulls. Coyotes and dogs, probably. He picked one up, a mandible, bleached by the sun, with a few sharp teeth still attached.

He looked around. Now he understood.

This cellar hole was definitely too wide for a human or coyote to jump across. But a doe, even a fawn, would have no difficulty leaping across. Especially if they knew it was here, hiding behind the stand of mountain laurel. Anything chasing the deer would end up down here, unable to get out. Trapped. These bones were the remains of previous victims.

So that was why the doe had stopped and let Ortiz draw closer. She had no intention of fighting in order to protect her fawn. She wanted to make sure that Ortiz did indeed follow right behind her, into the trap.

Ortiz had been prey, not predator.

He tossed the jawbone aside and went to the far wall. By forcing his feet and hands into the gaps between the stones of the wall, he was able to climb down. Standing on his tip toes brought his head up to ground level. He peered through the trunks of mountain laurel, scanning the landscape. He did this at each of the four walls.

Kozlov was nowhere to be seen.

But if the Russian did show up, he would ensure neither of them got out of there. Russell went to Ortiz and took hold of her uninjured arm.

She said something in Spanish that had the tone of complaint.

He loosened his grip on her arm but did not release her. He pulled.

She came to her feet with a pain-filled cry. She stood in one place, yet wobbled.

As a warning to himself, he said, "Pay attention."

It was her right arm that was injured. But at the reception, when he had inspected her clothing, he had learned she was left handed.

And Girard had paid dearly for touching her.

Russell would help her, but had no cause to trust her.

She flinched when he reached over and patted her buttocks and felt for the stone on the rear left thigh.

He pulled the stone from her pocket and tossed it aside.

She spoke, harshly.

He smiled at her. "What?" he said. "You're asking me to marry you? Wow! I'm honored, truly. But no can do. I'm already spoken for."

Her dark eyes were fierce.

He crouched down beside her.

Thorns protruded from her blood-smeared thighs and calves. Both shins were badly scraped and bruised. She was holding her left foot up off the ground; there was already severe swelling around the ankle.

He looked up at her. "Broken?" he asked.

Again she spoke words he didn't understand.

He made a snapping motion, and said again, "Broken?"

"Si! *Roto, muy malo*," she said. "Much bad."

He stood. He held onto her good arm with both hands, urging her to move toward the far wall.

She nodded excitedly. "Si! Si! Out."

He heard the cawing of a crow.

"Shhh!" he said.

The sound of a crow may have only meant that the bird was calling out in a squabble with other members of its flock. But there was also the possibility that it was warning of a disturbance of some sort. And that disturbance might be Kozlov.

Russell let go of Ortiz, which was a mistake.

She fell over at once, crying out in pain.

He went to the wall and raised himself up. His eyes were at ground level.

Kozlov was about fifty yards away. Judging by his position, he had been heading uphill. But now he was looking back in the direction of the cellar hole.

He must have heard her, because he turned and came running downhill.

Russell dropped back down. He picked up a stone and then pressed himself flat against the cellar wall. He looked at Ortiz. He put his finger to his lips.

"Shhh!"

Soon, the shadow of a human figure appeared on the dirt floor.

Kozlov was standing directly above Russell. But he wouldn't be able to see Russell unless he stood at the very edge of the cellar hole and looked straight down.

Russell could tell by the outline of the shadow that Kozlov was holding the spear in both hands.

Kozlov said something in Russian to Ortiz.

Ortiz, lying on the dirt floor, propped up on one elbow, shouted something back in Spanish.

"Deer?" Kozlov asked.

She motioned with her head toward the top of the mountain. "Up. Up."

"Bowen?" he asked.

"Bad," she said, and pointed at her leg. "Bad."

He laughed.

Russell watched Kozlov's shadow on the dirt floor. Kozlov was crouching down.

Russell couldn't wait any longer. The risk was too great.

Out here there were no rules, neither in benefit nor in burden.

And if Kozlov were to realize that Russell was in there, stuck down there, it would be, for Kozlov, like shooting an animal in a cage. Russell had to make the first move, a preemptive strike.

He looked up. Directly above him, he now saw Kozlov's leg dangling over the edge. Kozlov was about to climb down into the cellar hole.

Russell quickly stepped away from the wall, turned and threw the stone as hard as he could. He was so close to Kozlov it would have been difficult to miss him. The stone hit him squarely on the knee cap.

Kozlov let out a shriek of surprise and pain. He rolled away from the edge of the cellar hole.

Russell scrambled around, gathering up more stones.

The Russian had risen to one knee. He made a growling sound as he raised the spear.

Russell threw again, as hard as he could. This time he hit Kozlov on the shoulder.

Kozlov cried out.

Russell threw again.

Kozlov ducked down, out of view.

But Russell kept on throwing, one stone right after another, and then rushed back to the shelter of the wall.

Ortiz was crawling towards him.

He hurried to her, grabbed her hand and pulled.

She screamed in pain as he dragged her along the ground.

At the last, he let go of her hand and then pushed against her, literally rolling her over and over until she lay lengthwise against the base of the wall. It was the only place that offered any safety.

Russell picked up another rock. He made a quick, intense study of each of the four possible approaches: to the mountain laurel, then straight ahead, then to his right and finally to the ground in front of him where, before, he had seen the shadow of Kozlov.

Ortiz was sobbing.

Minutes passed. Russell continued the tense vigilance, his eyes never resting.

Perhaps Kozlov had gone away. Or maybe he was up there, close by, waiting.

Eventually, Ortiz was silent.

Russell cautiously scaled the wall until his eyes were at ground level. With his feet and hands pressed between the rough stones, it was an awkward perch. He could not see Kozlov. He looked behind him and to either side. Nothing. He lowered himself back down.

He helped Ortiz rise to her knees. He crouched down beside her, drew her unhurt arm around his neck and then assisted her toward the wall over by the mountain laurel.

He released her. She leaned her shoulder against the wall while holding her left foot up off the ground.

He pointed at her. "You do this?" He stood on tiptoes and reached up to grab onto rocks in the foundation wall.

She turned. She imitated him, leaning against the stone wall while standing on one foot.

He got behind her. He bent down by her unhurt leg. He put one hand against the sole of her foot and the other against her buttocks.

"No! No!" she cried.

He lifted slowly. "Just keep your leg straight," he said sternly. "Leg straight."

He strained. He pushed against her firm rear end.

She cried out. Then, judging by the tone, she was cursing.

"Hold on," he said. He now had both hands cupped beneath her foot. He thrust upward in one final, merciless push.

Her chest was against the top of the foundation wall. She was hanging onto a trunk of a mountain laurel bush with one hand.

Using the gaps between the stones in the wall for footholds and handholds, he climbed up beside her. He, too, grabbed onto a laurel trunk. He pulled himself up out of the cellar hole, took hold of her uninjured arm and hauled her up until she was on level ground. He then let go of her.

He stepped back.

Her cheek was against the earth. Blood oozed from her mouth. Tears spilled from her eyes.

He tried to help her up but she said something in a violent tone.

He backed away again. He looked about.

Where was the Russian?

Ortiz raised herself up between the laurel bushes. She rested on her knees with her left hand pressed to the ground. She held her hurt arm awkwardly beneath her as she knelt there. Her stomach moved spasmodically. She made a retching sound and then vomited, her entire body thrusting forward. She gasped for air and then put her forehead to the earth. She coughed. Her body trembled.

He wondered: "Shock?"

He looked around, but saw only clumps of grass, the loggers' discards and rocks. There was nothing to cover her with to keep her warm.

Far off, something moved.

He focused his attention on it. The object was so far away that it appeared very small, way up the mountain, beyond the wolf tree. He squinted and could then tell: Kozlov.

Kozlov was just leaving the open area of the wasteland, moving into the forest.

Ortiz moaned. He turned back to her.

She was now lying on her back. Her skin was pale. Her eyelids fluttered.

He pawed at the earth. He dug with his hands and then tossed the dirt onto her with the hope that it would help her body retain some of its heat. He tore at clumps of grass and piled them on her.

She sat up abruptly.

He was startled.

She immediately started brushing off the dirt and grass. She spoke quickly and loudly. Her tone said many things: she was angry, surprised and disgusted, all at once.

He backed away. "No, sorry...I was just trying to...."

She managed to rise, balancing on one foot. She continued to speak, now with a tone of reprimand. She waved him away. She shook a finger at him and continued her unintelligible harangue.

"You Mexicans sure do heal quickly," he said.

She raised a fist, as though to strike him.

He ran a short distance to a pile of discards. He searched for a straight branch. He found one and pulled on it, but it would not come free. He pushed, twisted, pulled again and when it finally did come free, he fell back with the momentum.

She laughed and then quickly cried out, as though her laughter had caused her pain.

He brought the branch to her. "A staff," he said.

She took it with one hand. She moved about, practicing. She held her right arm bent gingerly against her side. Her left foot was raised above the ground.

She looked at him. She nodded firmly.

"You were good," he said. "Very good."

"Si. Good, good." Then she turned and began moving back up the logging trail.

He caught up to her.

She started talking again. The words were quick and harsh. She waved him off and pointed up in the direction the deer had gone. "Deer! Deer!"

"But you can't...."

She gave him an amiable but sturdy smack with the staff.

He bent over and grabbed his shin.

She waved him off again, still talking rapidly, the words coming more sternly. Then she was shouting. "Deer! Deer! Go! Okay!"

"Road," he said and pointed down the mountain. He held out both fists, raising one while lowering the other, pantomiming someone turning a steering wheel. His lips flapped together as he gave a childish rendering of the sound of a sputtering car engine. "Road," he said, and pointed again.

She would have a much easier time of it if she just continued following the logging trail down the mountain. Eventually, it had to lead to the paved road. If she moved uphill, at some point she would have to cross the wasteland and with only one leg and one arm, that would be very difficult. Especially if she happened to meet up with Kozlov.

She nodded, and then waved him off again. "Vaya! Go!"

He held out the flaked stone he had taken from her. "Might need it," he said.

She took it from him. Her smile revealed blood red teeth. "Muchas gracias, Señor Bowen." She put the stone back in her pocket. She turned away. "Okay! Go! Deer! Deer!" she said, and then was ranting again in Spanish as she made her way slowly down the logging trail.

He watched her for a few moments and then he, too, turned away. He moved up, toward the top of the mountain, toward the place he had last seen the Russian.

CHAPTER 25

LOSING POISE

ussell was now at the very edge of the mountain, facing west. The loggers had not worked the edge, probably due to its inaccessibility. The trees here were enormous, mostly oak, maple and hickory. Behind him, the wasteland sloped down fairly steeply, but in front of him, the drop was precipitous; he saw huge boulders and sheer faces of rock. Down, way down, he could see the river Ian Rushmore had mentioned.

Beyond the river he saw a patch of forest and then a housing development. The houses had been built right next to one another in the flat of the valley. Smoke rose from chimneys. Cars moved along the interconnecting roadways. The development was close enough that he could hear the faintly audible sounds of barking dogs and the cries of children. It all seemed so tame, so pleasant, so... civilized.

Russell followed the rocky ledge upwards. At first, he was in sunlight, but soon had no choice but to be in at least partial shade, as he was once again in the forest. The wasteland was behind him now.

Dried leaves crackled beneath each footstep.

He was moving relatively slowly. He saw an occasional sign of deer, but his direction and pace were due more to assumption than to any clear trail. The doe had probably moved straight up the rough edge. The higher up she went, the greater her advantage. Anything that tried to come from behind her would have to do so while moving against the grade. And the grade was steep.

His body had cooled down when he had stopped to help Ortiz. He eased his way back to a faster pace, his competitive mindset returning as his body temperature rose.

The tracks he followed were occasionally visible, but only here and there, sometimes discernible in the leaf clutter, sometimes on the bare earth, sometimes not at all.

He stopped and stood akimbo as he stared at the ground, thinking.

This doe was clever, uncannily so. She had proven her stealth from the start, when he first encountered that morning; she had been quick to get the fawn away from the open area of the wasteland and into the forest, where it would be less visible. At the reservoir she had tried to lure both him and Nakamura into the water, where she had the advantage. When Nakamura was lying on the beach, she had dared to return and strike him on the head with her hooves. And Russell was convinced she had intentionally led Ortiz into that cellar hole. No experienced hunter or woodsman would believe any deer might be so...so calculating.

And yet, here she was, being just as wily once again. She was leading anything on her trail higher and higher up the mountain. If she were just permitted to ease her way up the mountain and nothing spooked her, then she had nothing to worry about. But if something were to frighten her, then....

He looked over the edge. He had moved so high that, although the river was still visible through the trees, it looked much smaller than it had before. He saw whitewater, but could not hear it.

The pitch was so steep and awkward that it would take a long time for him to get down to the river from where he stood. But a deer could negotiate such terrain with ease. So if nothing spooked the doe, she would probably just continue up along the edge. But if trouble arose, she would lead her fawn down there, down the steep side of the mountain where little else could follow with any competence.

He looked back toward the top of the mountain.

The doe was up there. The fawn was up there.

And Kozlov was up there. While tending to Ortiz, Russell had seen him moving in that direction.

He would use Kozlov against Kozlov; and use the stealth of the doe against the doe.

Point of assumption: Kozlov was up there and would spook the doe. She would run, but she wouldn't come back down toward where Russell now stood. Nor would she head out across the wasteland. She would go down the steep, rough grade to the river.

So that's where he should be, down by the river, waiting for her and the fawn.

This strategy was risky. What if she didn't go down there? He'd have an awful lot of mountain to climb back up. Much time and energy would be lost. It was a gamble, but one that made sense.

He began running back down along the mountain edge, in the direction from which he had just come. He stopped every once in a while to peer down at the river. If the doe and the fawn had already made their way down there, he couldn't see them.

The logging trail came back into view. Again he saw the wasteland of briar and rocks and clumps of grass and the loggers' discards. Then he could see the graveyard in its island of trees. Next he saw the old cellar hole into which Ortiz had fallen. From this approach, the man-made structure was obvious. Eventually, to his left, he saw the wolf tree.

Down along the rocky mountain edge he ran, slipping on leaves and falling, leaping rocks, ducking branches. He cut to his right, along a deer runway and down toward the river. He could now hear rushing water.

The runway was worn in an almost straight line, perpendicular to the mountainside. The pitch was steep and treacherous. He was moving downhill too quickly. He forced himself to the ground. He was now sliding on his rear end. He reached out for anything, a tree, a rock, a bush, anything to grab or at least slow his momentum. His back and his elbows banged against rocks before he finally came to a stop on level ground. He groaned in pain. He got to his feet slowly and went to the river.

The river was not particularly wide, but it looked fairly deep and the current was strong. The rushing water glistened in the sun. He knelt down. He splashed the chilly water on his face and cupped his hands and drank and drank and drank. He hadn't realized how thirsty he was.

Then he was moving again, along the riverbank. Soon he was in the shadow of the mountain. The rocky ledge he had just traveled was far above him, to his right. The air here seemed still, absolutely still, which was to his advantage.

The river was also to his advantage. If deer were nearby, they would be less likely to hear him due to the sound of the rushing water. So he stopped, looked ahead, moved forward, stopped, looked ahead, moved forward; again and again he did this, hoping to catch them unaware.

He decided to move a short distance up the grade of the mountain. This would increase the likelihood that, if he did spook them, they would cross the river rather than head back up the mountainside where he would have little chance of pursuing them.

He moved forward, stopped, looked ahead, keeping low, moved forward, hiding behind boulders and trees.

And then there they were, the doe and her fawn.

Something had scared them down off the mountain. Kozlov, probably.

Russell looked about, up to the sharp ledge, then to his left and then behind him. But Kozlov was nowhere to be seen.

Russell watched from behind a tree. The doe and her fawn were both facing in his general direction, but their tails were not up.

He did not move. He did not even blink. He waited until the doe looked away. The fawn lowered its head to browse on some greenery. He stepped out from behind the tree.

He cringed as he stepped on a fallen branch and it made a cracking sound. He froze.

But they did not respond. The river was too loud. They hadn't heard him.

So he started toward them again.

The doe raised her head.

Now both tails went up. The doe and the fawn turned and ran a short distance along the bank, leapt across the river and disappeared into the brush on the other side.

He jumped into the river. His body tensed at the engulfing cold. The current was stronger than he had presumed. He was being carried downstream. He swam, kicking hard with his legs and pulling hard with his arms before he could stand again. He came up out of the water onto the opposite bank.

Out of bounds.

He pushed through the brush and was now running through forest.

There they were, up ahead, running straight toward a clearing. She was leading the fawn toward the open area of the housing development, toward roads and cars and houses and dogs.

She was losing her poise. Perhaps.

Or perhaps she knew exactly what she was doing. Maybe she had yet another trick to play.

He saw a car pulling into the development along the paved access road, directly into the path of the deer. Tires screeched as the car came to an abrupt stop.

The doe did not change course. She leapt over the hood of the car. The white fawn veered to the left and passed behind the car.

From inside the vehicle came cries of fright and surprise.

Someone, a man, called out to Russell from the car, but not until after he had already run by. The words were indistinguishable, but the tone was clear. The message was both inquisitive and unflattering.

Up ahead, Russell saw that the doe and her fawn were committed to their course.

The houses of the development were identical to one another. A narrow alleyway separated one building from the next, and each alleyway terminated with a gate to the backyard. Each yard was of equal length and breadth, defined by a four-foot high chain link fence.

So, after getting by the access road, the doe and her fawn were confronted with a row of fenced yards. After leaping that first chain link fence, they could not move left because of the buildings. If they wanted to jump a gate and pass along one of the alleyways between the buildings, they would have to come to almost a complete stop so as to charge the alleyway with the necessary angle of approach. They would not move to the right. Russell was to the right, on the outside of the fence, running to their rear along the access road.

The only viable option left for the doe and her fawn was to do just as they were doing: keep moving straight ahead. They moved through every yard, leaping one fence after another. They jumped over picnic tables. They dodged barbecue grills, clotheslines and tricycles. Dogs barked. People paused from their chores and stared. Two women who stood talking over the fence between them squealed in joy and surprise as the doe passed by them on one side, the white fawn on the other. A golden retriever, sleeping in the sun, did not lift its head until after the fawn had already bounded over it.

People shouted.

Children cried out.

The doe and fawn remained in each yard for but a stride or two before they gracefully rose up to leap the fence into the next yard, on and on, right down the line.

"Oh my God, did you see that?! A white deer!"

"Hey, mister! What are you doing?"

Russell's course on the roadway was unobstructed. He was able to close the gap between himself and the deer.

The doe still had enough energy to pick up the pace and lose him.

But not the fawn.

He had chased them for hours earlier that day. Then Nakamura had pursued them. Then Ortiz. Then both he and Ortiz. Then, evidently, Kozlov had set them on the run. Now, Russell again had them running.

The fawn was weary. Its tongue dangled.

As Russell ran, he tried to anticipate the doe's next move.

It was unlikely that she would go left after the last fence. Cars moved along the road out there. Straight ahead was a brief stretch of open land and then another road. A work crew was on that road. A yellow backhoe slowly swung its enormous arm and dumped dirt into the back of an awaiting truck. Men in bright orange hardhats held pickaxes and shovels. Apparently, they too had taken notice of the commotion. They were all facing in Russell's direction.

To his right, on the other side of the access road, were more housing units. Those houses were still under construction, just shells of framing and roof surrounded by mounds of dirt yet to be back filled. Beyond these, there was open field, then more unfinished houses.

That's where she would go. She would cut right, directly across his path and simply try to outrun him.

He veered right in anticipation.

But she did not move to the right. After jumping the last fence, she and the fawn continued straight on.

He veered back to his left.

Members of the road crew had removed their orange hats and were waving them. They shouted and cheered.

Now the doe did move right, sharply right, so acutely that the fawn, unable to turn so abruptly, knocked into her and stumbled.

Russell again moved right to follow.

Losing her poise, she was losing her poise.

She and the white fawn turned right again, cutting across his path. They passed so close to him that he could hear the panting of the fawn. He reached out. His hand brushed against the doe's tail.

Hooves made a muffled clapping sound against the pavement.

She was leading her fawn back to the steep mountainside. He couldn't let that happen. If they went back up there, he would lose them.

People on the opposite side of the access road had come to stand at their fences. Some cheered. Some called out insults.

The road pavement ended. Now he was running on grass. Then he was moving between trees.

Back into the forest the deer ran, back into the shadow of the mountain.

When he came to the river, he simply jumped while running at full speed. He did not make it to the other side. He landed with his legs in the water and his chest on the riverbank. He scrambled to his feet, gasping for air.

He looked up.

The doe stood part way up the steep side of the mountain. The fawn was beside her, panting, its tongue dangling.

Both animals stared at Russell.

He was startled that they had stopped. If they had just continued upward they would have easily lost him.

He looked up beyond them. The mountain ledge at this point was only about twenty or thirty feet above him. And there, back-lit by the fading sun, standing with his spear at the ready, was Kozlov.

CHAPTER 26

MINE TO MAKE

*A*t such close range, the Russian Olympian, an expert with the javelin, could probably put that spear through either the doe or the fawn.

Or Russell.

Neither man nor animal moved.

The situation was not quite a stalemate. The doe could traverse the mountain side away from Russell, or even come back down to the embankment and follow the river. But she certainly wouldn't continue up the grade, not with the Russian up there.

Russell waited.

He watched Kozlov.

Then he looked to the doe.

She looked at him.

Somebody had to do something.

Kozlov could throw the spear at Russell, but then the doe and fawn would run away. If he threw the spear at the doe or fawn, he would then have to deal with Russell one-on-one. The next move, it seemed, belonged to Kozlov.

But then things got complicated.

When he looked up at Kozlov again, he saw that Kozlov was no longer interested in him or the doe or fawn.

Kozlov was now facing uphill with the spear held in a defensive posture.

Russell turned his head.

His eyes widened. His lips moved but he made no sound.

A large buck was only a short distance from where Kozlov stood.

Perhaps it was father to the fawn, because it was white. There were no patches of brown or black or gray— completely white. The eyes were brown, not pink, so it was not an albino. A true white. This was a massive, true white buck.

It seemed to be sizing up the situation, looking down at the fawn and doe, then at Russell, then back at Kozlov.

But what was it actually doing? It would have had no interest in the welfare of the fawn or doe. There was no 'family unit' among deer. Males did not hang out with their 'kin' once mating season was over. And the buck should have been scared off by all the commotion, not drawn to it. This was a sign of unusual aggression, holding its ground like this.

Judging by the shape and size of the enormous rack of antlers, there was little doubt: this was his forest.

Developing a rack that size took years. Should the horn of a mountain goat or an antelope animal break or become lost altogether, it would not be replaced. Horn was not regenerative tissue. Antlers, however, fell off each winter and then regrew throughout the spring and summer. Each year a buck managed to survive, its rack increased in size and grew more tines.

Antlers started out as soft tissue covered in a velvet-like substance. As the hours of daylight decreased in late summer, the supply of blood to the antlers stopped. The velvet was shed.

Then came the time of hardened antlers, when the soft tissue solidified into true bone. Sparring began. Sparring between bucks was more or less to test strength and size of antlers. One buck pushed his antlers against the antlers of another. Sparring served to initiate the younger bucks into the group as well as to reinforce the hierarchy of dominant males. It was not fighting. There was no intent to harm. It was more of a shoving match.

Days grew colder. Soon there were more hours of darkness than of light. The rut drew near. Perhaps an intruder male would come across the line of boundary and attempt to take control. Or a younger buck might rise up against the established dominant buck. There was no more sparring at this point. Antler contact was now a genuine battle.

This was why Russell was instantly certain that he was indeed looking at the owner of this territory. This particular buck had an unfair advantage.

Russell had seen a variety of antler racks. There were few rules as to configuration. He had seen the typical and the atypical. He had seen them with tines that were long and sharp. He had seen them palmated, like those of moose, with tines that were broad and dull. He had seen them with tines that flagged off to the side of each main beam. He had seen them with a mesh of branching tines, like tree roots, forked and crisscrossing. He had even seen a photograph of a buck with a third beam coming up out of its forehead.

To females, a large rack was sexually attractive, a sign of the male's fitness and longevity. The size of an antler rack probably also proved intimidating to other males.

During the mating season, antlers were used as both defensive and offensive weapons. Bucks lowered their heads and charged one another. If topography provided, each buck tried for the uphill advantage. Each tried to gore the other or somehow drive him away. Any disfigurement of antler, such as a broken tine, or even just a natural variation, might result in defeat. On rare occasions, the racks interlocked, permanently, and then the two bucks, snout to snout and head to head, were condemned to the long, slow death of the inseparable. More often, a clear champion emerged from these battles. Nature's intent was simple: female to the winner. Victory was a means of genetic passage.

The thick main beams of this magnificent white buck's rack grew in typical fashion. They sprouted up out of the brow, curved away from the forehead and then came arcing forward. The beams, and the tines they supported, were mirror images of one another. Russell counted ten tines, five rising from each beam. The first, or brow tines, those growing closest to the forehead, were short spikes, straight and sharp.

But the second tines were remarkable. They were extremely tall, much taller than any of the other tines. At the base, they were thick. As they rose, they tapered to a point and curved only slightly toward the center of the rack. Compared to the other tines, and to the tines of most white-tailed deer, these were like lances. With head lowered to meet the resistance of another buck, these two tines could slip right through the opposing antler rack. They would prevent another male from even getting close. These two tines could easily blind. Or slash. Or pierce. Russell imagined that any fight with this brute would end quickly. Such a configuration would not be easily defended against.

Yes, this was his forest.

During warmer months, perhaps this buck moved with a bachelor group, foraging and bedding down, with no obligation other than to increase the size and weight of body and rack. The activities of the year had all been building to the fall season. Now the buck was solitary. It moved alone in the chase. But the quarry had not yet presented itself. During this season, the buck was a prisoner of its own intent, a captive of a persistent and inescapable frenzy. It had rubbed the antlers against trees as notice of territory. It had scraped at the earth to leave signals of presence and status. Appetite for food had diminished. Sleep habits had been disturbed. There was only one motive now: to mate.

But it was early yet for does to be in estrus. The peak of the rut, the time of actual breeding, had not yet arrived. And this was its burden. This creature was a rage of hormones on four legs. The might of the forest surged through blood and sinew without release. The buck was now an absolute intensity of purpose, a purpose not yet attainable.

It was an enormous, imperial and unpredictable beast. Moisture dripped from its flaring nostrils. Its thick neck bulged. Its tail was raised in apprehension. It held its head straight and high.

Russell looked back at Kozlov.

The Russian was frozen in his defensive posture. Perhaps he was bewildered by the sheer size and apparent determination of the creature. Or perhaps he was simply afraid. He didn't thrust forward with the spear. He hadn't even raised it. He just stood there, holding the spear out in front of him.

The buck seemed to be sizing up the situation again, looking down at the fawn and doe, then at Russell, then back at Kozlov.

For a few brief moments, the only sound or motion was that of the river.

The buck forced a rush of air through its broad nostrils. Its ears went back against the neck. It grunted three times in rapid succession and then let out a strange wheezing sound. Then, in a display of anger and intimidation that made the animal appear even larger, the hair on its entire body raised up. It lowered and then lifted its head in the direction of Kozlov. It raised a front hoof and stomped the earth.

Kozlov dropped his spear, turned, and ran. He was limping, probably as a result of Russell hitting him earlier on the knee with a stone over by the cellar hole.

The buck surged forward with its head lowered. Those long sharp, tines were now aimed directly at Kozlov's back.

But the Russian was quick. He jumped to grab a tree branch and pulled himself up out of harm's way.

At the same time, the doe and fawn made their move. They went down toward the river and were once again running along the embankment.

Russell took off after them.

The doe and fawn disappeared among the brush and sapling trees.

Once again, Russell was running as fast as he could. His thighs ached. His lungs burned.

The doe and fawn came into view again. And yet again disappeared. The flow of water lessened as the river widened. The ground became soggy. Getting a foothold was now difficult.

The time between sightings of the deer increased. They were losing him. He was now in an area with few trees. The ground here was covered with ostrich ferns. Some had succumbed to recent frosts and lay pale and limp. Others were still green, their broad fronds obscuring the muddy ground beneath.

He was weary. He couldn't run any faster.

He saw the first sign of true bog: skunk cabbage.

The muck was up to his ankles now. It was difficult to run at all.

And then there it was.

He stopped. His chest heaved.

He saw where the fawn had made its last tracks, just before a fallen tree. It had apparently leapt over the fallen tree and landed with full force in the broad pool of muck. No skunk cabbage grew in there, just dark green and brown algae. The fawn was in it up to its shoulders. It panted and squirmed. But it appeared to be so weary and so mired that it could not advance.

The contrast was startling: a white fawn suspended in a pool of dark ooze.

He saw the path the doe had taken. Her tracks indicated that she had skirted this pool of muck, passing to the right of it.

She had made her mistake. Finally. She had probably intended for Russell to land in there, just as she had apparently intended for Ortiz to fall into the cellar hole.

The fawn had fallen into a trap intended for him.

He looked about for the doe. He didn't see her. He looked at the fawn. Was it sinking or just floating there? How deep was that sludge?

He got a stick, one that was taller than he. He started out toward the fawn. It was difficult to move through the muck. The dark, thick liquid reached to mid-calf, then to his knees, then his thighs. He took a firm stance and leaned forward, pushing the stick down into the bog as close to the fawn as he could reach. He figured the pool was about waist deep. The mud was so thick that when he released the stick it didn't fall over; it remained upright, like a straw in a milk shake.

He looked about for the doe. And Kozlov.

No sign of either.

He continued on.

The fawn bleated in distress. The noise was like the sound of poorly played kazoo.

It struggled but got nowhere.

He pushed his thighs through the thick slime.

Beneath his feet, the bottom dropped off. He was in above his waist.

One more sucking step. He groaned with the effort.

Now he was within reach of the fawn. It wasn't sinking, but neither did it seem capable of freeing itself.

He pushed his hand down into the muck and took the sharply flaked stone from his pocket. He wiped the stone clean on his chest.

With his left hand, he took hold of the trembling fawn. He pulled up on the lower jaw so that the back of the fawn's neck pressed against his ribcage. With his right hand, he brought the sharp stone to the exposed throat.

The fawn, now partially freed from the muck, kicked weakly with its front legs.

Russell spread his feet farther apart and braced himself. The muscles in his arms tensed. He looked down at the fawn's face. Its mouth was clamped shut by the pressure he was exerting on its jaw. Large blue eyes stared up at him. Though he still held the stone against its throat, the tension in his body relaxed.

The purity, the absolute innocence of the animal struck him to such a degree as to mystify him.

He braced himself again, concentrating his efforts, struggling against all hesitation. His leg muscles tightened. His left hand brought the fawn's jaw even higher.

But again, he did not kill.

Even with the animal pressed so closely to him, there was within him a sense of an acute distance from it, a sense of that which he could no longer reach, that which he could no longer encompass.

He held the stone away from the fawn's throat. He stared at the stone. He looked all around him. He saw his position as others might see it: a man standing in muck about to kill a fawn. His thoughts came in rapid succession, in silent argument.

The fawn! He had caught the white fawn!

"Then why...."

He looked down into the face of the animal.

It was strange to him, and powerful, that the awareness of such innocence was, by definition, an indication of absence from the same.

In his mind's eye he suddenly saw Nakamura lying on the sand. He winced, as if in pain.

He had known that Nakamura was injured, seriously injured.

And he had left him.

Inside him swirled feelings of disgust and loss and guilt. He let out a strange whimpering sound, a sound that conveyed vulnerability and confusion.

And sorrow. He had left a man to die. The sorrow pierced him.

"*Tasukete*...," Nakamura had called.

Russell strained, and once again the fawn struggled against his grasp.

He was suddenly overcome with revulsion for himself, and for the game. The stain was within him, coursing through his veins.

But leaving Nakamura was part of the game, just part of the game. And the point of the game was to win! Anyone else would have done the same thing.

Besides, Nakamura was a mean, arrogant bastard who had tried to kill him. He had hit Russell in the head with the pine branch, kicked him, punched him and then left him lying on the forest floor. When the positions were reversed, why should Russell have been expected to act any differently?

To win is to leave the wounded where they fall.

Yes, yes, of course.

"And now I am one of the wounded," Sarah had said.

No...no...not Sarah....

"*Tasukete....*"

No...stop! No! There were no rules out here, no rules in this game.

If there were no rules, then he could do as he chose. Yes, of course. It was that simple.

And if he could do as he chose, then the game was his to make.

"Yes, yes," he said. "Mine to make."

And he had made a game that was heartless. He had made a game that was depraved. He had made a game of greed.

"*Tasukete....*"

But how else was he to win?

"And now I am one of the wounded," Sarah had said.

His sense of loneliness was sudden and extreme.

Again he argued against himself. Nakamura *knew*. He had been warned, multiple times. He understood the risks. He had signed all those waivers and disclaimers.

And certainly none of Russell's intentions could have possibly come as surprise to Sarah. They had talked about the game for years. She had been with him through all of it. She *knew*. What more could he be expected to....

Once again, the sorrowful whimpering sound rose from deep within him. He was stunned and horrified by his unrelenting self-righteousness.

Even so, in an act of defiance, he tightened his grip on the white fawn.

He was so close to winning, so close! All he had to do now was cut the fawn's throat. He could then use the flaked stone to slice the animal open, anus to breastbone, and remove the entrails. This would make it significantly easier to deal with, much lighter to carry. It would then be no more than an object, no longer a fawn but a dressed carcass, mere meat and bone. He would carry the dead animal down the mountain to the finish line.

And, strangely, killing the fawn seemed like the merciful thing to do. Never again would it have to flee from man or dog or coyote. Never again would it have to seek food and shelter, or suffer through another winter.

But the miraculous creature was still breathing, and this obvious and severe definition struck at his very core.

He released the fawn.

It eased forward, back down into the muck, still unable to escape.

He clenched his hand around the stone, making a fist, and then forcefully drove his fist into the muck.

The fawn bleated and squirmed.

He saw that he was in a frenzy, a frenzy of too many thoughts, too many options, too much hesitation. Too much frustration. Emotions roiled. Thoughts came and went.

He could leave the fawn here, mired in the mud. It would starve, or drown, or be attacked by predators. It would die here.

Or he could lift the fawn up out of the muck and set it free.

But Kozlov was still out there somewhere. The fawn was vulnerable. The Russian would have little trouble catching it in its exhausted condition. He knew Kozlov wouldn't hesitate to kill it and then head straight for the finish line.

So to leave the fawn here meant death.

And to let it go meant death.

Or he could end its suffering right here and now. He could cut its throat. Or hold its head under the muck until it suffocated.

"Yes," he said.

"No," he said.

He looked about.

"*Tasukete…*," Nakamura had called.

Russell put the stone back in the pocket.

His hands shook in response to the cold. His teeth chattered. And yet he lowered himself until he was up to his neck in the revolting muck.

He took a deep breath and closed his eyes. He lifted his feet from the bottom of the pool and slowly submerged.

Now he was entirely engulfed by the thick, liquid earth.

He was suspended, neither sinking nor rising, without sense of sight or sound or smell. His muscles were tense, straining against the cold slime. He forced his body to relax and he was then able to extend his arms outward, his legs straight ahead.

Now, he was without intent. For a moment he was without thought or sensation. For a moment he did not distinguish, nor to the forest or the fawn or the Russian or the clouds or the sun or the wind was he distinguishable. This was a means to absolute control, the cessation of all but the beating of his heart.

Then body gave notice of its need: breathe.

Tension returned to his muscles. His mind filled with intent. He put his feet down and pushed and brought his head above the algae covered surface.

He gasped for air. He shook the slime from his head and wiped it from his eyes. He shivered violently.

The fawn's left front hoof appeared at the muck's surface, and then was gone; the right hoof appeared, and then was gone, followed quickly by the left hoof again. The fawn, the beautiful white fawn was trying to swim away. It bleated. It thrust its head sharply from side to side. But it could not free itself.

He had forced it to this fate. He could free it of this fate.

The game, Russell now saw, was indeed his to make.

He must choose.

He, too, was easy prey, standing here like this.

He would not drown the fawn. He would not cut its throat or break its neck.

And neither would he let it go.

CHAPTER 27

LITTLE GHOST DEER

*W*hile still standing in the pool of muck, Russell reached into the rear of his shorts for the fishing line that he had taken from the tree branch over by the reservoir. He cut three pieces from it with the stone. One piece was longer than the other two. He shoved the remaining bundle of fishing line back in his shorts. He knotted a loop at either end of the longer piece of clear plastic line; one loop was larger than the other. He passed the larger loop through the smaller loop and thus had fashioned a type of choke collar, like those used on dogs. He slipped it over the fawn's head and down onto its neck.

"Just in case," he said.

He bent his knees and was once again up to his neck in the slimy muck. He moved his hands through the muck, feeling for the fawn's hind legs. Once he had located them, he wrapped another piece of the fishing line around them, binding the two legs together, and then tying a knot. This was awkward because the mud was cold and thick and he had to do it all by feel. As he went through the same procedure with the front legs, his eyes were just inches from the eyes of the fawn.

He could feel the fawn's warm breath on his cheek.

It tried to kick but could not. It bleated in his face.

Now, with its front legs bound together and its rear legs bound together, the fawn could not run. He tried to lift it up, but couldn't, not only because he was so fatigued, but the dark mud sucked against his intention. So he simply moved the fawn through the muck, one hand under its belly, one hand on its back, like a parent ushering a young child through its first swim.

Now in shallower mud, he slipped his arms under the fawn's belly and brought his hands up around the other side. He pulled the fawn up against his chest and straightened his legs.

Up it came out of the muck.

He walked to dry land and eased the fawn onto the ground. His body shook with cold. The fawn, too, was trembling.

He did some pushups and then hopped up and down. He flailed his arms.

The fawn bawled and bleated in rapid succession. It was announcing its distress, just as a baby tries to elicit response from its mother by crying. Russell knew this might draw the doe. It might even attract other deer that happened to hear the call. They would come to investigate, and perhaps even try to protect the fawn.

He pulled the coil of fishing line from his shorts again. He cut off a piece and tied it around the fawn's snout, closing its mouth and silencing the calls of distress. He didn't like doing this, as it was further cruelty to the frightened animal. But it would lessen the chances that he and Kozlov, or the doe, or some other deer, would do battle.

He doubted that the fishing line would come free of the legs. Above and below each binding the leg bones widened, so unless the knots came undone, the bindings could not slide, neither up nor down. But though the hard plastic line did indeed apply the necessary pressure, there was no grip to it. It was smooth and slippery, so it could slide off the tapered muzzle at the slightest urging. But for now, it would have to suffice.

He looked about. There was still no sign of the doe. Or Kozlov.

He carried the fawn as he would carry a bundle of firewood, the fawn's belly against his forearms, his elbows slightly bent as he hugged the animal against his biceps and chest. When he came to where the river once more ran clear and clean, he put the fawn down on the ground. He looked about. Then he cupped both hands together and scooped water onto the fawn. He cleaned the muck from its legs and underbelly, from its chest and tail. This would make it less slippery to carry. But also, he wanted to see.

He pulled gently on the mouth, revealing the teeth and gums: on the rear lower jaw the first premolars, and the first molar partially erupted. He guessed it was only about three months old. Which meant it had born quite late in the season, as recently as August.

He stood. He stared down at the white fawn. It was so sleek, with thin legs and narrow face, its ears now back against the neck. Built for speed.

The blue eyes were wondrous.

"Little ghost deer," he said softly.

He looked about, then flailed his arms again, warming himself.

He considered jumping into the river, to clean off the muck, but decided against it. Getting wet again would only increase the chances of hypothermia. He was already too cold. Besides, if the muck dried on his body, maybe it would act as an insulator and help him retain body heat.

Again, he looked about. He had to get moving again.

He lifted the fawn high over his head and then brought it down slowly across his shoulders. The bound front legs came down the right part of his chest, the bound hind legs came down the left. He could feel the animal's warm, heaving belly and its rapidly beating heart against the back of his neck. He took hold of the front legs with his right hand, the rear legs with his left hand. He rubbed his cheek against the smooth, snowy flank.

This was absurd.

This plan was foolish. Insane. Suicidal. Kozlov was still out there. So was Girard. Either of them could easily destroy him.

The argument in his head continued as, with the ghost fawn across his shoulders, he took his first step towards the finish line.

CHAPTER 28

NO LONGER A PLACE OF PURSUIT

ussell was now moving east, up the last of the rocky mountainside and away from the noisy river.

He passed through some crowded pines. Because the trees grew so close to one another, creating shade, there was little undergrowth. His feet made no noise on the thick bed of pine needles. But the old dead branches still attached low on the trunks were hazardous. They were rigid, and sharp as spikes. They did not give way when he brushed against them. Instead, they scratched and jabbed at him. He had to duck and weave as he moved, cautious of himself as well as the fawn. He paused to rest. He knelt and then leaned forward slowly so as to ease the fawn from his shoulders onto the ground.

The blue eyes stared back at him.

He stroked the animal, drawing his hand over the top of its head and down along its back.

Crows and blue jays squawked in the distance, uphill from where he rested. He stood and looked about. Something or someone was moving around up there.

The mountain was no longer a place of pursuit, but of evasion.

Point of assumption: Kozlov knows the fawn has been caught. Kozlov is watching. He is waiting.

Russell tried to imagine the Russian's situation. Kozlov had survived the bitter morning cold. He had run and chased all day, subjecting himself to briar and bramble and stone and branch. His body ached. His wounds burned. The cold air was returning. Irritation had escalated to anger. Soon it would be dark and the temperature would plummet. Snow would fall. Time was running out and Kozlov had no deer.

But Russell did.

Someone had the prize and had not yet crossed the line.

So if Kozlov knew that Russell had the fawn, then he was showing evidence of control. He had not come charging down at Russell. He was waiting. He would choose his moment. Kozlov was letting Russell do the work of carrying the fawn down the mountain.

If Kozlov could stay in control and not let the anger and frustration slip into rage, then he would indeed be formidable.

Russell considered evasive maneuvers. Going back uphill would do him no good. Heading west, back to the housing development was equally useless.

He turned. He would do what he had advised Ortiz to do. Go straight down the logging road. Somewhere down there, it had to eventually intersect the main, paved road. Also, carrying the fawn on pavement would be much easier.

He shivered. The slime and mud were drying on his flesh.

He did some quick push pushups. Then he knelt, lowered his head to the ground and drew the fawn against the back of his neck. It struggled weakly, trying to kick its legs.

He straightened his back, strained and stood.

"Hold on, little one."

He moved downhill among the lengthening shadows cast by the falling sun. Soon the road came into view. From where he stood, the paved road looked like a dark serpent winding through the valley.

He looked about. This was awkward now, with the fawn across his shoulders. He couldn't just turn his head. He had to twist his entire torso.

His eyes scanned.

Nothing moving.

He continued on.

He stopped. He began to turn to look behind him when he saw it out of the corner of his eye.

A spear was coming directly at him.

CHAPTER 29

OUT OF BOUNDS

ussell saw the straining of arm and leg muscles as Kozlov charged toward him. Russell had been lucky in that there had been enough time for him to react. He didn't move to the left or right to avoid the spear. He dropped straight down, into a squat. The spear passed harmlessly over him and the fawn. But only by inches.

Now he leaned forward and let the fawn slip from his shoulders onto the ground. While pulling the stone from his pocket, he stood to face Kozlov.

Kozlov made no noise as he approached. His expression was stern. His eyes were wide and glaring.

Russell held his position. Kozlov had the uphill advantage, so Russell would wait until the Russian was close before making his move.

Kozlov stopped. He reached one hand behind him.

The knife glinted as he brought it forward.

Russell took a step back.

The knife looked small, perhaps a paring knife, with a short blade and dark handle.

"No rules," Russell said. "And yet you still managed to cheat."

Kozlov's smile was cunning and vicious.

Russell skirted to his left and up the grade, taking the uphill advantage. "Two men, one prize," he said.

He motioned to Kozlov with his hand, urging him forward. "Come on, you Russki bastard."

Kozlov took a quick step forward, and just as quickly stepped back.

Russell smiled. He slipped the flaked stone back in his pocket. He wasn't going to need it after all. Maybe Kozlov was strong and an exceptional athlete, but when it came to fighting, he clearly didn't know what he was doing. Instead of holding the knife as he would hold a sword, low and out in front of him, he held it in a clenched fist, up high by his ear. Of all possible strategies for a man wielding a knife, this was the least effective, the easiest to defeat.

Kozlov charged.

Russell reached up and caught the Russian's raised arm by the wrist. With his other hand he drove a right body blow, swift, powerful, just below the ribs.

Kozlov grunted and dropped the knife.

Russell threw another hard punch to the same spot of the belly.

Kozlov exhaled a sudden rush of air. He bent at the waist.

Russell jerked his knee upward with all his might. His knee met the Russian's cheekbone with an awful cracking sound.

Kozlov cried out and fell back against the earth, barely conscious. His eyes were closed. He moaned.

Russell shouted: "You cheating...you...you Russian!"

He picked up a large rock and hoisted it high over his head. He would crush the man's skull. It would be like killing a snake. He could do it.

"And there isn't a cop or lawyer or judge that can do anything about it!" he yelled.

His arms trembled with the weight of the rock.

He let out an anguished cry.

But he couldn't do it.

He wouldn't do it.

But Kozlov wanted the fawn. Kozlov would kill for that fawn. As soon as he was able, he would chase Russell down again. So it would be stupid not to incapacitate him somehow.

Still holding the enormous rock up high, Russell positioned himself at the Russian's legs.

As a defensive act, to make sure Kozlov would not be able to follow after him, he would crush every bone in the man's feet.

Russell took a deep breath.

The Russian deserved what he was about to get. He was the enemy. He was a cheater. Russell didn't even need to throw the rock down. The rock was so large that if he just let it fall from his hands onto the ankles, the world-class athlete would probably never walk again.

Kozlov stirred. He was coming to.

Russell gasped in angered frustration.

And suddenly Kozlov was up and running away, limping as he went.

Russell tossed the rock and watched it bounce harmlessly down the mountainside, hit a tree and come to a stop.

He fell to his knees, exhausted, bewildered.

"What the…what are you doing out here if you're not willing to…."

He crawled around until he found the knife. He held it up high for the Russian to see. He shouted, "Go back to Vald…Vlad…os… is… tovo… ok… ah, hell! Go back to Moscow, you bastard!"

He laughed, a mad cackle.

He placed the knife on a rock and pounded another rock on top of it, again and again. The plastic handle shattered. The blade broke. He tossed the remnants of the knife helter-skelter.

He retrieved the spear. He balanced it between two stones and dropped a third stone on it. But the spear would not break. It was white ash, the same wood used to make hockey sticks: strong yet flexible. Much too strong and flexible.

He smacked it as hard as he could against a tree trunk, repeatedly, but still it would not break. In frustration, he tossed the spear into the woods. He had little doubt that Kozlov was watching him. He was equally confident that once the Russian's head had cleared, he would retrieve the spear and come after him with it. But there was nothing else Russell could do. The spear wouldn't break, and he couldn't carry both it and the fawn.

Russell went to the fawn. He raised it above his head and then brought it down gently across his shoulders.

He trotted among leaves and brush along the side of the logging road. He purposely avoided the logging road itself because the dirt there was soft and his footprints would be easy to track.

He stopped and looked back.

Kozlov was up there, somewhere, watching him.

Russell momentarily removed his right hand from the fawn's legs. He waved. "God-bye Yuri!" he shouted. "God-bye!"

The fawn bounced up and down on his shoulders as he continued his descent.

He came to the end of the wasteland. He was in forest again. It was dark and cool. Soon, ahead of him, he saw where the logging trail emptied out onto the paved road. He moved west, to his right, between the trees. And then headed back uphill, looping.

Kozlov would be coming, that had to be assumed. Russell would much rather have him to the front than to the rear. If Kozlov remained behind him, Russell would not only have to look where he was going but also continuously look to the rear. That would be difficult, especially with the fawn. By looping, he would let Kozlov get in front. Then Russell would only need to be concerned with what lay ahead.

After moving uphill for a while in his loop to get behind the Russian he stopped, dropped down and lay flat against the earth and waited. From here he couldn't see the logging road itself, but he would be able to see anything that moved along it.

The fawn was on the ground beside him. He stroked its head. Whenever he moved now he felt the tug of the dried blackish green muck on his flesh.

It wasn't long before he saw Kozlov moving slowly down the logging road. As expected, the Russian had retrieved the spear. He held the spear in both hands as he looked from side to side, apparently trying to track Russell. At one point he stopped and disappeared from view, probably crouching down to inspect the ground. Then he stood up again, looked about, and continued down the mountain.

Russell waited for a few minutes, letting Kozlov gain on him.

It was stupid not to have crushed the Russian's leg or foot when he had the chance. It was stupid not to have broken his arm or….

He stood and hefted the fawn back onto his shoulders.

Point of assumption: Kozlov had searched about and determined or just guessed that Russell was still on the mountain. Perhaps the Russian was waiting near where Russell stood right now, just a short distance down the logging trail. Or maybe he had gone to the base of the mountain, to the intersection of the logging trail and the paved road. Russell chose not to go back to the logging trail, even though it would have led him directly to the road. He headed straight down the mountain, through the woods.

Eventually, he came to a steep embankment. At the bottom was a culvert that separated the mountain from the paved road.

How strange!

Civilization.

He sat, with the fawn across his shoulders. His legs dangled over the edge of the embankment. He remained very still.

A car was approaching.

He waited.

The car passed by. A car!

He looked to either side. Then he twisted slightly to look behind him and, as he did so, the earth beneath him suddenly gave way. He went sliding down the steep embankment, out of control, bouncing over rocks and bumping against tree trunks. He tried to stop himself by straightening his legs, hoping to brace myself, but the pitch was too great. He was tossed sideways and then onto his stomach. The fawn was jarred from his grasp but continued to slide with him. He kept a hand pressed against it, desperate, to ease its descent as much as he could.

He came to a stop in the culvert. He groaned in pain. He swore.

His abdomen was badly scraped and bleeding.

He inspected the fawn, rolling it over, stroking it, talking to it. He found no evidence of injury.

It bleated, again and again. The binding had slipped from its snout.

He ran a short distance back up the embankment, searched around until he found the small loop of fishing line. He brought it back to the fawn and slipped it back over the snout.

He hunkered down as another car passed by.

Then, once again he hoisted the fawn gently onto his shoulders.

He came to the guardrail, which reached to about mid-thigh. He looked behind him, then to the left and right. He stepped awkwardly over the guardrail, into civilization.

And out of bounds.

He was on pavement. Now he could move with greater ease toward the driveway that led up to the old house and the spectators and hot drinks and bonfires.

And the finish line.

He trotted. His bare feet made smacking sounds on the dark pavement.

Something moved.

Up ahead, on his left, near where the logging trail met the main road, something in the roadside shrubbery had moved.

He assumed it was Kozlov. He stopped and looked about for avenues of escape. He could turn around and simply move along the road, but seeing as it was flat and unobstructed, Kozlov would easily catch up to him. Going back from where he had just come, down into the culvert and up the embankment again, was not a viable avenue of retreat. It was too steep. Any escape would have to be to his right where there was another guardrail, then another embankment, and then a forest of thin trees.

He looked to where he thought he had seen something move. He waited. He could hear only his rapid breathing.

Up from the culvert ran Kozlov, spear in hand. Quick and agile, he leapt over the guard rail.

Why hadn't Russell finished him off when he had the advantage....

He heard a car approaching from behind him.

Kozlov moved to the middle of the road. His legs were bent deeply at the knees. He held the spear out toward Russell. The right side of his face was horribly swollen from where Russell had kneed him. There was a cut on his cheek. He looked as though he was grimacing, jaw straining, teeth clenched, eyes narrowed.

Russell turned to see that the approaching car behind him had stopped. The woman in the driver's seat looked bewildered and frightened. She kept her eyes on him as the car began backing up and then stopped with a jolt as it met the front bumper of a pick-up truck that had also stopped in the roadway.

Two men were in the truck. The driver got out and stood on the pavement. He kept his hand on the open door. His passenger had opened his door and now stood on the running board. Neither man seemed disturbed by the minor accident. Both concentrated their attention on Russell.

The woman in the car locked the doors and closed the windows.

Russell turned again.

Kozlov was moving toward him.

Now a car came up behind Kozlov.

Russell could see the odd configuration on the roof of the car behind the Russian. It was a police cruiser.

He walked backwards as Kozlov approached.

The Russian jabbed the air repeatedly with his spear.

From behind Russell came the sound of a male voice. "Hey, buddy, what's this all about?"

Russell continued to back up, away from Kozlov.

The lights on the roof of the police car came on and began spinning. They sent rotating shafts of red and blue onto him and Kozlov, onto the trees, onto the embankment, the pavement, onto everything.

He watched Kozlov.

If Kozlov had taken notice of the police lights, he showed no indication of having done so. He did not take his eyes off Russell.

Suddenly, Kozlov charged with the spear held out in front of him.

A male voice shouted, "Stop! Police!"

Russell turned and ran. With the fawn heavy on his shoulders, he stepped up onto the bumper of the woman's car and then leapt onto the hood.

Kozlov was quickly there.

Russell saw a ferocious absence in his eyes.

Kozlov jabbed at him with the spear, trying to stick him in the legs.

Russell danced, lifted a leg, hopping from one foot to the other.

Kozlov's spear caught him on the thigh—not a direct hit, but enough to draw blood.

Evidently, the fishing line had once more come free. The fawn bleated.

Russell moved up onto the car roof.

The policeman's voice was loud and vehement.

"You! With the spear! Drop it! Now!"

Russell felt the vibrations of the woman's screams passing through car roof.

"I said drop it!" the cop yelled.

Kozlov continued to pursue.

Russell stepped from the roof of the car down onto the trunk.

"Stop or I'll shoot!" the policeman shouted.

But Kozlov did not stop.

The fawn bawled loudly in Russell's ear as he jumped from the trunk of the car onto the hood of the pick-up truck.

The two men scurried back into the truck and pulled the doors closed.

Kozlov swung the spear like a baseball bat, trying to hit Russell's legs.

Russell jumped as well as he was able. The fawn was heavy. His muscles ached. His lungs burned. The spear passed beneath his raised feet. He came down heavily on the truck hood. He heard shouts from the men inside the vehicle.

A gunshot sounded.

If the policeman had been aiming at Kozlov, he missed. If it had just been a warning shot, it had no effect.

The woman in the car was now shrieking.

The Russian made a snarling sound as he jabbed at Russell with the spear.

Russell kicked his feet out and landed with his butt on the truck fender. He cried in pain and slid off the truck out of control against the guardrail.

He looked back.

Kozlov had raised the spear and was now bringing it down as a club.

But Russell was out of reach.

The spear smacked hard and loud across the hood of the truck.

Shouts of indignation came from the men in the truck.

The bawling fawn struggled to free itself.

Russell, now on the pavement, headed toward the rear of the truck on the passenger's side.

Kozlov, too, moved toward the rear of the truck. But the driver opened the door abruptly, using it as a weapon. The door caught Kozlov on the shoulder, knocking him backwards. He grunted from the blow and dropped the spear. He moved to pick it up but a shiny black shoe stepped on it, pressing it down on the blacktop. Kozlov looked up into the barrel of the policeman's pistol.

"Flat on the ground! Hands behind your head! Now!"

Russell saw the expression on Kozlov's face change from that of frenzied attacker to that of bewildered captive.

Kozlov said something.

The cop shouted, "English? No speak English?"

Kozlov shook his head.

The cop put a hand on the Russian's shoulder and pressed.

Kozlov lay flat.

Now the policeman pointed at Russell. "You! I want you to...."

But Russell turned away, made the awkward step over the guardrail and ran off into the woods.

CHAPTER 30

AMBER EYES

*R*ussell stopped running when he thought he was a safe distance from the road. He knelt on the forest floor, panting.

He could see Kozlov being led to the patrol car with its lights flashing. He lay flat when the two men from the truck approached the guardrail and looked out in his direction.

The fawn tried to kick its legs.

For whatever reason, it had stopped bleating. It lay on its side. The large blue eyes stared up at him.

He reeked of drying algae and muck, a deeply pungent odor of earth. Every inch of his body ached. His arm was sore where he had fallen on the discards early in the day. Hooked thorns of black raspberry and wild rose protruded from his calves and thighs. His forehead hurt where Nakamura had struck him. In his lower neck, where Nakamura had also hit him, there was a dull throbbing. The flesh on his abdomen had been scraped raw when he had slid down the embankment into the culvert. His leg burned where Kozlov had speared him; red blood mixed with the blackish green muck. He pressed dirt against the wound to stem the bleeding.

He watched as the police car and the other vehicles left. They had their headlights on.

The sun was down. He could see the sky through the trees to the north. Clouds were gathering. It would be dark soon.

The wind had shifted to the northeast. He sniffed the air. Rain was coming.

He picked up the fawn and carried it with both arms under its belly and his hands pressed against its flank.

He moved east, parallel to the road. He walked slowly through the forest. There was no hurry now. He needed to gather strength. And he needed to think.

Of the five original contestants, only two were left now. He assumed Girard was still waiting at the finish line.

He began to plan.

He noticed a light through the trees. He came to an open field and could now see that the light was a flood light on the garage of a house. Across the road from it was the driveway leading up to the house by the starting/finish line.

He moved to his left, through the field, northward, toward the main road.

The growling stopped him.

Had it been a coyote, it would have been easily spooked if he had simply made a sudden move toward it. But this was not a coyote. This was someone's pet dog. He saw a collar with identification tags dangling. The animal probably belonged to the people who lived in the house.

It looked to be about 90 lbs. He recognized the breed. Sleek silvery-gray coat, docked tail, floppy ears—a Weimaraner. Fierce, alert, swift dogs. Bred to hunt large game in the forest—boar, bear...and deer.

And Russell had brought a fawn into its territory.

The dog raised its muzzle and sniffed the air. It growled again.

Russell backed away slowly.

The dog barked.

"Shhh...."

Russell continued to back away.

The dog stepped toward him. It snarled, baring its teeth.

Russell crouched down. He lowered the fawn to the ground, easing it onto its side.

The dog cocked its head.

Russell remained crouched down low. Perhaps this would be interpreted as a less threatening stance, maybe even one of submission.

His movement was slow as he reached for the stone in his pocket.

The dog growled and moved toward him.

The fawn bleated and squirmed.

This seemed to excite the dog even more. It moved as if to go around him.

Russell raised his arm in an abrupt, threatening gesture.

The dog backed away and came toward the fawn from a different angle.

Russell rose and stepped toward the dog, stomping his foot. "MINE!"

Now the dog moved in a circle, a wide circle, out of reach. Then it moved back and forth before once again circling, each circle smaller than the previous circle, coming closer and closer, head lowered, sniffing, then lifting its head and snarling.

Russell whispered, "Nice doggie."

The dog lunged and bit him on the wrist, piercing the flesh and causing Russell to drop the stone.

The dog backed off.

Russell would not give it a second chance. He leapt onto the dog. He grabbed it by the collar. He rolled with the animal and when they stopped rolling in the tall grass, the dog was on top of him, scratching at him with its claws, snapping and growling, trying to bite him in the face. He held the dogs face just inches from his own. He pushed against the animal's throat.

Drool dripped from the dog's mouth.

Eons glared from the amber eyes.

Russell used his left hand to punch the dog on the nose. Though blood came out of one nostril at once, the Weimaraner seemed undeterred. It surged with power.

Russell brought his left knee up into the dog's belly. The dog did not whelp or cry out, but the momentum helped Russell roll over on top of it. He punched it again. Still no effect. He twisted on the collar with all his might, turning it, tightening it against the dog's throat. Judging by how much harder the dog struggled, this was having a definite impact. The dog was being strangled.

He grabbed the dog by its collar, and then turned in circles, swinging the dog through the air, around and around. He let go. The dog went skidding along the ground through the tall grass. It scrambled to its feet. It made hacking sounds.

Russell pointed at it: "Next time, I kill you."

It came right back at him.

Russell braced himself.

The dog came running at him and at the last moment, leapt up.

Russell shot his right leg backward and bent his left leg forward. As he did this, he brought his right arm forward. The heel of his hand slammed against the dog's chest.

The dog fell to the ground. It lay there flat against the earth, gasping. Its chest heaved.

Russell searched about for the flaked stone. He found it and put it back in the pocket. He picked up the fawn. He carried it in both arms and scurried toward the road.

He stopped at the sound of a whistle. He turned.

The Weimaraner was just getting to its feet.

A male voice called out. "Mako! Maaaako!"

The dog looked toward the lighted house and then back at Russell.

Now the whistle was loud, with more demand. "Come, Mako!"

Russell waited.

The dog moved toward him.

The fawn bleated. Russell clamped its muzzle shut with his hand.

An inquisitive "Mako?" was followed by a single loud clap of hands and then a harsh, "Mako! Get over here right now!"

The dog stopped, turned and went limping slowly off in the direction of the house.

Russell let out a sigh of relief and sat, again easing the fawn onto its side.

He looked at his latest wounds. He counted four punctures. There were also numerous impressions where the dog's teeth had not pierced the flesh.

He had been through ten years of hell in one day of chase.

He groaned as he stood. He lifted the fawn and headed toward the road. Cars passed. Their lights bounced through the growing darkness.

The wind had intensified, out of the northeast. The first raindrops fell. He felt them on his shaved head. He could hear them landing on the fallen leaves.

He tried to get up the embankment to the road but could not manage the grade and hold onto the fawn at the same time. He kept slipping back down.

He looked at the fawn. It should have been a carcass by now. He should have gutted it, lightening the load. He could then have just dragged it along behind him.

But it was still alive and he would do his best to keep it that way. To save his own life, yes, he would kill it. But for no other reason. No. Not even to win.

So he simply moved along the grade in the direction of the lighted house until a more favorable approach to the road appeared.

Holding the fawn under one arm, he grabbed hold of the guardrail and pulled himself up and over. He slipped on the wet pavement but did not fall. He saw the driveway the bus had travelled to deliver them to the starting line earlier that morning, which now seemed so long ago.

Soon, very near the actual driveway, the forest was easily accessible. He moved uphill, under the cover of white pine.

He was back in bounds. But after the Russian and the policeman and the dog, being in bounds somehow seemed safer than being out of bounds. There was a certain comfort to it.

He moved up the base of the mountain with the wind at his back. It was twilight. The sky had clouded over. He was beneath a thick canopy of pine. It was not complete darkness, but he found it difficult to see. He turned and sniffed the air. He listened.

But…it couldn't be. It wasn't possible.

Al Girard had to be up at the finish line. Ortiz, Nakamura and the Russian were all accounted for.

So he continued on for a little while and then stopped yet again. And yet again, he turned and sniffed the air. Once more he listened, listened intently.

It was impossible. And yet he was certain. He didn't know how he knew, but he knew.

He was being followed.

CHAPTER 31

HARD TO HOLD

F ire. He yearned for fire.

He was crouched at the outside corner of the waist high stone wall.

Glimmering fire pits dotted the land.

He saw hundreds of vehicles parked in the fields. He saw the glaring stand lights of the media, and large bonfires still raging near the bleachers at the finish line.

At this distance, the spectators were small and featureless, as a colony of insects, with some moving in this direction, some moving in that direction, while others huddled in groups, each to an indecipherable duty or pleasure that from this vantage point seemed a confusion of activity, mysterious as to cause or intent.

Between here and the finish line, the land was relatively even, almost without contour. If he just followed the stone wall from here, he would eventually arrive at the finish line. But there was a good chance that Girard would intercept him. In his present condition, he wouldn't stand a chance against the giant on the flat. He had to approach him from a point of advantage. He had to come downhill toward the colossus.

He continued uphill, north of the finish line, and then cut east, to his right. He came to a massive maple tree. It was really more than one tree because the main trunk erupted from the earth to splay into three trunks, each, in and of itself, worthy of being called a tree. The division began close to ground level. The trunks grew close together and then spread apart as they rose. In all, it formed a vase shape, narrow at the base and then flaring at the top, each trunk arcing away from the center and flowing outward into limbs and branches. Because of this great breadth at the top, its leaves would create a broad shadow in summer light. Thus, the ground around this tree was its own, the shade having prevented all but the least of competition.

Through the crowd of now frost-pale and drooping ferns, a narrow ribbon of worn earth curved beneath the tree. This was the footpath made by the owners of the property.

All he had to do was follow that path due north to the finish line.

Easy enough.

Except for Girard.

He sat with his back against the trunk of the tree, laying the fawn on the ground beside him. The wind brought the scent of smoke and charred meat and the occasional sound of human voices.

He shivered. He rubbed his arms and legs to encourage circulation. Where he was wet from the rain, the once dried muck was slimy again.

He looked at the fawn.

"It's almost over, little one."

Once again, he had the uneasy sense that he was being watched or followed. He looked about, but saw nothing unusual.

He figured that Girard was cold, anxious and hungry. He was probably also frustrated to the point of anger. Boredom was just as much a demon as the cold. He probably wanted to go home. But he couldn't justify doing so until everyone had come in. He has waited this long, he would wait a while longer. His body might not be weary, but his muscles had to be tense and tight from the cold. His anger and frustration might well work to his advantage against someone as weary as Russell. Girard was massive and strong. And itching for a fight. He'd come at Russell, deer or no deer.

The fawn bleated.

He quickly reached over and pressed its upper and lower jaw together.

He gently stroked the fawn as he slowly released his grip. He then tied the last of the fishing line around the muzzle. He tied it as tightly as he dared. He saw it digging into the creature's flesh.

If the giant had heard the fawn, there was little doubt that he would have come charging up there. And there was also little doubt that if he got his massive hands on the fawn, he would snap its neck.

Russell walked down toward the finish line. As he drew closer to it, he crawled on his belly.

Now he could see that Girard was indeed still down there, pacing back and forth, flailing his arms, muttering angrily to himself.

Russell moved silently back uphill. He found a spot where there was a break in the canopy, where the rain fell directly on him. He lifted his face to the rain, and opened his mouth. His throat was so dry. Then he hunched forward and let it sprinkle on his back. It was not a drenching, just enough to moisten the dried muck. Just enough to make his flesh slippery. And hard to hold.

He then moved straight down the path toward the finish line.

Soon, he again saw the pacing silhouette of Girard.

Though Russell was only walking, hardly exerting himself, his heart was pounding in his chest.

He knew that if his plan didn't work, he was a dead man.

He saw Girard stop.

He heard the huge man call out. "I see you, pal. I see you!"

Behind Girard there was now much commotion and calling out from the bystanders.

"Someone's coming!"

"They're coming in!"

Russell continued down the slope. Now he was so close to Girard he could see his features in the dim light.

Russell thought the giant was a fool to let him get this close. It would be so easy. Pull the stone from his pocket, lunge, grab him by the leg and slice open the femoral artery. And that would be the end of it.

"Who's there?" Girard asked. "Who is it?"

"Bowen."

"Bowen? Hell, I was hoping for the Jap." He let out a rueful laugh. "What happened to you? Fall into a tar pit?"

Russell said nothing.

"Jesus, I can smell you from here," the giant said, and then looked beyond him.

"You can smell me? Ha! That's a laugh. The entire forest can smell you, you overgrown Canuck. You reek of stale deer piss."

"Shut up, you little twerp. The deer. Where's the deer?"

Russell made no response.

"Still playing that turtle game, eh?" Girard asked angrily, and stepped toward him.

Russell took two steps back and said, quickly, "Kozlov is in."

The giant stopped advancing. "The Russian?" He smirked. "I've been right here all day. The Spanish chick limped in from the road, I know that much. But no one else has gotten past me. Not the Russian. Not the Jap."

"Nakamura is dead. Over by the reservoir."

"Dead?"

"Yes."

"You kill him?"

"No."

"Then how...."

"Kozlov was picked up by the police."

The giant grunted. "Cops?" he said. "What are you talking about?"

"Down on the road."

Behind Girard, Russell saw the low hanging hemlock boughs. These were the boughs he had parted, like curtains, just after the start. But the giant was not in the right place. He had to be centered on the finish line for Russell's plan to work.

Russell stepped as if to get around him.

But Girard moved to block him. "Not so fast, pal."

Perfect. Now he was right where Russell wanted him.

The giant drew his head back, grimacing. "You really stink, you know that?"

Russell breathed in deeply, exhaled, breathed in deeply, exhaled.

The crowd was calling out in excitement.

From far up the hill came a delicate but definite sound.

The fawn was bleating its call of distress.

The giant looked beyond him. "What was that?"

Russell rushed forward, thrust both hands against the huge man's chest and pushed with all his might.

Girard stumbled backwards. He waved his arms about as he attempted to retain his balance. "Whoa!"

Russell hunched his back, lowered his head and continued pushing. He could feel Girard pawing at his back, grabbing at him. But Russell's flesh was wet with slime. The giant could not get a grip. His hands kept sliding off.

Girard brought a heavy fist down on Russell's back.

Russell's knees momentarily weakened with the blow.

Now Girard grabbed Russell's biceps. And squeezed with tremendous force.

Russell cried out in pain. But he continued to press the heels of his hands as hard as he could into the giant's chest. He could feel Girard trying to lean forward, trying to change the momentum. Russell moved his feet more quickly. He felt the tree's boughs scraping over him. The finish line was near.

Girard pressed his thumbs into Russell's biceps. He tried to pull Russell to him.

Russell kept his arms locked in their straightened position.

"Son of a bitch!" the giant growled.

When Russell dug his heels into the earth, his forward momentum stopped abruptly.

But the giant continued moving backwards. The wet muck prevented him from retaining a hold on Russell. His hands slipped down along the biceps, then slipped along the forearms and wrists, and suddenly the two men were free of each other.

Girard's massive bulk continued backwards until, with a loud curse, he was through the gap in the stone wall.

And across the finish line.

He fell onto his rear end as the crowd quickly cleared from his path.

People booed. Others cheered.

Ian Rushmore called out, "Albert Girard has crossed the finish line."

With assistance, Girard got to his feet. He shook off the helping hands and bellowed in a mixture of French and English, "*Injuste*! He can't do that! *Injuste*!

"You are done, Mr. Girard," Ian Rushmore said mildly.

The giant moved toward the break in the stone wall, back toward Russell.

Ian and two of the reeves stepped in to block his intent.

"It's not fair!" Girard shouted. "*Non*! *Non*! He pushed me across!"

"Love and war, Mr. Girard," Ian said. "It's all fair. You have crossed the line twice. Once to start, once to finish. You are done. *Finis*!"

Once again, Girard moved toward Russell. The reeves stepped forward. One took hold of his left arm, another took hold of his right arm. The massive man shook them off like flies.

Ian held his ground and said, stiffly, "Your contract no longer applies, Mr. Girard. You are now subject to the laws of this land. Do you understand?"

Girard roared back, "I waited there the whole damn day!"

"Do you understand what I just said, Mr. Girard?" Ian asked.

The giant spat on the ground. He pointed at Russell. "I'll get you for this, Bowen! I'll get you!

Russell felt a momentary tinge of sympathy for the Canadian. Girard had hugged the finish line all day with hopes of at least some opportunity to do battle for the prize. And Russell had simply pushed him out of the game. It was done.

But Girard was also fortunate. If Kozlov had been this close to victory, Girard might not have fared so well. The Russian would have been happy to spear him like a fish.

Russell didn't feel any fondness for Girard, but he did hold a certain admiration for him. Girard was the only one who had complained openly about the cold. Running brought considerable warmth to those who chased. But Girard did not chase. Yet he had endured, true to his station. He had outlasted all but Russell.

Now, Girard was finished.

Russell raised a hand of acknowledgment to him.

In response, the giant held up his middle finger.

Russell shrugged.

He turned away. He passed between the low hanging hemlock boughs and walked back into the forest to retrieve the fawn.

CHAPTER 32

ON THREE LEGS

*A*s Russell drew nearer, the bleating and bawling of the fawn grew louder. These were intense sounds of anguish, high pitched notices of the predator's grasp intended to draw maternal protection.

Russell crouched down. He stroked the fawn's head. It quieted at once.

The fawn was not where he had left it. He saw the trail of disturbed ferns and guessed as to what had happened. The fawn must have squirmed against the leg bindings, although its legs were still bound. In doing so, it had slid downhill and away from the huge maple tree. The fawn had managed to remove the binding on its snout, probably by rubbing its face back and forth against the earth. The knotted piece of fishing line Russell had tied around the muzzle lay on the ground near the fawn's head.

He sat next to the fawn. He continued to stroke it.

"They're waiting for us, little ghost deer."

He considered:

Nakamura.
Ortiz.
Kozlov.
Girard.

All were accounted for.
The chase was done.
All that remained was to cross the finish line.

He would sound the victory horn. He would warm himself by the fire. Then he would head home to celebrate with Sarah. They would dream of how their lives would be changed by the prize money.

He heard a disturbance.

Something was moving about.

He stood and looked. In the dim light, he made out the outline of the doe. She had apparently drawn close to her fawn, lured by the bleats of distress. But now his eyes followed her raised white tail as it bobbed in retreat through the darkness.

Had he done something to spook her? He had just been sitting there. He hadn't moved till now.

Suddenly a blur of white came at him from the uphill advantage. He whirled around, holding his hands out in startled defense. The hard cold of antler bone forced him backwards and downhill. The white buck had its head down, and the tines rattled against the protective cup in his shorts. Russell's feet moved at a frantic pace. He was running backwards, trying to retreat from the advancing force.

He pushed away and to the side, barely avoiding being gored. He went totally limp, letting his body relax as he fell to the ground. But as he rolled away along the forest floor, his right leg was trampled by the heavy hooves. He cried out at the pain.

He scrambled to his feet.

The white buck had stopped, turned, and was again in chase.

Russell did not even try to defend. He ran with every bit of energy he had left.

He heard hooves pounding the earth behind him.

He dove to his right, rolled and then was up again, running.

He ducked under the low dead branches of a white pine tree. He scampered to the trunk on his hands and knees.

He turned to look.

The buck had stopped. It wasn't far from him, but it couldn't advance because of the dead pine branches protruding like spears from the tree trunk.

The buck lowered and shook its head, tossing its antlers fiercely from side to side. Stiff dead branches of the pine tree cracked and shattered.

The buck was clearing a path to him.

Russell tried to climb the tree, but the dry branches snapped beneath his weight.

Once again he ran, and once again he heard the pounding of hooves behind him.

He dove to his left, rolled heels-over-head through the wilted ferns, and then scrambled to his feet again.

He did not look back.

He continued on toward the massive maple tree.

In desperation, with no other means to safety, he leapt with total abandon, knees high, elbows and forearms and fists tucked in, for a split second coasting through the air. He passed between two of the diverging trunks of the maple and then landed hard in the crotch of the tree. His forward momentum slammed him into the third trunk. He thrust his arms out at once to prevent himself from falling backwards onto the ground.

He cried out as he felt a burning pain in his right side. He looked down and saw the sharp antler tine just as it was withdrawing from his confined space among the three tree trunks.

The buck had lunged at him. The tree trunks were so close together that the deer's entire rack could not pass between them. But the long lance-like tines, being close to the center of the head, had not been blocked. One had pierced his flesh. The lunge had been well aimed. Had the buck hit slightly lower on the tree, not even those tines would have been able to fit between the narrow space separating the trunks.

Russell looked up. The three trunks were almost straight in their rise. The first branches were fifty or sixty feet above him. The bark was rough and furrowed. He considered climbing. But the trunks were too thick and offered nothing to hold onto. If he should fall....

He huddled in the middle of the trio of trunks. The space was cramped. His naked shoulders pressed against the rough bark. There was barely enough room for one foot in the crotch of the tree. His position was excruciatingly painful, as his weight pressed his foot down between the forking trunks. He did his best to brace myself, moving upward in his confinement and forcing the soles of both feet outward against two of the trunks. In this manner, he was able to apply pressure and suspend himself above the crotch. He hunkered down as low as he could, with his chest pressed against his sharply bent knees.

The buck paced around the tree. Its tail was held high. It kept its eyes on him.

Russell turned his body so as to follow the buck with his eyes.

The buck snorted. Steam rose from its nostrils.

It backed away. It moved around the tree.

Russell again turned his head so as to follow.

The buck lifted it front hooves off the ground and lunged forward. Russell felt the tree shudder from the impact. There was a snapping sound as one of the shorter tines broke off the beast's rack. But once again, the breadth of the antler rack was too great to fit between the trunks.

The buck had tried every available approach. It could not reach him.

Now the animal backed away, its tail limp. It stared at him.

Russell heard several gentle grunts from behind him. He recognized their source and understood the message being conveyed. They were grunts of position. They had come from the doe. Low and subtle, they announced: "I am here."

He turned in the tree to look.

She was there, by her fawn. Her tail was high. Her ears were erect. She was facing in his direction.

The fawn bleated. The doe lowered her head and licked its face.

Up until this point, he thought the buck had just been crazed, attacking him for no other reason than the fact that he had invaded its domain. He assumed it was simply frenzied by the hormonal rage of the late pre-rut. But at the sight of the returning doe, he was less certain.

Anyone who had studied deer knew there was no 'family unit' among deer. The buck would have no interest in the welfare of the fawn, especially not at this time of year. There was territory to protect. There were trees to rub. There was earth to scrape. The buck's only impetus was to mate. Once they had mated, the doe alone cared for her offspring.

No, it was not possible that the buck would have come to the fawn's defense.

And yet, here they both were.

The doe had proven her cunning all day. She had acted like no other deer he, or as far as he knew, anyone else, had ever encountered.

The buck, too, had acted like no other when it charged at Kozlov over by the river. Now, out of nowhere, it had attacked him.

"You are insane!" Russell shouted at the buck. He turned to face the doe and shouted at her, too. "Insane! Deer don't do this!"

Earlier, he had the sense that he was being followed, but, no...it was not possible.

It was just not possible that the buck would come to the fawn's defense, and it was equally implausible that the doe had acted as a decoy, drawing Russell's attention to her fleeing white tail, thus allowing the buck a clear shot at him. No. The buck and the doe simply would not act cooperatively in an attempt to regain the fawn. It was inconceivable. Deer simply did not behave that way. Ever.

And yet....

He heard movement. He turned his head.

The white buck was now moving with the ease of inherent majesty. With its right foreleg lifted and held parallel to the ground, the animal took two steps forward. It then lowered the hoof, lifted the other foreleg, and took two more steps forward. It continued to circle the tree in this fluid, regal interchange of front limbs. The shifting of weight from one leg to another was a seamless transfer, with no halting of motion. It was an elegance that certain purebred show horses attain only after years of training. This creature, bearing the massive rack upon its head, and of such bodily bulk, was suddenly a ballet of weightless precision.

Russell maneuvered his body in the crotch of the tree so as to watch. He risked exposure by craning his neck and bringing his head beyond the limits of his confinement. Just to see.

The buck continued in this same delicate trot, holding up a bent leg while taking two steps, then holding up the other leg while taking two more steps, as round and round the tree it went.

Their eyes were fixed on one another as the creature moved in its effortless, graceful symmetry.

The temperature had dropped. The forest was darkening. The rain had sharpened into sleet. But Russell did not feel the cold. His wounds were silent. He forgot his fear. He was, in all manner of mind and body, captive of the beast.

The buck stopped. It stomped the earth. Steaming air rushed from its nostrils. Then it rose up on its hind legs and moved toward Russell, both front legs scratching at the air.

Russell pressed his back against the tree bark. He looked up and to the side and behind him. There was nowhere to go. He was trapped.

On its hind legs like this, the buck was monstrous, over three hundred pounds of uncontrolled rage. It rested one hoof against the tree and used the other to paw at him, repeatedly, like a cat reaching into the bird cage.

Russell held his arms up to protect his face and head.

The hoof clubbed him, tearing the flesh on his shoulder.

Russell cried out in terror and pain. In trying to evade further injury, he leaned too far backwards and fell out of the tree. He jumped to his feet, started to scramble back into the protection of the tree when he saw that there was no need.

He came around to where the buck stood.

The buck shook its head. It snorted.

The magnificent and powerful creature had been subdued by such simple means.

It now stood on three legs.

Perhaps it had happened when the buck was swiping at him while raised up on its hind legs. Or when the buck tried to drop back down onto all fours.

But now its left foreleg was wedged in the narrow space between two of the diverging trunks.

Russell was cautious to claim deliverance. He reached out and drew a hand along the white flank.

The buck tossed its angry head. A rear leg kicked back.

Now Russell was certain. The enormous animal was stuck.

Russell looked about. The doe was still nearby, but paid no heed. Its head was down as it continued licking the little ghost deer.

He turned back to the buck.

The scene was absurd. This tremendous beast was held captive by one hoof, one hoof caught in the crotch of a tree.

Russell saw its muscles tense. The buck was trying to pull straight back on the entrapped limb. It then moved forward just slightly, as though to either push or raise the foreleg.

It snorted. Otherwise, it made no noise. It just stood there. And would stand there until death.

The predicament was simple and complete. The buck was easy prey.

Russell took a deep breath. His astonishment was equal to his relief.

His teeth chattered. He convulsed with sudden shivering. The sleet had changed to snow. He was weak and he was hungry.

He listened. The forest was an absolute silent stillness.

Once again, Russell saw his position as others might see it: a nearly naked man in the woods. A huge white beast with its hoof caught between forking tree trunks. A fawn, bound fore and aft. And a doe, protecting her fawn.

He looked down to the doe.

"Either I borrow the little one or steal the big one," he said. "Which will it be?"

As he took his first step, he realized his pain. The buck had trampled one leg and ravaged the knee of his other leg. He hobbled forward.

The doe stepped between him and the fawn. She stomped the earth. A rush of air came from her nostrils.

He raised his arms. As he hobbled toward her, he shouted and screamed and flailed his arms to scare her away.

Her ears went back. She raised her head up high and stared at him with her dark eyes.

He recognized the posture. She wasn't going to run off. To the contrary, she was going to attack. She too would try to club and slash him with her hooves.

"I'm warning you," he said. "If you rise up, I will take you down."

He took a cautious step toward her.

Just as the buck had done, she rose up on her hind legs. Her front hooves scratched at the air.

He stepped back and waited. Just as she was coming back down, he charged. By the time her front hooves hit the ground, he was on her. He grabbed her around the neck and wrapped his legs around her middle.

His momentum knocked her down. He clung to her. Her thick coat was a soothing warmth. He could feel her racing heart.

She kicked her legs and shook her head.

He knew she wouldn't be able to stand, not with his weight on her.

But she did stand with his weight on her.

She writhed and bucked and then began to run.

He hung on for few strides and then let go. He hit the ground and, as fast as his weary and damaged legs would carry him, rushed to the fawn. He picked it up and clutched it against his stomach and chest.

He turned to face the doe.

She would not attack him now. She would not risk hurting her young.

"I win," he said softly.

She kept her distance. Her ears and tail were erect. A forelimb was raised. She was absolutely motionless, a majestic tension among the ease of falling snow, obviously confused as to fight or flight.

The fawn bleated. The doe made no move.

Russell hugged the fawn for its warmth. He backed away slowly from the doe.

Then he turned and ran, wobbling from side to side, teeth chattering and body shivering, towards the finish line.

CHAPTER 33

FIRE

*A*s he crossed the finish line, he tried to hold the fawn up high for everyone to see, but he was too weak. Instead, he laid it gently on the ground at the feet of Ian Rushmore.

Cameras clicked and flashed. People cheered and clapped and crowded in to see Russell and the white fawn.

Ian grabbed Russell's wrist, as if to raise his arm in the declaration of his victory. But Russell shook loose of Ian's hold. He was wild with a single intent. He pushed his way through the crowd.

"Move!" he pleaded. "Move!"

People cleared a path.

He whimpered at the sight of it.

Fire.

Sparks floated upwards against the falling snow.

His body went limp with the warmth. He fell to his knees and let out a series of moans that quickly turned into racking sobs.

People gathered around him, but no one spoke.

The fire crackled and roared.

Otherwise, the only the sound was that of Russell weeping.

One of the reeves draped a coat over his shoulders. A reeve brought him a hot drink. But he was shivering so violently that the hot tea spilled out onto his hands, and he dropped the cup.

A medic came and crouched down beside him with his box of supplies.

Russell shook his head. "I'm not done yet," he said. He stood.

The medic held the coat for him as he put his arms through the sleeves. He zipped it up and pulled the hood up over his head. He made his way back to the finish line as people took pictures, pointing and expressing awe at the white fawn.

Ian followed him. "It's not an albino," he said. "It has blue eyes."

"Nakamura …. Nakamura is dead."

Ian's eyebrows went up. "What? But…where is he?"

"His body is over by the reservoir."

"I'll call it in on the radio," the medic said. "Better get someone over there."

"Go," Ian said.

Russell asked, "Does anyone have a knife?"

One of the reeves stepped forward and handed him a pocketknife. He opened it and crouched down by the fawn.

"Hold it down for me, Ian."

Ian knelt and pressed both hands against the fawn's body.

Russell tried to cut the bindings but was shaking so much he was afraid he might cut into its legs. "Someone else," he said.

The reeve cut the bindings on the front legs.

The fawn kicked at once and tried to stand.

The reeve cut the bindings on the rear legs. "Okay!" he shouted.

Ian pulled his hands away.

The fawn stood.

"…*but none to keep*," Russell whispered as the white fawn bounded off.

People gasped and cheered, and rushed to the stonewall on either side of the line to watch the animal as it disappeared into the forest.

Ian took hold of Russell's hand and held it high. "Russell Bowen!" he cried. "Kincaid Champion!"

People crushed around him. They patted him on the back. They cheered and clapped.

Reporters shouted questions. Cameras flashed.

The instrument case was brought out. Ian opened the case and handed Russell the horn.

Russell took the horn in his hands and aimed to the heavens. He struggled against the shaking of his lower jaw. He put his chapped and swollen lips to the mouthpiece. And blew.

He didn't do a very good job of it. Because he was so weak and cold, his effort produced more of a sputtering than a clarion call. But the crowd's applause and cheering were vigorous.

The press shoved microphones in his face.

"How does it feel to be the youngest Kincaid Champion in modern history?"

"Why was that deer all white?"

"Where is the Japanese runner?"

"You're covered in blood and some sort of...muck. What is that stuff, Mr. Bowen?"

Other reporters stood in front of video cameras, chattering away in their monologues.

Someone handed him a bottle of water, and he gulped the contents down.

Ian took the horn from him. "Into the house," he said. "Let the medic attend to you."

But Russell said "Not yet."

He wasn't quite finished.

He crossed back over the line, into the forest.

CHAPTER 34

LIKE THE REST OF US

*R*ussell went around the buck so as to approach it from the front. He thought this would be safer for both of them. The less frightened the buck became, the less likely it was to panic and make a desperate move. Its trapped limb would break easily.

It was a strange, pathetic sight, the magnificent creature just standing there with snow collecting on its back.

Russell leaned into the crotch of the tree.

The buck's muzzle was right there in front of him.

"Look at you, Mr. Ghost Deer," Russell said as he peered down into the darkness between the tree trunks. "Just like the rest of us."

He could see where the deer's foreleg flared to the hoof. It seemed that just the hoof itself was caught. "A victim of your own reach," he said.

The buck kicked back with a rear leg.

"Easy," Russell whispered. "Be easy."

He reached down into the narrow space. He could get no more than two fingers beneath the trapped hoof, and therefore could not apply enough upward pressure.

He raised his eyes to the buck. "You wait here," he said. And laughed.

He reversed his way from the crotch of the tree.

He hobbled about, continuing to talk in a soothing tone to the buck as he searched for a branch of the appropriate length and thickness.

"People would pay good money to have your big white head on their wall," he said. "But I'll make sure that doesn't happen."

He gathered up several branches and brought them back to the tree.

"That doe is quite the character, eh?"

He ran his hand over the buck's beautiful white flank.

"Easy," he whispered. "Eaaassy."

He crouched down to the side of the buck and cautiously tried to slide the branch beneath the trapped hoof. It wouldn't fit. He tried another and another until one finally fit. He moved to the opposite side of the tree.

He pulled the stone from his pocket. He shook it at the buck. "You know, I could kill you and eat you, mister."

He tossed the stone away and then leaned into the tree crotch.

It was too dark to see the branch he had placed beneath the hoof, but he could feel it. One end of the branch was beneath the hoof to the front, one end beneath the hoof to the rear. He took hold of each end and jerked upwards several times.

The hoof came free.

Russell lifted his head and smiled

as the magnificent white buck disappeared among the falling snow.

He then went hobbling back down toward the finish line with two intentions in mind.

He would go home to Sarah. And he would sit by the fire.

But when he arrived back at the finish line, the police were there waiting for him.

CHAPTER 35

WHOLE THAN FIRST

*J*t was disorienting to look in the mirror and not recognize his own reflection. In his hair and on his face, even on his eyelids, on his chest and between his fingers, all over his body, the layer of blackish green muck had dried and cracked like old leather. No one had offered him an opportunity to clean up. To the contrary, the point had been made that he was not to clean anything off his body because doing so might destroy evidence.

He was sitting in the interrogation room of the Burwick Police Department. The dried muck tugged at his flesh as he leaned forward. The room was too warm. He removed his coat and laid it on the table. On the floor beside him lay a pair of crutches, given to him by the detectives who had questioned him for hours, hours ago. His right leg, grotesquely swollen and sensitive to the touch, was wrapped with a bandage and propped up on a chair.

And so there he sat, as he had begun, with no coat or shirt or shoes or socks or hat or gloves; just the deerskin shorts.

The video camera up in the far corner made him nervous.

A woman entered the room. Her high heels made a rhythmic clicking sound against the floor as she approached the table. She didn't speak to him or even look at him.

He watched her, studying her.

She was tall and slender, graceful. Her short hair was black, a bundle of tightly sprung curls. She wore a white blouse beneath the blue blazer. The blouse had a lace collar, buttoned tightly at the neck.

She put a leather satchel down heavily on the table, opened it and pulled out a laptop computer and a stack of papers. She crossed the room, the high heels once more making their rhythmic clicking sound against the floor.

She sat down at the table, looked up into the small camera in the corner near the ceiling, and said,

"Jesse McCormick, Office of the Chief State's Attorney, with Russell Bowen. Case number…" She looked down at her papers. "Where is that… here it is…Case number 4008312." Once again she looked up into the camera. "November 11th, 2020." As she turned away she glanced at her watch and said: "10:50 p.m."

Now, for the first time, she looked at him. The thick lenses of her glasses magnified the piercing certainty of her eyes.

He waited.

She glared.

He waited.

At last she said, "Just what did you people think you were doing on that mountain?"

"Am I under arrest?"

"No one is being arrested yet," she said. "But I am holding the whole lot of you."

"You can do that?"

She nodded. "Think of it as a form of collective liability. Each individual is being held responsible for the actions of the group. Understand? You are all suspects in the death of Mishima Nakamura."

"I don't think you…."

"You've been apprised of your rights, Mr. Bowen?"

"Yes."

"And you realize that you don't have to talk to me?"

"Yes."

"And you understand that you have a right to legal counsel?"

"Look," he said, "I'd like to know...."

"I'm the one asking the questions here, Mr. Bowen."

"Yes, I understand that I have the right to a lawyer."

"You also understand that our conversation is being recorded?"

"Oh yes," he said, and looked to the camera. "Big Brother has a glass eye."

"For your protection," she said.

He looked at her again. "It's a little late for that."

"You're referring to your leg?"

"No," he said. "I think that will heal."

She looked at him askance. She pointed to his leg. "But it's obviously badly injured. Yet you refused further medical treatment. Are you sure you don't want a doctor to...?"

"Of course I want to see a doctor. But first I want to go back to the hotel to get my car so I can go home."

She leaned towards him and said, "Not yet, Mr. Bowen." Now she grimaced and waved a hand in front of her face. "Whew! You smell like swamp."

She leaned back, with her shoulder against the wall, folded her arms across her chest. "I watched the video of your statement to the police."

"And...?"

"You get high marks for creativity," she said, and smirked. "Mishima Nakamura was killed by a deer?"

"Yes," he said. "A white-tailed doe."

She moved to the table. She opened the computer, typed on the keyboard, looked down at her papers. "I saw you cross the line this morning."

He drew his head back in surprise. "What?"

"A 'secret' location?" she said, with a sniff. "Did none of you make it beyond first grade?"

"I don't...."

"We were waiting for you, Mr. Bowen." She flipped through some of the pages in front of her. "Once we learned that the game was going to be held in Burwick, it was not difficult to find out where. We just sent people door to door asking if anyone had been approached by The Kincaid Committee." She looked up at him.

"Did you think it was a coincidence that a police car just happened to be there when Kozlov was on the road running around with his spear? We had police cars driving around that mountain all day long."

"I see."

"Listen. I'm with the Office of the Chief State's Attorney, Mr. Bowen. We are responsible for the statewide administrative functions for the division of Criminal Justice. As late as last week, we were still trying to stop this game from taking place. But no judge was willing to issue an injunction based on what was in The Kincaid catalogue. Even the implied intent of that so called 'Covenant' was vague. It wasn't as if you and the others had agreed to duel at dawn, which would have been illegal due to the intent. 'Combat by agreement' is how we refer to it in Connecticut courts. You may well have been willing to kill one another, but a *willingness* to violate the law is different from an intent to break the law. No crime. Understand?"

He nodded.

"In all," she said, "the State didn't sanction the game, but neither could we prevent it from taking place. So I was stationed here a few weeks ago. My boss wanted to pounce on this thing. Be ready to grab those passports, he said. Don't let anyone slip out the back door. If anything happened, that is. Well, guess what, Mr. Bowen? Something did happen. A man is dead. It's highly doubtful that Nakamura died of old age, wouldn't you agree?"

"I told you...."

"I've talked to the others," she said, raising her voice. "Girard. Kozlov. Rushmore. We picked up Ortiz at the hospital. She's in a wheelchair with a broken foot. She also has a broken arm and a fractured jaw. And I thought I was having a rough day! By the way, she says you're a fool."

"Oh?"

"Yes. Ms. Ortiz told us you stopped to help her."

"No rule against it," he said.

"Quite," she said. She sighed. "All right then, Mr. Bowen. We have people running around playing caveman. We have reeves and coaches and trainers. Reporters and bystanders. Language barriers. Telephone calls to embassies, and ambassadors contacting senators. International flights already booked." She paused, as if for effect, then said, "And a body in the morgue." She looked at him. "Small town, big mess."

"And?"

"This incident could attract a lot of attention, Mr. Bowen. International attention. I know from experience that once the wheels start turning in the big cases, there's no stopping them." She put her hands on the table and leaned in close to him. "And, given the chance, I'm going to roll those heavy wheels right over you."

He adjusted his position in the chair, which hurt his leg, which made him wince. "I felt safer in the woods," he said.

"You begin to understand," she said, and backed away.

"I haven't done anything illegal."

She cocked her head. "Now that's an interesting choice of words," she said. "People in your situation typically claim that they are innocent. But they also typically say 'I haven't done anything wrong.' That's not what you said. Perhaps you misspoke? Or maybe...."

"What is it that you want from me?"

"Okay," she said, "here's the deal. If you lied in your statement to the police, this is your chance to clean it up. A preliminary autopsy is being performed on Mr. Nakamura as we speak. If a more detailed autopsy is needed, so be it. If the evidence connects you to the cause of death in any way, I will crush you, Mr. Bowen. Crush you. But if you want to admit to something now, before those results come in, I will go a little easier on you. Understand how it works?"

"As I told the detectives...."

"Yes, yes, of course. The deer killed him. Do you actually expect me to believe that?"

Russell made no comment.

"Doing that turtle thing, are you, Mr. Bowen?"

He nodded. "You've been thorough."

"Oh yes," she said, with triumph. "I've done my homework. Leaving fire. Tyrants and turtles. Flake a stone and chase? Or make a spear? Frenzy and 'No Takes.' Fawns and does and rutting bucks. I didn't stay all day with the bystanders, so I didn't see you come in. But I heard that you brought a white deer across the line, Mr. Bowen. Was it a true white? Or was it just an albino?"

"I get your point."

"Your picture will be in newspapers all over the world tomorrow, Mr. Bowen. From Connecticut to London to Moscow. Not only because you won, but also because of that white fawn. That pictures will sell a lot of copies."

"Maybe so."

"Title 26," she said. "Connecticut Statutes. Section 26-86(f), to be exact. Even during hunting season, *'No person shall hunt, wound or kill or remove from the wild any fawn deer at any time….'* I think you see where I'm going with this."

"Then arrest me for hunting a fawn."

"I could," she said. "But I'm not interested in anything quite so trivial."

She strolled back and forth, and when she spoke again, she had eased into a more accommodating tone. "The law sometimes makes exceptions for what might otherwise seem to be criminal activity, Mr. Bowen. Perhaps you honestly believed you were not committing a crime when, and if, you struck and killed Mr. Nakamura. Perhaps it was a legitimate case of self-defense. Has a crime even been committed in the death of Mr. Nakamura? That's what I'm trying to determine. State of mind is crucial here. This so-called 'Covenant' you all agreed to tells me a lot about your state of mind. You can clarify it for me even further by answering some questions."

"What kind of questions?"

"Did Ian Rushmore ever tell you that he had received permission from any sort of governmental body to run this contest?"

"No."

"At any time, did Ian Rushmore lead you to believe that he was a lawyer?"

"No."

"Did he lead you to believe that the documents you signed were in any way legally binding?"

"I assumed they were legally binding on my own accord."

"Answer the question."

"That is my answer. Of my own free will, I considered those contracts to be legally binding."

"Seriously?" she said. "You actually believed that a group of people could just gather around a table and make up a bunch of rules?"

He shrugged. "Isn't that how it's usually done?"

Muscles along her jaw tensed and relaxed, tensed and relaxed. Her intense eyes narrowed. "Did you honestly believe that your contract with these other people was not subject to the laws of the State?

"I expected the laws of the State to permit me the right not to be protected by the laws of the State. Yes, I honestly did believe that."

"But did you think that you could commit a crime and not have to pay the consequences?

"The contract between us dictated that there could be no crime. Anything was possible. We all understood."

"Look Mr. Bowen. You seem like a fairly intelligent person. How could you have possibly believed that?"

"Because I chose to. And so did they. We gave our consent. It was an agreement among ourselves. We weren't going to rape and pillage through town. We chose to enter a competition in which certain rules did apply, and others did not apply, just like in boxing and hockey and football. No one else was at risk. I don't understand what...."

"These documents you signed?" She stepped to the table and opened a manila file. "*These* papers. These aren't contracts, Mr. Bowen. They are just pieces of paper with writing on them. They're worthless."

"I considered them to be contracts. Don't I have the right to...."

"No, you don't, Mr. Bowen. You can't give someone else the right to break the law. It's preposterous. You think two thugs on the street can agree to battle to the death and not expect the law to have something to say about it?"

"We agreed only to a possibility."

"Unalienable rights, Mr. Bowen," she said, and let out a sigh of frustration.

She flipped through the papers in the file, roughly, quickly. "You were the one who told the medic the location of the body?"

"Yes. The medic called the police."

"And you knew the location because...?"

"I told you. I saw the...."

"You saw Mr. Nakamura killed by a deer? Do you *really* want to stick with that story?"

"I saw it happen."

"A world-class athlete, a professional baseball player, was killed by a *deer*? Not gored by the antlers of a crazed male deer, but killed by a sweet and gentle doe? And this doe even pummeled his head with her hooves?"

"I never said she was sweet and gentle."

She leaned down, looked at the computer screen. "In your statement to the detectives, you said that after Nakamura was injured, you ran off."

"Yes."

"But about an hour later you went back."

"Yes."

She looked over at him. "Why did you go back?"

"The doe. She had looped back in that direction. I was following her."

"And Nakamura was still lying there?"

"Correct."

"You stopped?"

"I did, yes."

"Why did you stop, Mr. Bowen?"

He said, without hesitation, "Because I had failed to protect myself."

McCormick frowned and drew her head back. "Because you...what?" she said. "Because of guilt, is that what you're saying?"

"Worse than guilt," he said. "Loss."

"Oh?"

"There's redemption for guilt," he said.

"You need to explain this to me, Mr. Bowen."

He nodded, slowly and continued. "Yes...loss. It was so quick, all encompassing ... a part of me, something... it was gone... I don't know why... out there in the forest, when I saw him still lying there...it was such a strange sight.... And at that moment, it dawned on me that somehow...somewhere I had come to believe it was acceptable to leave an injured man lying in the woods."

"But that's part of this game, isn't it, Mr. Bowen?"

"Of course it's part of the game," he said. He averted his eyes. He cleared his throat. "If I say so."

As she moved away from the computer screen, she shook her head, as if she didn't understand. "But...but you didn't go immediately to tell Ian Rushmore or anyone else that Nakamura had been injured?"

"No," he said. "No, I didn't."

"When you went back to him, he was dead?"

"Yes."

"You've had medical training?"

"He wasn't breathing. He had no pulse. From where I come from, that means you're dead."

"You touched the body?"

"I shook him. I felt for a pulse, put my ear to his chest. I..."

She pointed at him. "That gash on your forehead looks serious," she said. "So does the wound on your stomach. And then that leg...."

"They hurt."

"I'm sure they do," she said. "Did Nakamura give you any of those wounds when you fought with him?"

"Very clever Ms. McCormick, but I never said I fought with him."

"*Did* you and he fight?"

"Like I told the police, I won't talk about anything that happened between Nakamura and me. They asked me how Nakamura died. I told them what I saw. And I've told you the same thing. Without an attorney, that's all I'm going to say about it."

She stared at him silence.

He shrugged. "Just playing the game," he said.

"The law is not a game," she said.

"Oh, please, spare me," he said. "In this corner we have a prosecutor, and in the other corner, a defense attorney. Each has tactics and each has a strategy. At the bench sits our referee, wearing a black robe. The

winner will take home a favorable verdict as the prize."
He shook his head. "I don't want to cross the line into
that game. You guys play too rough."

Her eyes narrowed. Her lips pursed. She lowered
her head, studied something in the paperwork and
then looked up at him again. When she spoke again,
her tone was calm, somber. "At the very least, you
were all reckless and irresponsible," she said. "Even
Nakamura."

"Huh?" he said, and in the enthusiasm of disbelief
he tried to sit up straight, but his injured leg wouldn't
allow it. He winced in pain and slouched back down in
the chair.

"Every one of us," he said, "including Nakamura,
we were all in agreement and we documented that
agreement two, three, four times. We agreed that there
would be no referees. We agreed that there would be
no penalties. We agreed that there would be no
arbitration, no lawsuits, no appeals.

Want the thrill of a lifetime, Attorney McCormick?
Want the fear of a lifetime? Take *complete* responsibility
for yourself. Believe me, you'd look about. You'd do
your best to take care of yourself. It's the beauty of the
game. From start to finish, it's a lost art, having no one
to blame but yourself."

"Complete responsibility, as you define it, is not
legal."

"That's no excuse," he said.

"You can't...."

"It's so simple," he said. "Don't like heights? Then
don't climb mountains. Don't like being around sick
people? Then don't work in a hospital. No one forced
us. We *chose*. Each and every one of us chose."

She lowered her head, and pinched the bridge of her nose. "In a way, there's nothing new here. Good people doing stupid things. But this time, a man *died* as a result of your group's actions."

"He chose."

She set those piercing eyes on him again. "You think that justifies his death?"

"It doesn't justify anything. But I don't blame the game, if that's what you're getting at."

"No? Then who should be blamed for the death of Mr. Nakamura?"

"Nakamura."

She put her hands on the table and leaned in toward him again. "You show a fundamental lack of appreciation for the legal system," she said. "You don't seem to understand that it's the law's job to protect you, even from yourself."

He sat forward in the chair, closer to her. "Do me a favor," he said. "Tell me more about the law that protects me from myself."

"Don't mock me," she said, and backed away.

"I'm not mocking anyone. I am the most dangerous person in my life, just as you are the most dangerous person in your life."

"I don't think I...."

"It's true," he said, and smiled, the dried muck tugging at his skin. "In the world of boxing they put it this way: protect yourself at all times. Because it's understood that you're the problem. *You* are your greatest threat. It's not something that the law...."

"Please!" she said, looked to the ceiling, then back at him. "Please... Mr. Bowen, let's stay on point."

"But this *is* the point."

"State of mind, Mr. Bowen. State of mind. May I?"

"Ask away."

"While you were playing this game, none of you had any obligations of any sort except for the rules you all agreed to in advance. Correct?"

"God, Conscience, and Nature. Just like it says in the Covenant."

"So, after this...after this 'leaving fire,' as you call it, you believed you could do whatever you wanted to Nakamura and the others because the laws of the State no longer applied."

"There's no such thing."

"No such thing as what?"

"Leaving fire."

She moved back to the table. She leaned down and typed rapidly on the computer keyboard. "I advise you to be careful here, Mr. Bowen. This may well be the very premise of any defense you might offer. Maybe you...."

"It's a myth."

She looked at him with a victorious smirk. She stood erect, turned away from the computer and while glancing up at the camera in the corner, said, "Please explain that to me, Mr. Bowen."

"I didn't like Nakamura," he said. "Then again, I'd be surprised if his own mother liked him. Talk about being the most dangerous person in your life.... He was a real bastard. Aggressive, overbearing, with a genuine mean streak. But...but that doesn't matter. Understand? Yes, he knew there were no rules between us. He understood. I know he did. And, yes, he was there when Ian Rushmore warned us that if we got injured, no one was likely to come to our aid until the night of the second day. Once we crossed that line, we were on our own, in every sense. Nakamura knew all of this. And yet none of that matters. "

"Mr. Bowen...."

"Leaving fire?" he said, and let out a disparaging laugh. "It's a myth, maybe only a wish. Nakamura and Girard and Ortiz and Kozlov.... I watched each one of them as they arrived at the hotel parking lot. I searched for their full character in every nuance. I studied their every move at the reception, the dinner, the Charge, what they wore, how they spoke. My arrogance? I judged everyone... but myself. That's why I could leave a man to die like that. So... and we... for all of us... being in the game changed nothing. We were the same on that side of the line as we were...." He laughed again. "You know what happens when you cross the line? You go with you. Understand?" He tapped side of his head. "You can't get away."

"No, I don't understand."

"That's why it's Nakamura's responsibility that he ended up dead. He shouldn't have tried to take the doe like that, grabbing her tail. Of course she was going to kick back with her hind legs. What else did he expect her to do? It was his own fault. And it was his fault that he was out there in the first place. It was his fault that he signed the Covenant. It was his fault that he crossed the line. *He* was *his* responsibility, all the way. And yet somehow none of that seems to matter, ultimately. None of it." He took a deep breath. His lower lip trembled. "Nakamura got hurt. He called out to me for help. I left him." He looked at her.

"And for the rest of my life, I'll be telling myself it was just part of the game."

"There is no law concerning 'duty to rescue', Mr. Bowen, not in Connecticut."

"Law?" He shook his head. "I'm not getting through to you."

"Bingo!" McCormick said. She rolled those menacing eyes and let out a long sigh. "Okay...so you left Nakamura lying on the ground. Later, you had an encounter on the road with Kozlov."

"And?"

She began to pace. "Like I told you, it was no accident that you ran into the police. They were driving around the mountain all day, keeping an eye on things. So far, Kozlov has been charged with assault with a deadly weapon, reckless endangerment, and refusal to obey an officer of the law. You're aware of this?"

"The detectives told me, yes."

"The arresting officer claimed that the person in the dispute with Kozlov was not only carrying a white fawn across his shoulders, but was also covered in some sort of tar or mud or makeup which made identification impossible. Judging by your appearance, I'd say that other person was you."

"And?"

"State of mind, Mr. Bowen. As far as you're concerned, was it right that Kozlov was arrested?'

"Yes."

She stopped pacing and looked at him. Her manner of accusation returned, quick and direct. "But you've told me that the agreement you all made with each other was binding."

"Yes."

"You all agreed that there was...." and she lowered her head to read from pages on the table. "...there was...and I quote...'neither benefit nor burden'...of laws....' *except those of God, of Conscience, and of Nature.'* Isn't that correct?"

"Yes."

She raised her eyes to him again. "And yet you agree that Kozlov should have been arrested?"

"Yes."

"You're contradicting yourself, Mr. Bowen."

"No, I'm not," he said.

"But you..."

"He was out of bounds."

She pursed her lips. Her eyes narrowed. "What?"

"Kozlov was out of bounds," he said. "The contract between us was null and void until he was back in bounds."

"So...honor among thieves. Is that what you're saying?"

He smiled, and once again the dried muck tugged at his flesh. "I didn't steal anything," he said.

"Back to Nakamura. He was 'out of bounds' when he was killed. True?"

"Yes, that's true."

"And if, if... if you fought with him when the two of you were out of bounds, would it be correct to say that both of you were then subject to the laws of this State, despite the Covenant?"

"Yes. Out of bounds is out of bounds."

She stared in silence at the computer screen, then looked at him.

"I have to admit, it's all very innovative." She was now genuinely smiling, although this did little to lessen the forbidding look in her eyes. "The white-tailed defense."

"All right," Russell said. "Charge me with something and put me in front of a jury. They'll come to the same conclusion. The competitors were adults. No one else was at risk. It was a game. We all knew what we were doing. What business is it of the government's?"

She snapped the laptop computer shut and put it, along with her papers, in her briefcase. She moved to the door, put her hand on the knob.

"Last chance," she said. "Is there anything about what you've told me or the police that you want to change?"

"Nothing."

"Anything you want to add?"

"What will happen to Kozlov?" he asked.

"Not much, probably. He's an Olympian. Any judge will look favorably on that. If he has....

"Olympian," he said, making no effort to conceal his disgust.

She cocked her head. "Care to elaborate on that?"

"No.

"All right," she said. "State's prerogative. But if Kozlov has no prior record and nothing links him to Nakamura's death, he'll probably be fined and shipped back home."

"And the others?"

"If nothing connects them directly to the death, they go free. Anything else?"

He nodded.

"Speak it," she said.

"I'd rather finish whole than first."

She sighed, with obvious impatience. "Mr. Bowen...."

"Okay, okay. Umm...yes. I'm hungry."

"I'll see to it."

"And I could use some more aspirin."

"Yes, all right." She opened the door and left the room.

Food and water were brought to him, along with the aspirin.

After a while, Attorney McCormick returned.

"You're free to go, Mr. Bowen."

"I am?"

"The evidence collected so far is not inconsistent with what you told us."

"What you're really saying is that you don't think you could convince a jury of my guilt, isn't that right?"

"A police officer will escort you back to the hotel," she said.

"Nakamura," he said. "What did he die of? Was it a broken neck?"

"A stroke, possibly."

He let out a quick laugh of disbelief. "Stroke? He wasn't even 30 years old. How could have possible died from...."

"A stroke occurs when the brain is deprived of oxygenated blood."

"Yes. And?"

"The force that drove Nakamura's head back and to the side...whatever caused it...that force was considerable. As a result of extreme rotation and hyperextension of his neck, the coroner said his left carotid artery scraped over cervical vertebrae, maybe C2 and C3, causing a tear in the artery. Blood clots formed. Eventually, one or more of those clots broke off, traveled, got stuck, and blocked the flow of oxygenated blood to his brain. Voila. Was it the cause of death?" She shrugged. "Maybe."

"Did..."

"But... but...he also had epidural bleeding on the right side of his head. According to your statement, the doe pounded Nakamura in this area with her hooves as he lay on the ground. Whatever the cause, his temple was crushed. It says here, *"blunt force trauma fractured the skull and caused bone to break, rupturing a meningeal artery, probably causing immediate unconsciousness."* However, sometimes...."

"But he spoke to me. I heard him. I can still hear him: *Tasukete!* Loud and clear. How could...."

"If you'll let me continue...."

"Oh. Okay, sorry."

"...sometimes the loss of consciousness with this type of injury may be indeed be immediate, but also may only be temporary. A phase known as a 'lucid interval' may follow. The injured person can be alert and talking, even as increasing pressure is building around the brain as blood continues to leak from the wounded artery. 'Talk and die' is the colloquial phrase.

Sometimes it lasts hours or days, and sometimes it lasts only minutes, depending on the severity of the damage. So, yes, Nakamura may well have been able to speak before he once again lost consciousness." She nodded. "And that's it. A debilitating, life threatening situation for Nakamura...a stroke, brain swelling, ever increasing pressure within the skull, ...not a good scenario. But the exact cause of death isn't known yet. This was just a preliminary autopsy, Mr. Bowen, a result of superficial observations and diagnostic imaging. But the Burwick facility is just a small, country hospital. A more sophisticated medical environment is needed."

336

"Could…" he began, and then cleared his throat. "Do you know…could he have survived …if he had received medical attention right away?"

McCormick stared at him in silence for a few moments before she said, slowly, accentuating each word, "I can't save you."

"No…."

"Now, as I said, you are free to go."

"Okay."

"There are a lot or reporters out there, Mr. Bowen. They really want to talk to you. As do the men with the truck. And the woman in the car."

"What?"

"The incident with the Russian," she said. "On the road…."

"Oh, right, I forgot about the car and the truck. They both got dented, didn't they?" He looked up at the video camera.

"I accept responsibility, but will not admit to any culpability, for damages done to said truck and car. However, I will offer to reimburse the owners for any repairs needed."

With the aid of the crutches he rose awkwardly from the chair. He looked at McCormick. "How was that?"

"Goodbye, Mr. Bowen," she said, and left the room.

CHAPTER 36

FIRELIGHT

For what he had surrendered and for what he had gained, he knew both intense anguish and intense joy. And in mind and body, he had never felt so thoroughly exhausted. Yet somewhere in him he was relieved, because he had finally arrived home.

Home.

It was terribly late.

But through the front windows of the house, he could see that a fire was burning in the fireplace.

He got out of the car and moved slowly on the crutches along the walkway.

He looked up and saw that Sarah had opened the front door.

She waited at the threshold, silhouetted by the flickering firelight behind her.

THE END

ABOUT THE AUTHOR

*B*orn under a bad sign in Boston, Patrick McKenna Lynch Smith grew up in Connecticut. After attending the Protracted School, he worked at many jobs, and many other jobs, including belaboring the point.

On several occasions, he arrived where he started and knew the place for the first time. He was married, widowed, and married again. He lives with his wife Bet in the quiet corner of northeastern Connecticut.

Leaving Fire is his first published novel. In 2013, he published a memoir entitled *Leaving the Life: A true story of love, loss and gratitude*. It was a bestseller in his own mind.

His articles and poems have yet to be published in *The New Yorker*.

ALSO BY
PATRICK MCKENNA LYNCH
SMITH

LEAVING THE LIFE: A TRUE STORY OF LOVE, LOSS AND GRATITUDE: 2013

WARNING: THIS IS NOT FICTION. You may wish it was, as then these events would not actually have happened. Leaving the Life is a brutally honest account of **true love, loss and the struggle for survival.** It is a beautifully written, tragic **love story** filled with courage, compassion and hope.

This page-turner will move, touch and inspire you. Go inside the private lives of an ordinary couple as their world is turned upside down by a **terrifying diagnosis.** Their journey will leave you **grateful** for what you do have, and for what you do not have. You will cling closer to your loved ones. There is a **surprise happy ending** that not even the author saw coming.

"I don't have words to express my gratitude, my awe, not only for what you have lived through, but the elegant humanity of your writing. I was moved to tears." ~ Lisa Davidson

It is very sad, but also extremely well written. The book made me think about what marriage vows really mean, about sickness and health, about courage, and how I want to live my own life. I couldn't put it down. The ending was surprising and heartwarming." ~ Kay G, Cancer survivor

A MESSAGE FROM THE PUBLISHER

If you found *Leaving Fire* worth reading, please help share it with others.

- **Recommend it.** Help others find this book by recommending it to friends, readers, groups and discussion boards.
- **Review it.** Please tell other readers what you thought of *Leaving the Life* by **reviewing it** online on Amazon, Goodreads, or elsewhere.
- **Email the author.** If you do write a review or have other feedback, the author would be very interested in hearing from you. Email contact@patrickmlsmith.com, or visit www.PatrickMLSmith.com.
- **Note:** Leaving Fire is available in paperback, and as an eBook on Amazon. You do NOT need a Kindle to read Amazon eBooks. Amazon offers free apps that will let you read Kindle eBooks on just about any computer; tablet or smartphone.

Thank you and good night.

www.ingramcontent.com/pod-product-compliance
Lightning Source LLC
Chambersburg PA
CBHW060354260626
47160CB00006B/2308